To my darling children,
Beatie, Trevor, Todd, Nick,
Samantha, Victoria, Vanessa,
Maxx, and Zara,

May you always be happy
  and safe, above all,
may your adventures be rewarding,
  your partners loving,
may you be wise, lucky, and blessed,
and may you lead long, happy lives.

With my greatest love,
Mom/d.s.

SPY

Danielle Steel has been hailed as one of the world's most popular authors, with nearly a billion copies of her novels sold. Her recent international bestsellers include *Lost and Found*, *The Dark Side* and *Child's Play*. She is also the author of *His Bright Light*, the story of her son Nick Traina's life and death; *A Gift of Hope*, a memoir of her work with the homeless; and the children's books *Pretty Minnie in Paris* and *Pretty Minnie in Hollywood*. Danielle divides her time between Paris and her home in northern California.

By Danielle Steel

Spy • Child's Play • The Dark Side • Lost And Found
Blessing In Disguise • Silent Night • Turning Point • Beauchamp Hall
In His Father's Footsteps • The Good Fight • The Cast • Accidental Heroes
Fall From Grace • Past Perfect • Fairytale • The Right Time • The Duchess
Against All Odds • Dangerous Games • The Mistress • The Award
Rushing Waters • Magic • The Apartment • Property Of A Noblewoman
Blue • Precious Gifts • Undercover • Country • Prodigal Son • Pegasus
A Perfect Life • Power Play • Winners • First Sight • Until The End Of Time
The Sins Of The Mother • Friends Forever • Betrayal • Hotel Vendôme
Happy Birthday • 44 Charles Street • Legacy • Family Ties • Big Girl
Southern Lights • Matters Of The Heart • One Day At A Time
A Good Woman • Rogue • Honor Thyself • Amazing Grace • Bungalow 2
Sisters • H.R.H. • Coming Out • The House • Toxic Bachelors • Miracle
Impossible • Echoes • Second Chance • Ransom • Safe Harbour
Johnny Angel • Dating Game • Answered Prayers • Sunset In St. Tropez
The Cottage • The Kiss • Leap Of Faith • Lone Eagle • Journey
The House On Hope Street • The Wedding • Irresistible Forces
Granny Dan • Bittersweet • Mirror Image • The Klone And I
The Long Road Home • The Ghost • Special Delivery • The Ranch
Silent Honor • Malice • Five Days In Paris • Lightning • Wings • The Gift
Accident • Vanished • Mixed Blessings • Jewels • No Greater Love
Heartbeat • Message From Nam • Daddy • Star • Zoya • Kaleidoscope
Fine Things • Wanderlust • Secrets • Family Album • Full Circle • Changes
Thurston House • Crossings • Once In A Lifetime • A Perfect Stranger
Remembrance • Palomino • Love: *Poems* • The Ring • Loving
To Love Again • Summer's End • Season Of Passion • The Promise
Now And Forever • Passion's Promise • Going Home

Nonfiction

Pure Joy: *The Dogs We Love*
A Gift Of Hope: *Helping the Homeless*
His Bright Light: *The Story of Nick Traina*

For Children

Pretty Minnie In Paris
Pretty Minnie In Hollywood

Danielle Steel

SPY

MACMILLAN

First published 2019 by Delacorte Press
an imprint of Random House
a division of Penguin Random House LLC, New York.

First published in the UK 2019 by Macmillan
an imprint of Pan Macmillan
The Smithson, 6 Briset Street, London EC1M 5NR
Associated companies throughout the world
www.panmacmillan.com

ISBN 978-1-5098-7788-1

1 3 5 7 9 8 6 4 2

A CIP catalogue record for this book is available from the British Library.

Typeset in Charter BT
Printed and bound by CPI Group (UK) Ltd, Croydon, CR0 4YY

"Every great dream begins with a dreamer. Always remember, you have within you the strength, the patience, and the passion to reach for the stars to change the world."

—SOURCE UNKNOWN

SPY

Chapter 1

Thinking back on it later, the summer of 1939 was the last "normal" summer Alexandra Wickham remembered. It had been five years since her celebrated first London "Season" at eighteen, an event her parents had anticipated with excitement and expectation since she was a little girl. She had looked forward to it as the experience of a lifetime, a defining moment when she would be presented at court with all the other daughters of aristocratic families. It was her official entry into society, and since 1780 when the first Queen Charlotte's Ball was held by King George III to honor his wife, the purpose of "coming out" and being presented had been to allow aristocratic young ladies to catch the eye of future husbands. Marriage was supposed to be the result in a relatively short time. Although modern parents in the 1930s were less earnest about it, the hoped-for outcome hadn't changed.

Alex had been presented at court to King George V and Queen Mary, and had come out at Queen Charlotte's Ball, in an exquisite white lace and satin dress her mother had had made for her by Jean

Patou in Paris. With her height and delicate blond looks, Alex had been a stunning beauty, and she didn't lack for suitors. Her older brothers, William and Geoffrey, had teased her mercilessly about being a debutante, and her subsequent failure to land a husband within the early months of the Season in London. Being at parties, balls, and social events was a major change for Alex, who had been horse-mad, like the rest of her family, since her earliest childhood. She'd been taunted into being a tomboy by her brothers, as a matter of survival. Wearing elegant gowns every night, and proper dresses at every luncheon in London, had been tiresome and sometimes even hard work for her.

She'd made many friends among the other debutantes, and most of them had been engaged by the end of the Season, and married shortly after. Alex couldn't imagine herself married to anyone at eighteen. She wanted to go to university, which her father thought unnecessary, and her mother inappropriate. Alex was an avid reader and student of history. A flock of diligent governesses had given her a thirst for knowledge and a love of literature, and honed her skills with watercolors and intricate embroidery and tapestry. Her own gift for languages had helped her learn French, German, and Italian almost flawlessly. She spoke French and German as well as she did English, which no one considered remarkable, and her Italian was almost as good. She enjoyed reading in French and German. She was also a graceful dancer, which made her a highly desirable partner at the balls she attended with her family.

But there was more to Alex than the quadrilles she danced effortlessly, her love of literature, and her gift for languages. She was what the men she met called "spirited." She wasn't afraid to voice her opinions, and had a wicked sense of humor. It made her a wonderful friend to her brothers' male companions, but few of them could imagine marrying her, despite her beauty. Those who wanted to accept the challenge, Alex found fatally boring. She had no desire to be locked away in Hampshire where her parents' manor house was located, doing needlepoint by the fire at night, like her mother, or raising a flock of unruly children, like her brothers had been. Maybe later, but surely not at eighteen.

The five years since her London Season in 1934 had flown by quickly, with Alex traveling abroad with her parents, riding in the local hunt or others she was invited to, visiting her friends who had married and even had several children by then, going to house parties, and helping her father on their estate. She had more interest in the land than her brothers, both of whom had fled to London. William, the oldest, led a gentleman's life and had a passion for flying machines. Geoffrey worked at a bank, went to parties every night, and was known as a heartbreaker. Her brothers were in no hurry to marry either.

Geoffrey was twenty-five, and William was twenty-seven and went to air races in England and France at every opportunity. He was a proficient pilot. Alex thought her brothers had a lot more fun than she did. She was something of a prisoner of the rules of society, and what was considered appropriate for a woman. She was the fastest rider in the county, which irritated her brothers and their friends, and her gift for languages came in handy on their family travels. By twenty-three, she had been to New York several times with her parents, and considered American men more liberal in their thinking and more fun than the Englishmen she'd met. She liked talking politics with her brothers and father, although they urged her not to do so at dinner parties, so she wouldn't frighten the men who might want to court her. Her response to her brothers' comments on the subject was sharp.

"I wouldn't want a man who didn't respect my opinions, or to whom I couldn't speak my mind."

"You'll wind up a spinster if you don't curb your tongue and your passion for horses," Geoffrey warned her, but both of her brothers were proud of how brave she was, how intelligent, and how bold and clear in her thinking. Their parents pretended not to notice, but they were secretly concerned that she hadn't found a husband yet, and didn't seem to want one.

She listened to all of Hitler's speeches in German on the radio, and had read several books about him. Long before the events of the summer of 1939, she had predicted that war would be inevitable. By that summer, her brothers and father agreed with her. It seemed unavoidable, and they were dismayed but not surprised when war was declared on September 3. They gathered to listen to King George's speech on the radio, urging Britons everywhere to be strong and courageous and defend their country. Like most of the population, the Wickhams' response was immediate. Both of Alex's brothers enlisted in the RAF, William in the Fighter Command, which suited him as an ace pilot, and Geoffrey in the Bomber Command. There was no hesitation. They reported for duty and training shortly after, as did most of their friends. It was what was expected of them, and they went willingly.

Alex remained quiet about it for several weeks, and then startled her parents when she announced that she had joined the voluntary First Aid Nursing Yeomanry shortly after Willie and Geoff had left for training. Her parents had made their own decision about how to contribute to the war effort. Her father was past the age of enlisting, but they had volunteered to accept twenty children from London into their home. The evacuation of children from the cities was being encouraged, and many parents were eager to find safe homes for their children in the country. Alex's mother, Victoria, was already busy preparing the building where they housed the household staff and stable hands. Their male staff would be greatly diminished by conscription anyway, and they had other quarters in the house for the women. They were setting up bunk rooms for the children. Three of the housemaids were going to help care for them, and two girls from the village, and two teachers from the local school were going to give them lessons. Victoria was going to teach them as well. She had been hoping that Alex would help her, but then Alex announced that she was going to London to drive lorries and ambulances, work as an aide in the local hospitals, and do whatever other assignments they gave her. Her parents were proud of her, but concerned about her being in London. Bombing raids were expected, and she would have been safer in the country, helping to take care of the children. The children the Wickhams would be housing were from poor and middle class backgrounds, and families all over the country were taking them in.

Alex had studied her options carefully before volunteering for the First Aid Nursing Yeomanry. She could have joined the Women's Voluntary Services to do clerical work, which didn't interest her, or the Air Raid Precautions, or worked on a female pump crew for the fire service. The Women's Voluntary Services was also organizing shelters, clothing exchanges, and mobile canteens. She could have joined the Women's Land Army to be trained in agricultural work, about which she already knew a great deal from their estate, but Alex didn't want to stay in Hampshire, and preferred to go to the city.

The Auxiliary Territorial Service offered more of what she hoped to do, with driving and general duties, but when she contacted them, they suggested clerical work, which would keep her cooped up in an office. She wanted more physical work. She had also spoken to the Women's Auxiliary Air Force, about deploying barrage balloons. But in the end the First Aid Nursing Yeomanry sounded as if it was the best suited to her skills, and they said there would be other opportunities for her once she joined.

Her brothers teased her about it when she wrote to them, and said they would keep an eye on her when they went to London. Her mother cried when she left Hampshire and made her promise to be careful, but she was already busy and had her hands full with the children billeted with them. The youngest was five, and the oldest was eleven, which Alex thought would be much harder work than whatever she would be assigned to do in London.

She arrived in town in October, a month after war had been declared. The king had spoken again, thanking the entire country for their response to the war effort. Alex felt like she was finally engaged in something important, and she thoroughly enjoyed her month of training with women of all ages, from all walks of life, and every part of the country. She felt that someone had thrown open the doors and windows of her life to a broader world, which was what she had hoped to find at university, and had longed for, for so long. She wrote letters to her parents and brothers constantly, telling them about what she was doing and learning.

Geoff came to London during a break in his own training and took her to dinner at Rules, one of their favorite restaurants. People smiled approvingly to see them both in uniform. She was excited when she informed Geoff about everything she'd been told. She already knew that she would be driving supply lorries as her first assignment, which would free up the men to do more important things.

"Just what I've always dreamed of," he teased her, "having a sister who's a lorry driver. It suits you, Alex. Thank God you never got married."

"Oh shut up," she said, grinning at him with eyes full of mischief. "And I didn't 'never' marry, I just haven't married yet. I probably will one day."

"Or you could drive a lorry after the war too. You may have found your true calling."

"What about you, when do you start flying?" she asked, with a look of concern, hidden by their constant teasing.

"Soon. I can't wait to bomb the hell out of the Germans." William was already flying missions. The two brothers had always been fiercely competitive, but William had more experience as a pilot than Geoff.

As always, they had a good time together, and Geoff dropped her off at her dorm after dinner. Blackout rules were already being enforced, and windows were covered. Shelters were being built. London was buzzing with activity and young people in uniform, as wartime regulations and conditions were announced. Food rationing hadn't begun yet, but they'd already been warned by the Ministry of Food that it would start with sugar, butter, and bacon in January. Everyone knew that life was going to change radically, but it hadn't yet. And holiday meals would remain much the same.

On their way back to Alex's dormitory, Geoff warned her of the dangers of fast men who would be trying to take advantage of young, innocent women, and that pregnancy or venereal disease could be the result. Alex laughed at what he said.

"Mama didn't mention any of that when I left home."

"She's too polite. She probably doesn't think she needs to, and that you're too well brought up to misbehave." He gave her a stern, brotherly look.

"And you think I'm not?" She raised an eyebrow at her brother.

"I know men. And if you fall in love with some randy bastard, he could talk you into something you'll regret."

"I'm not stupid," she said, looking mildly insulted.

"I just don't want anything to happen to you. You've never lived in the city, or met men like some of the ones you'll be meeting now. They can be pretty bold," he warned her again, determined to protect his baby sister.

"So can I," she said confidently.

"Well, just remember, if you get pregnant, I'll kill you . . . and you would break our parents' hearts."

"I'm not going to do anything like that," she said, shocked that he'd even suggested it. "I came here to work, not to find a man, or go to bars and get drunk." She knew that some of the girls in her dormitory flirted with every soldier they saw. It wasn't her style. "Maybe I should have joined the army, or the RAF like you and Willie. I thought about it. Maybe I will, eventually."

"You're doing enough as it is," he said, with a warm expression. "People say good things about the First Aid Nursing Yeomanry, and a lot of it's not about nursing. It's heavy work. Just don't get kicked out," he teased her again, "by mouthing off to a teacher or your superiors or something. I know what you can be like!"

"Just mind your back and make sure you get the Germans before they get you," she warned him. They hugged each other, and he left her outside her dormitory. He had to be at his base by midnight, and he had a ride back.

She was pleased to have seen him. She missed her brothers, and her parents, but she was happy to be in London, being trained to be useful. She couldn't wait to start work. She had almost completed her training, and was proud to be part of the war effort, although she wondered if she should be doing more. Both of her brothers were part of the Advanced Air Striking Force of the RAF, and would be flying bombing missions over Germany. Reconnaissance missions had started as soon as war was declared, and Alex's lorry or ambulance driving seemed meager to her in comparison to her brothers' more dramatic contributions. But at least she wasn't sitting at home in Hampshire, she told herself.

She and Geoff had talked at dinner that night about going home for Christmas. All three of them had gotten leave to do so, and Geoff had said it might be the last chance they'd have. They were excited about it, and other men in Geoff's Bomber Command were going home too. Their superiors were being lenient with them for this first Christmas of the war. It was something to look forward to. There had been no major action, or very little, in the war so far. It was mostly preparations and plans, and getting ready for what was to come. Canadians, Australians, and Americans had come to volunteer too. There were even two Canadians and an Australian woman in Alex's group. Alex liked getting to know them. They all seemed much freer and more independent than the English girls Alex knew, and she admired them.

When Alex, Willie, and Geoff got back to Hampshire in time for Christmas, it looked no different than it had in other years. The countryside was as peaceful. The only change was that with blackout regulations, windows were covered so one couldn't see the Christmas tree lights shining brightly from the homes, or shop windows in the towns. And there was anti-blast tape on store windows in Lyndhurst, their favorite market town. Petrol rationing had been introduced, so people weren't traveling long distances to visit their families. But food was plentiful and Christmas celebrations were the same as before. Restaurants and hotels were full. People were in a festive mood despite the war.

Hundreds of thousands of children had been sent from London to homes in the country, and the government discouraged sending them back to London for the holidays, and urged the host families to keep them in the country, as many might not want to leave their parents in London again if they went home. Their parents were told not to visit them, for the same reason. And since railway travel was to be kept to a minimum, the children who had been sent away had to adjust to their first Christmas without their parents. Victoria and her helpers were determined to make it a happy time for them.

The Wickhams were making a big effort to entertain the children and have Christmas be special. Victoria and the girls who helped care for them had knitted and bought gifts for all of them. Victoria had stayed up late every night herself sewing a teddy bear for each child. Alex joined her when she got home, helping her finish the final ones by tying bright red ribbons around their necks. Victoria had knitted a sweater for each child. She and almost every woman in the country were knitting constantly, and following the various government schemes about how to save money on clothes. Restraint was being encouraged but not enforced.

The Wickhams had two dinners on Christmas Eve. First, an early one for the children, where they received their gifts, and squealed with delight over the teddy bears. Miraculously, all the sweaters fit, the navy blue ones for the boys, and the red ones for the girls, and there were sweets for each of them from the shop in Lyndhurst. Later that night, the family had their traditional Christmas meal in the dining room. They dressed formally in black tie and evening gowns, as they always did. They exchanged gifts that had been thoughtfully picked out. Victoria had knitted a pink angora sweater for Alex and also gave her a pair of pale blue sapphire earrings, the same color as her eyes. They exchanged their gifts at midnight after dinner. Alex had bought her mother one of the stylish new large handbags in London. It would be practical for carrying ration books and even her knitting. They were becoming very popular in London, one of the first noticeable fashion changes of the war.

On Christmas morning, Alex shocked her family with another, when she appeared for Christmas lunch wearing trousers, which were also the latest rage in London. Her brothers looked horrified, and her parents startled.

"*What* are *those*?" William asked with obvious disapproval, when she walked into the drawing room before lunch. She'd been riding her horse that morning, and barely had time to change. "Is that part of your uniform?"

"No, it's not," she said staunchly. "Don't be so old-fashioned. Everyone is wearing them."

"Should I have worn a dress?" he asked.

"Only if you want to. Trousers are comfortable and practical. Gabrielle Chanel has been wearing them in Paris for several years. They're very fashionable. Besides, you wear them, why shouldn't I?"

"Can you imagine Mama wearing trousers?" he said as though their mother weren't in the room. Their father smiled.

"I hope not. Your mother looks lovely dressed as she is." He glanced warmly at his wife. "If Alex wants to try out a new fashion, she might as well do it here. She's not hurting anyone," their father said generously, and William was upset, as Geoff laughed.

"Good one, Alex. Willie needs a little shaking up," Geoff commented. Her hairdo was new too. She was wearing her long blond hair in a bun, instead of the braid she'd worn since her childhood. There was a neat roll in the front, and she had on bright red lipstick, which was new too. After three months in London, she appeared more grown up and sophisticated, and even more beautiful.

"That's why women have uniforms," Willie persisted, "so they don't show up in ridiculous outfits like that. Trousers are for men, dresses and skirts for women. Alex seems to have gotten confused." William was stiff and disapproving. He was far more conservative than his younger brother.

"Don't be such a stuffed shirt," Geoff scolded him, and eventually William relaxed and they enjoyed the meal of pheasant and goose. In the civilized atmosphere of their dining room, with the family portraits gazing down at them, it was difficult to believe there was a war on. The only visible difference at their table was that all of the young men who worked for them had enlisted in the armed forces, and the maids were serving, which would have been considered improper before the war. It was a necessity now. All of the women were doing volunteer work in the neighboring towns, or had joined the Auxiliary Territorial Service, the Women's Voluntary Services, or the Observer Corps. Everyone was involved in some way in the war effort, but on a peaceful day like Christmas, nothing showed, except the blackout shades and fabric on the windows. The tree was brightly lit in the drawing room during the day, and the children had been brought in to admire it the day before. They were in awe of how tall it was, and how lavishly decorated with all the beautiful ornaments the family had used for years, with the antique angel at the top.

After lunch, the family took a walk together, and avoided talking about the war. Nothing new and dramatic had occurred since September except that the first German aircraft, a Heinkel He III bomber, had been shot down over Britain at the end of October. Winston Churchill had been consistently outspoken about what was to come.

But the Wickhams talked about local news as they walked the grounds of their estate. The boys bantered easily as they went ahead, and Alex joined them after staying with her parents at their pace for a while. Victoria was enjoying having children with them in Hampshire, although she admitted it was a lot of work to have so many young children to be responsible for. So far, they had given her no trouble and weren't as homesick as they had been in the beginning.

"What are you two talking about?" Alex asked Willie and Geoff as she caught up with them, still wearing the trousers that had outraged her oldest brother.

"Fast planes and loose women," Geoff quipped with a grin at his sister.

"Should I leave you to it?" she asked him.

"Not at all. Are you behaving yourself in London?"

"Of course," she said, remembering Geoff's advice. And in fact she was. She was busy with her volunteer work, and the assignments they gave her, mostly driving so far. She was responsible, reliable, and a good driver. She'd been driving in Hampshire for years, after one of the stable hands taught her when she was seventeen. "Are you behaving yourselves?" she asked her brothers, and William nodded, while Geoff hesitated.

"I'm not going to tell my baby sister about my love life," he said, laughing, and both his siblings rolled their eyes.

"Don't brag," Alex said, and that time William chuckled.

"His fantasy life, more likely. What woman would put up with him?"

"Scores of them," Geoff said confidently, and then chased them around the same trees they had played near as children. There was something so peaceful and restorative about being at their home in Hampshire. They all loved it. Alex thought it too dull when she lived there, but now that she was in London, coming home seemed like a gift, as it did to all of them.

Their parents watched them chasing one another like children and they smiled. It was a familiar scene, and Edward put an arm around his wife. For an instant, it panicked her, watching them, hoping they would all be safe, and Edward could sense his wife's thoughts. "They'll be fine," he whispered to her, and she nodded, with tears in her eyes. Her fears stuck in her throat like a fist. She hoped he was right.

They walked back to the house when it started to get dark, and then went to visit the children, who had had a good day, playing with the girls who took care of them. One of the teachers had spent the day with them too, since her own sons hadn't come home from their far-away bases for Christmas. The children from London were a blessing for them all.

William was the first to leave, three days after Christmas. He had to get back to his base. He wasn't allowed to tell them why. Geoff left the morning of New Year's Eve. He had plans in London that night, and was taking an early train. After thanking his parents and kissing his sister, he promised to take her to dinner again in London soon.

Alex left on New Year's Day. Her leave ended that night. Her mother held her close for a moment, and then looked in her daughter's eyes.

"Be careful, Mr. Churchill says things will get rough soon." Victoria believed him.

"I'm fine, Mama. They trained us for everything, and there are bomb shelters everywhere now, with wardens to get everyone underground as soon as the air raid sirens sound." Victoria nodded, with tears in her eyes. It had been a precious Christmas, for all of them, and she prayed it wouldn't be their last. In peaceful Hampshire, it was hard to believe there was a war on, and she couldn't bear the thought that her children would be in danger and she could lose one of them.

Alex hugged her again, and then waved, as one of their old farmers drove her to the station. Her parents stood outside her childhood home, waving at her, as the children from London came rushing out and stood around them, and Alex saw her mother stroking a little boy's hair with the gentleness that Alex loved about her. She knew the image would stay with her forever, wherever she went. Once the house was out of sight, she was excited about going back to London, where everything was happening. She could hardly wait. She waved to their old farmer once she boarded the train, and a few minutes later, it rolled slowly forward and the Lyndhurst station disappeared from view.

Chapter 2

The war began to gain momentum in the early days of 1940, like a slowly growing dragon, flashing its tail in warning. Missions were flown, planes were shot down on both sides, but no major battles were fought. Thousands of men were drafted into the army after the early volunteers of the months before. Alex was surprised when she was brought in by her superiors and questioned about her language skills. It had become apparent that she was completely at ease in French and German, and fluent to a considerable degree in Italian. She was asked if her parents were either German or French, and she said they weren't. When interrogated further, she explained that she had been taught all three languages by her governesses, growing up. Nothing further came of it, and she forgot about the interview. She assumed they just wanted to confirm her allegiance to Britain, and once they knew her parents were English, they felt no concern.

She had dinner with Geoff several times, and William once. She got home to Hampshire in April for a long weekend, but her brothers hadn't been back since Christmas. Her father particularly missed William's help running the estate. He had an older man to assist him, but Edward was essentially running it all alone now that William was in the war.

The children from London were thriving under her mother's watchful eye. Victoria knitted constantly the whole time Alex was there, making sweaters for them, for people at the hospital where she volunteered, and another sweater for Alex. It seemed to be a national pastime. Even in London, Alex saw women knitting everywhere.

Winston Churchill became prime minister, and told the country to be braced for attack. His warnings became all too real when the Battle of Britain began on July 10, and Hitler unleashed the demons of war on them with full force. The country held up staunchly and was well prepared. The bombing of London and other cities was constant, and Alex managed to call her parents to tell them that she was all right. She heard from both her brothers in the ensuing days. A month later, the Luftwaffe attempted to gain air superiority over Britain, with heavy losses on both sides, but more among the Germans, who failed in their mission. It had been a hellish few weeks since the Battle of Britain began. Churchill addressed the nation on the radio. Alex spent every night in the air raid shelter, with screaming babies, sweating men, and crying women, but there was a kind of solidarity between the people of London that she had never known before.

By day, she drove over rocks and rubble in the lorries and ambulances she was assigned, sometimes carrying the wounded to hospitals, at other times loads of bodies to where they would be identified and claimed. Buildings crumbled around her, the sight of the dead and injured became familiar, along with the stench of death and the plaster dust that choked her as she drove.

In August, two days after the Luftwaffe's fiercest attack when they failed to dominate the British in the air, the matron of her dormitory came to get her as she dressed for work. She asked Alex to come downstairs. When she followed her, she saw one of the leaders of William's fighter squadron waiting for her with a somber face. She knew the moment she caught sight of him, and fought not to show how violently she was shaking, trying not to faint. His words were quick, William had been shot down during the battle with the Luftwaffe on August 13. It had been declared a British victory. He had died a hero's death, at twenty-eight. She nodded and thanked the squadron leader, and went back upstairs to sit on her bed, feeling dazed. All she could think of were her parents, and how they would take the news. Their oldest son was dead. She wanted to talk to Geoff, but knew she couldn't reach him. He was flying missions every day, like William.

The matron gave her half an hour alone, and then came upstairs and told her that she had five days' leave, if she wanted it, to go home to see her parents, if she was able to get there. Alex nodded, with tears streaming down her cheeks, thanked her, and then packed a small bag and left a few minutes later.

She was able to get a slow train and arrived at Lyndhurst at dusk. She found a man with a car at the station, who was willing to drive her home for a small fee. It was dark when she got there and she knew her parents would know by then. The house seemed empty when she arrived. She walked into the library, and found her parents sitting like statues, too shocked to move, too brokenhearted to speak, until they saw her, and then all three of them sobbed in each other's arms. They had all known that people die in wartime, and William was a fighter pilot, but somehow they had been so confident in his abilities, he was so young and strong and sure of everything, that none of them had thought he would die. They sat together until midnight, and then went to the kitchen. Alex made them something to eat, but they weren't hungry. The vicar of the local church had come to see them earlier that night, Alex couldn't remember a word he had said. William was gone, in a stupid war that never should have started, caused by a lunatic in Germany. It made her realize now how many young men could die, and she still had one brother flying. Suddenly everything about the war seemed so wrong, no matter how brave they all were.

Alex put their untouched food in the icebox, and stayed with her parents until they went to bed. It was her mission to take care of them now. They were the children and she the parent. Word had spread of William's death, people in the area had brought food. The children they were housing had left little bunches of flowers on the front steps, not knowing what else to do. Some of them had already lost their parents in the bombing raids on London. Alex understood it all better now, the senselessness of war, and the losses they would sustain before it was over. It was all too real.

She laid down on her own bed after her parents retired for the night. She hoped that they would sleep, but doubted that they would. She lay there wide awake all night, thinking of William, how serious he had been, even as a young boy, the role of eldest son, which he took so much to heart, and the land and home and responsibilities he would inherit. Now Geoff, ever the clown and family jester, would have to step into his shoes, and take over from their father one day. Geoff had never prepared for it since William was the heir. Everything raced through her mind. She saw the sun come up, and heard the front door open and close. She tiptoed to the stairs, and looked down to see her brother standing there, thunderstruck, exhausted, with dark circles under his eyes as he looked up at her. They had given

Geoff leave too. She raced down the stairs and flew into his arms, and clung to him as they both burst into tears.

She followed him into the kitchen, and made him something to eat. Rationing had finally begun to bite, and she used the eggs they still got from the farms on their property, toast with a little bit of the foul-smelling margarine they had now instead of butter, and the jam her mother made, with a cup of weak tea. He ate it as they talked about William and what happened. It seemed strange now that there were only the two of them, and not three. Their family seemed suddenly unbalanced, like a chair without a leg.

By the time Geoff finished eating, their parents joined them, and they sat together in the kitchen for a long time. The vicar was coming back to see them, and they were going to plan a small funeral service to be held at the church the next day, before Geoff and Alex had to go back to London. He would have been buried in the family cemetery on their estate, but there was no body. So in time a headstone in his memory would bear his name, with no remains beneath it.

Alex took their mother upstairs to help her bathe and put on a plain black dress, while Geoff and their father went outside to get some air and go for a walk. Edward tried to tell Geoff some things about the estate, since he would inherit it now. That possibility had never occurred to either of them before. Geoff couldn't bear listening to his father talk about it, it made William's death much too real to both of them. Geoff was relieved when he stopped.

Time was moving at a snail's pace, in slow motion. It all felt surreal. William was gone. Alex walked past his room on the way to her mother's, and was grateful that the door was closed. She couldn't have borne seeing all his familiar things just yet, not now.

When the vicar came, they arranged everything for the service.

Victoria said what music they wanted. The vicar told her the choir would sing. Alex volunteered to arrange the flowers herself. After that, the rest of the day crawled by until it was evening again. Her father drank too much scotch before he retired for the night. Victoria went to bed as soon as the sun went down, and finally Geoff and Alex were left alone. He poured her a drink from what was left of the scotch, and one for himself.

"I hate this stuff," she said, making a face as she sipped it.

"It'll do you good." He drank his neat and poured himself a second one. "I figured I'd be the one to die in this war. He was such a good pilot. I was sure he could outrun every German."

"If you die, I'll kill you," Alex said grimly, taking another sip of the scotch, and he smiled at her.

"I'm not going to die, I'm just a gunner, dropping bombs out of a big bomber. There's no fancy footwork. They said William died a hero. What difference does that make? Who goddamn cares if he died a hero? He's gone. He took himself so seriously," he smiled at the memory, "even as a boy. He was the oldest son to the core. I don't even know how to run this place. He would have. He knew everything about it."

"You'll learn after the war," Alex said firmly. "Papa will teach you." He was eager to get started already now, with William barely gone.

"I don't want to learn. I want Willie to come back," he said and then started to sob, and Alex put her arms around him, wondering if any of them would ever be the same.

They sat together until three in the morning, until Geoff was thoroughly drunk, and Alex was exhausted. Then she walked him upstairs, and put him to bed with his clothes on. She went to her own room, lay down for a minute on her bed and fell sound asleep until the sun streamed into her room the next morning. As soon as she was fully awake, she realized what the day was. They had William's funeral to get through. Everything about the whole concept seemed so wrong. His funeral. Not his birthday, or something to celebrate. Her big brother Willie was dead. She'd always been so proud of him.

The family gathered in the front hall at ten o'clock that morning, her mother in another somber black dress, with red-rimmed eyes, clutching a handkerchief and wearing a hat Alex had never seen before. Alex was wearing an old black dress, with black stockings. The day was unusually hot. Her father was wearing a dark blue suit, a white shirt, a black tie, and a homburg. Geoff looked severely hungover and was in his uniform. Alex drove them to the church, and when they got there, they all stared for a minute. They hadn't expected anyone to be there. Word had spread from one family to another, and all of their employees and tenant farmers were there, all the families they knew, the locals William had grown up with, those who weren't in the army. And if they were away, their parents and sisters were there. There were easily three hundred people crowded into the tiny church and spilling out of it, while the Wickhams made their way through the silent crowd that stood there in respect for the family's loss and heartbreak. At the sight of them, the Wickhams had tears pouring down their cheeks, as the crowd parted and they made their way to the front pew, and took their places. Alex was relieved there was no casket. It would have put her over the edge, and killed their mother. It was easier not having anything.

The service was simple and respectful. The choir sang in their pure voices. Vicar Peterson spoke of William as a boy and a young man, of his skill as a pilot, and how much he would be missed by everyone. He reminded the assembled company that William had given his life for king and country, and had been a hero to the end. He had no sweetheart that they were aware of when he died. Geoff knew he'd been seeing a girl in the Women's Auxiliary Air Force, at the base, but he didn't think it was serious. William hadn't wanted to get deeply involved with anyone after the war started, unlike Geoff who wanted to go out with all the women he could lay his hands on.

The vicar handed Victoria a single white rose from the arrangements Alex had carefully made the night before, and the family walked out of the church into the bright sunlight. Months later, there would be a new headstone in their family cemetery on the estate, but for now there was no reason to go there. They stood looking lost outside the church, as people filed by to shake their hands or embrace them, and when it was over, Alex drove them home. There were services like this one all over England, particularly since the Battle of Britain had begun a month before, and now they were part of the bereaved families who had lost their sons to this terrible war.

They got home at lunchtime, and the children had made a wreath of wildflowers and placed it on the door. Victoria smiled when she saw it. They went into the kitchen, and Geoff and Edward sat at the kitchen table, while Alex and Victoria made a simple lunch, which they attempted to eat but could barely swallow.

Victoria went to take a nap after that, and Edward walked upstairs with her. Alex and Geoff took a walk all the way to the pond at the far end of the property, where they had played as children and chased the ducks and geese.

"Remember when the bastard pushed me into the pond on New Year's Day when I was seven?" Geoff asked her and she nodded with a wintry smile.

"You cried all the way back to the house, and Papa shouted at him and said he could have drowned you. I was only five, but I still remember it perfectly." They both smiled at the memory, although it had seemed traumatic when it happened.

"I can't believe he's never coming back," Geoff said softly. "I keep expecting him to walk in and tell us it was all a mistake." They both wished it had been, but it was beginning to sink in.

The four of them stayed close together that night and the next day. The day after that, Geoff had to leave and report back to the air base. He and Alex clung to each other when he left, and their mother sobbed openly, begging him to be careful. Alex spent another day with them after Geoff went back, and then she had to leave too. She sat on the train, staring at her feet, and thinking about her brothers and her parents, when a man in uniform stepped into the first-class compartment and sat down. He was wearing the familiar RAF uniform she knew so well, and she avoided his eyes, once she recognized it. She didn't want to talk to a pilot, and have to explain about her brother. It was all too fresh to mention to a stranger, and he didn't speak to her either. He just sat down and stared out the window. Eventually he took a book out of the bag he was carrying. She didn't bother to look at what it was. But she noticed that he was tall, good looking, and had dark hair and warm brown eyes.

They'd been traveling for an hour, when they stopped at a station, and he glanced up from his book, saw the sign on the platform, and smiled at her. They were stopping at every station, which made the trip seem endless.

"It's going to be a long journey at this rate," he commented, "if you're going back to London too." She nodded, and he picked up the book again, and then closed it half an hour later. "Visiting friends or family in Hampshire?" She hadn't seen him when they had boarded the train, but he had noticed her. It would have been hard not to. A pretty blonde with a good figure. She was wearing her hair in a knot again, with the neatly pinned roll in front, and the bright red lipstick she wore every day now. It was her look ever since she'd moved to London. She was wearing a simple black suit, black stockings, and high heels, and wasn't in uniform, since wearing it off duty was optional because the First Aid Nursing Yeomanry was voluntary. She wore her uniform proudly at work, but rarely off duty, except when she went out to eat right after work with some of the other women.

"My parents," she answered his question. "I grew up in Hampshire," she said quietly.

"I came to visit friends, but they had to go to a funeral while I was there," and as he said it, he noticed the black suit and black stockings and wondered if that was why she had gone home, and if the funeral his friends had gone to was somehow connected to her. They lapsed back into silence as he glanced at her sympathetically, and then the train stopped at another station a short time later. "I'm sorry," he said softly, remembering that the funeral had been for a young RAF pilot. "Your brother?" he asked, and she nodded, as tears filled her eyes and she looked away. He could easily imagine that even his uniform was painful for her, and he wasn't wrong. "I'm Richard Montgomery," he introduced himself, and held out a hand. He didn't want to intrude on her, nor be rude either.

"Alexandra Wickham," she said politely as they shook hands, which jogged his memory again. The young pilot's name had been Wickham.

"It's an ugly war," he said with a hard look in his eyes, and then he left her alone, and didn't talk to her again. She fell asleep, and didn't wake until they reached London. He helped her carry her bag onto the platform. “Will you be all right on your own?” He was worried about her, she looked so devastated. She nodded and then smiled at him.

“I’m fine. Thank you. Where are you stationed?” she asked, just to be polite, and when he said it, it was the same place Geoff was based.

“I have a brother there too, in Bomber Command. My brother who died was a fighter pilot.”

“I lead a fighter squadron.” She could see that he was older than her brothers, though only by a few years. He was thirty-two.

“I’m with the First Aid Nursing Yeomanry,” she said, and he nodded.

“You must work hard,” he said, walking her into the station. Then he handed her her bag. “Take good care of yourself, Miss Wickham,” he said kindly.

“You too.”

“Maybe we’ll run into each other again,” he said with a hopeful look, but they both knew it was unlikely. London was a big city, teeming with people in chaotic circumstances now. “What’s your brother’s name in Bomber Command, in case I run into him at the base?”

“Geoff Wickham.” He smiled at her again and they both walked away. He turned and waved at her, and then hurried for the exit, and she took a bus back to her dormitory. She was tired when she got there and signed in, and told the matron she would report for work the next day. She gave Alex a little pat on her shoulder and Alex went to her room. All the other girls were asleep in their bunks and she was grateful she didn’t have to talk to anyone that night.

She reported for duty, in uniform, at six o’clock the next morning, for her assignment as an ambulance driver. It was an early shift. She finished work twelve hours later, too tired to think, which was a relief, and was surprised to find a note on the message board for her. It had a captain's name and a phone number. She didn't recognize the name, and wondered what it was about. It sounded official, but it was too late to call by then. She had a later shift the next day, so she tried the number the next morning before she left for work at eight A.M. She was back on ambulances again. The name on the message slip was Captain Bertram Potter. He answered the call on the first ring.

"Miss Wickham?" he asked, and she confirmed it. "Good of you to call me back. I'm calling from Special Operations Executive. We've been in existence for about a month, since we got Cabinet approval in July, and I'm sure you haven't heard of us yet. I'd like to have a chat with you, if you have the time. One of your superiors at the Yeomanry recommended you. You have some language skills that might be helpful to us. Do you have time to stop around sometime today?" She had no idea what he wanted, or why anyone had recommended her, but he sounded pleasant.

"I'll be working till about eight or nine tonight."

"What time do you start tomorrow?" he asked her.

"Eight A.M. if I'm on ambulances, slightly later if I'm driving lorries."

"Is a seven o'clock meeting too early for you?"

"No, it's fine," she sounded surprised that he was so eager to see her.

"Good. We're on Baker Street." He gave her the address and told her to come to the second floor, and ask for him. "I'll have some strong coffee for you. Thank you for coming in at that hour. I like to get an early start."

"Not at all." After she hung up, she wondered if they wanted her to do translations for them, since he had mentioned her language skills.

Other than that she knew nothing and had no idea what to expect. She asked the matron in her dormitory what the Special Operations Executive was, and she said she had no idea. There were so many special offices and volunteer bureaus being formed that she couldn't keep up with them.

Alex got up at five-thirty the next morning in order to get to Baker Street on time, and she was there promptly at seven, in her uniform. She had to report at lorries at eight-thirty, but it gave her an hour with Captain Potter before she'd have to leave, which ought to be enough if he wanted to give her some translating to do later. She could do it at night in her dorm, in bed with a torch, if the lights were out.

She asked a woman in uniform at a desk for Captain Potter and after she went to tell him Alex was there, he came out and escorted her to a small barren office with no windows and nothing on the walls. He was austere looking with thinning blond hair and piercing blue eyes. He looked to be about forty. He was wearing an old tweed jacket. She looked around and wondered what they did there. There was no clue in the decor.

"We just opened the office a month ago in July, as I told you on the phone. We're not fully set up yet, but we are efficiently staffed. We're a fairly large group of operatives, many of them women, who take on special assignments of a confidential nature. Some of it can be quite dangerous work, and some of it is less so. It can be as simple as translations, and we understand that you are flawlessly fluent in French and German, which could be very useful to us. You might be asked to translate radio transmission codes, fill out documents, or you could be asked to do forgeries, work in code or invisible ink. If you're willing, we may ask you to go behind enemy lines and bring back information, create reconnaissance maps, or get forms for us to fill out, to use as papers for our agents in the field." Alex was watching him closely in fascination, trying to understand what he was saying and where this was leading.

"How would I get behind enemy lines?" she asked in nearly a whisper.

"In a variety of ways, by train, or we might parachute you in, in certain instances. Some assignments are more extreme than others. Sometimes sabotage could be involved. You would be trained of course in weaponry, self-defense, and how to defend yourself specifically behind enemy lines. Mostly you would be sent on reconnaissance missions, to bring back information, and to aid Resistance groups in enemy areas and occupied zones." France had fallen to the Germans two months earlier.

"Are we talking about espionage?" Alex asked with a look of amazement. He didn't answer for a minute, and then he nodded.

"Yes, we are. You're a perfect candidate for us because of your excellent French and German. Does any of this sound interesting or possible to you? You would have to be unfailingly discreet, no one can know that you're working for us, or what you do. That could be awkward if you have a fiancé or a boyfriend, who would wonder where you disappear to periodically and question you. You would have to agree to keep your work for us a secret for twenty years, even from your family, or spouse, or children later on. We're a top-secret commando unit, and officially we do not exist. You would have a high security clearance, particularly if you'd be willing to go behind enemy lines for us. And of course, you'd have a cyanide pill, if things go too wrong. But, with a good set of papers, and your German skills, you're much less likely to run into trouble." Alex sat and stared at him for a long time.

"You're asking me to be a spy?" She didn't know if she should be flattered or terrified, or both.

"An agent," he corrected, "of the SOE. We have big plans for our branch, and a considerable number of operatives signed up already, recruited from other bureaus. We're getting them from the military and some of the volunteer groups. You fit our profile quite perfectly," he said coolly. "The beauty of what we're doing is that we can do things military personnel cannot. We have more leeway."

"My brother was just shot down and killed by the Germans," she said grimly.

"I'm sorry to hear it, but in a way that's immaterial in this job. We're asking you to perform missions with precision and training, not emotion. Your reasons for joining us are your own, but at no time can you allow your personal feelings to interfere with an assignment. You need to be clear about that before you start. If you want to work with us, that is."

"I've never thought of doing something like this. I volunteered with the Yeomanry because I wanted to help the war effort."

"I'm sure you are helping, but someone else can drive an ambulance or a lorry. Not everyone is able to do what you can, with your fluent French and German. You'd be the perfect operative to send behind enemy lines, if you can keep a cool head. But you and we will both know more about that once we train you. And if you work for the SOE, you would be paid in cash, so there is no trace of it. It's not an exorbitant amount given the risks. We don't want you suddenly having a large amount of money you can't account for. It's a reasonable sum. I assume you're supported by your parents." She nodded. Alex looked at her watch then and saw that it was almost time for her to leave for work, and she wasn't sure if he wanted her to make a decision on the spot. He was asking for a big commitment in an obviously high risk operation. She would have liked to discuss it with someone, like her father or brother, but the captain had made it clear that she couldn't. She would have to make her mind up on her own.

"You're welcome to give it some thought, if you feel you need to do that." He saw her hesitation. "There's no question, these aren't ordinary missions, and some of them can be dangerous. But they're exciting and interesting too, and you'd be making a *real* difference to the war effort, bringing us vital information we need, and wreaking havoc on their side. That's what we all want, and what we need to win the war." As he said it, in spite of his earlier warning, she thought of William shot down by the Germans, and suddenly she wanted to take the job he was offering, not as revenge, but for justice. The Germans could not, should not, win the war. And if she could help her country win it, she wanted to do that. Hitler had to be stopped, before half the children in Europe were dead or orphans.

"I'll do it," she said in a single breath. "I want to. When do I start?" There was a fire in her eyes that he had hoped to see, and now it was there burning brightly. It was passion, love of country, and wanting to do more than drive a lorry over what remained of a building. They needed people just like her, who were willing to die for their country, so others could be free. She looked like a brave girl to him. What he needed were agents with immense courage, determination, and a passion for freedom. After talking to her, something told him that Alexandra Wickham was just that kind of woman.

He stood up and shook hands with her then, more than pleased with their meeting. "Say nothing to anyone, Miss Wickham. If anyone asks, you can say I was looking for volunteer nurses' aides. And after this, do not discuss anything you heard today. Your friends and family don't need to know you've left the Yeomanry. If they discover it, you can say you're working with the pumpers on the street, helping to put out fires, or with the air raid wardens, getting people into shelters. They can never know you work for us from now on for the next twenty years, even after the war ends. Can you live with that kind of secret?" She nodded affirmatively and looked as though she meant it. It was for a good cause, the best one of all, the survival and freedom of England.

"Yes, I can. I don't need to tell anyone."

"We'll advise you when to report for training. You'll live with other female agents, in a barracks, all of whom appear to work for a variety of volunteer services, and all of whom will have top secret clearance like you. From now on, what you do, where you go, who you know, what you see is a secret. Even among other agents. And if you suspect someone you know or are related to is also an operative, you never ask. When you see an agent you know is one on the street or anywhere, you never greet them. You can expect to hear from us sometime in the next month. We're putting a class together now. We'll expect you to come within hours, after we call you. And if you do have a boyfriend, you can't tell him anything either. You need to come and go freely with no explanations to anyone. Understood?"

"Yes, sir." She stood up, smiling at him, and wishing she could start at that moment, and not wait to be called.

"Take care of yourself in the meantime." He sat back down at his desk then, and she left his office, stunned by everything that had happened. She was twenty-four years old, and she had just become a spy for the British government. All she knew was that she was working for the SOE now. She hoped that her brother would have been proud of her, since there was not a soul in the world she could tell. From now on, whatever happened, she was on her own.

Chapter 3

As Alex had been instructed, she said nothing to anyone about her meeting with Bertram Potter. Geoff came to London to have dinner with her the following week, and he was still deeply depressed by their brother's death, and obsessed with killing Germans now. It was all he talked about, and Alex was sad after having dinner with him. He was suddenly bitter and angry, and fixated on revenge. He barely spoke of anything else.

The following night, she was lying in her bunk still awake at midnight, thinking about her meeting with Captain Potter and wondering when she'd be called, when the air raid sirens went off. They were all used to it by now, the blackouts and curfews, and air raids at night. She and fifty other women went rapidly down the stairs in their shoes and bathrobes to the shelter underground. It was always stifling and crowded. They all kept something by their bedsides to wear if they had to evacuate in a hurry. The important thing was wearing solid shoes, and she did. There were always rocks in the street now, and debris from buildings that had been bombed. She rushed down the stairs with the others in orderly fashion, left the building, and hurried up the street to the bomb shelter they went to almost every night. They could already hear the planes coming and the first bombs drop several miles away, as they arrived at the bomb shelter, where easily another hundred people had already found their way. Others had gone to the Tube stations underground, the subways, which had a greater capacity.

There were naked bulbs hanging from the ceiling, a floor of planks had been set down, there were benches throughout. Some volunteer group had left blankets because it got very cold and damp at night, and there were some toys for the children. Sometimes it was hours before the all clear would sound if the Luftwaffe pelted them all night. Alex thought of her brother in his downed plane again as she hurried down the stairs in an old pair of brogues she had worn ten years ago as a young girl. They were the most solid shoes she owned and she had brought them from home for this purpose. She sat on a bench with a group of other women, several of them had babies in their arms. A few of them nursed them to keep them quiet.

Most of the men sat on the wooden planks on the floor. She noticed a few men in uniform, who had obviously been out late, visiting someone, probably their girlfriends. She noticed a dark haired, broad shouldered RAF officer with his back to her, and paid no particular attention to him. It was late and everyone was tired, and there was always the question of what would remain of the houses they lived in. What if they came out of the shelter and found them destroyed? It was a possibility they had to face every day, the prospect of losing everything and even the people they loved. It made Alex long for Hampshire for a few minutes, and her parents' peaceful life there.

They could hear the bombs dropping and feel the walls of the shelter shake, and it was two full hours before the all clear finally sounded. The Luftwaffe had emptied their full load and were heading home.

There were fires everywhere when they came out of the shelter, and pumping crews doing their best to fight the flames. A building had collapsed and there was debris all over the street. Alex helped a woman with two children who said her husband was in the navy. And as she assisted one of the children to step over the rubble, and dodged an ambulance with its headlamps covered for the blackout, the dark haired man in uniform spoke to her.

"Miss Wickham?" She didn't know who he was at first, and then recognized him as the man on the train when she'd come back from Hampshire a few days before, after Willie's funeral service. He had said he hoped their paths would cross again and now they had. She looked up as she pulled her dressing gown around her, but she didn't recall his surname. He was Richard Something, but she couldn't remember what. She was too tired to search her memory now. She had to be at work in six hours.

"Oh, hello," she said, looking tired and distracted, as the mother reclaimed her child's hand, thanked Alex, and left. It had been a long night and that was familiar now.

"Richard Montgomery," he said, supplying his name for her. "Are you all right? Where do you live? I'll walk you back."

"Thank you, I live in a dormitory just down the street. I'll be fine." There were fire trucks trying to approach the scene, and crews shoveling the debris of the fallen building out of their path.

"It was a bad one tonight," he commented, as he took her arm to steady her, when she stumbled on a rock. "I was visiting a friend and about to head back to the base, when the sirens started. I have to be back in a few hours." She nodded, and wondered if he was flying a mission that day. Most of them were at night, unless they needed daylight to hit their target more precisely. There had been some mistakes made at night.

"We've lost three buildings on this street since I got back," she said, sounding tired. "They never let up." She felt desperately sorry for the people who lost their homes, or dug frantically through the rubble looking for people they loved who hadn't gotten out.

They were at her dormitory by then, which once again had been unharmed. It was no thing of beauty, but it was home for now. He looked at her when they got there.

"This is a terrible time and place to ask," he said, apologetic. "But I don't know how to reach you. Would you have dinner with me sometime? Say day after tomorrow?" She felt a shiver run down her spine as she realized that if he didn't show up, it would mean he had been shot down. But that was the way things were for now. You never knew who would die today or tomorrow, or still be alive next week, let alone in a year. He gazed at her pleadingly as though it was important to him, and she didn't have the heart to turn him down, although she had other things on her mind. This was no time for her to get involved with a man, with the job she had just accepted with the SOE as a spy. And what if they called her for training tomorrow night? Then she would stand him up.

"I'll try," she said. "Sometimes I get called in to work at the last minute, or have to work all night." It wasn't really true, but if the SOE called her and she didn't show up, she needed some excuse. She would have to start lying now and become good at it. "Is there somewhere I can leave you a message if I can't make it?" He jotted a number on a piece of paper and handed it to her. She tore off a corner and wrote down the number of the dormitory and gave it back to him.

"You can leave a message for me here if you need to. Where shall we meet?" He gave her the name of a fish restaurant she'd been to. It wasn't fancy, but it was clean, the food was good, and it was a quiet place to talk. It wasn't too crowded or too noisy, and they were open for dinner in spite of the blackouts and rationing. Some restaurants were only open for lunch now.

"Seven o'clock?" he suggested.

She nodded. "I finish at six. I'm starting at six in the morning that day."

"Don't worry, if you're late, I'll wait for you." She wanted to clean up at least a little before she met him. She was sorry he hadn't suggested her day off, when she'd have had time to wear a decent dress and heels. "See you then," he said smiling at her, and she saw that he had kind eyes. She had noticed that on the train too. There was a gentleness about him despite his obvious strength, the broad shoulders, and his height. He was handsome, but that seemed less important now. She waved as she disappeared into the dormitory, and hoped that his mission went well. If not, it would be one more loss to add to countless others. She already knew so many people who had died, not just her brother.

She reported for work a few hours later, and forced herself not to think of Richard. She couldn't afford to invest much emotion in anyone now. Their lives were all too ephemeral, particularly his as a pilot, and hers when she went to work for the SOE.

There was no air raid that night, miraculously, and she worked a twelve-hour shift the next day driving an ambulance and barely had time to wash her face and brush her hair and put on a skirt and blouse with a red jacket before she met Richard at the fish restaurant. She looked pretty and young despite the haste with which she'd dressed, and he was happy to see her. His whole face lit up when she arrived. He was waiting for her when she got there, which meant he was still alive and hadn't been shot down, which was something to be grateful for. He looked just as relieved to see her.

"These days, you never know who's still going to be around from day to day," he said, and then was embarrassed when he remembered her brother. "I'm sorry, I shouldn't have said that."

"Why not? It's true," Alex said simply. "I don't like to think of it that way, but several of the girls I work with have been killed in air raids when buildings collapsed, and my brother . . . there's no predicting who's going to survive all this. I've seen people climb out of the rubble who you'd never have thought would survive it, like a man the other day who told me he was eighty-five. And then a bomb drops, and a hundred people are killed, including women and children."

"My sister, Jane, was killed in one of the first air raids," he said quietly. "She was on a pump crew, trying to fight a fire. She was a teacher, her students loved her. She was helping an elderly neighbor to the shelter, the woman could hardly walk. They never got there, and they were both killed. War teaches us a lot about destiny, and that you can't predict anything. I fly bombing missions over Germany almost every day, and I'm still alive, for now. And she's not."

"Your parents must be devastated," Alex said sympathetically, thinking of her own, still in shock over William's death just a week before.

"Both of my parents died before the war. Maybe it's just as well. They were killed in an accident, together. Maybe that was better than all this." There was something very serious about him, and his eyes were so gentle. "Tell me about yourself before the war," he said, smiling at her, and she laughed.

"There's not much to tell. A quiet life in Hampshire, too quiet for me. I rode my horse every day. I love to hunt with my brothers. We're all mad riders. I came out six years ago, and had a proper London Season, which seemed somewhat ridiculous to me, although some of it was fun. Lots of parties and balls and people to meet and pretty dresses, and then after six months it's all over. I failed to find a husband, and didn't want one, so I went back to Hampshire with my parents, which was something of a relief. Then boredom set in. Watercolors and needlepoint, and I have a passion for books. I know more about the crops on my father's property than he does, but I don't want to be a farmer either. I signed up as a volunteer and ran for London almost as soon as the war started, and I've been here for almost a year now. I'll have a hard time going back to Hampshire when it's over. I like the hustle bustle of London, and feeling useful driving a truck. I don't suppose that's a career I could embrace either, but I have no training for anything else. I wanted to go to university and study literature but my father wouldn't let me. I was brought up by governesses and tutors at home, and I always wanted to go to a normal school."

"If you have a passion for reading, you probably learned more at home than you would have at school," he said, smiling at her. His father had been a gentleman farmer, but after hearing about her London Season, and being schooled by governesses, he could tell that she far outranked him in the hierarchy of British society, and he suspected her parents wouldn't approve of him. They obviously had greater aspirations for their daughter, which she didn't seem to share. She seemed to be very pleased not to be married, and was enjoying her life in London, despite the perils of war. "Do you think you might stay in London afterward?" he asked, curious about her. He had a feeling she was headstrong, and had her own ideas, which didn't include languishing in Hampshire, especially now that she had tasted city life on her own. There were a number of young women in London like her, and Richard had a strong suspicion that society as they knew it was going to undergo some drastic changes after the war.

"I'll certainly try to stay," she said, "although my parents won't like it and will put up a fight for me to come home. They're willing to let me be here for king and country, as part of the war effort. But after that, they'll want me back where I was, and where they think I belong." It occurred to her as she said it that they certainly didn't expect her to join a top secret commando unit as part of her volunteer work, and become a spy.

"I think a lot of women will be in your situation. They're an important part of the workforce now, and they won't want to give that up when the men come home. They've gotten some independence, even if they're not paid as well as men. That's not fair, but at least they've gotten out of the kitchen, and into offices and factories. It's a big step for women." She was surprised by how liberal and modern he was. He seemed to like the idea of women working, if they wanted to.

"I'd have to go to university if I want a decent job," Alex said. "I don't think driving a lorry after the war would be challenging enough for me," she said and he laughed.

"I can see that would be the case." She was an extremely bright young woman with a fine mind and a number of ideas that didn't include sitting by the fire in Hampshire doing petit point and embroidery. But she hadn't figured out her future path yet, or how to get there. First, they all had to survive, which was by no means a sure thing at the moment. They were grateful to be alive every day.

They talked about the travel she'd done with her parents, and her visits to New York and Boston with them. They had gone to Egypt, on an archaeological study trip, and had toured extensively in Italy and Spain. She had never been to Asia but thought it would be fascinating.

Richard's life before the war had been much smaller, although he had gone to Cambridge after eight years in a boarding school in Scotland, which he said had been exactly like prison. His sister, Jane, had gone to a very good boarding school for young women. He had been properly brought up and educated, just not quite at the social level of her parents, which she didn't care about, but Richard felt sure they would. People of her parents' generation and background expected their daughters to marry within the aristocracy, and preferably someone with a title, not a gentleman farmer with a good education, no title or fortune and a very small farm. In their real world, after the war, he had nothing to offer her that they would approve of. Knowing that didn't stop him from wanting to spend time with her, and the war gave them opportunities to meet and get to know each other that they wouldn't have had otherwise. He was thirty-two, eight years older than Alex, which didn't seem like a problem to either of them.

They had a lovely evening together, and then he took her back to the dormitory, and she thanked him for dinner. He asked if she could dine with him again on Saturday, which was going to be his first full day off in a month, and she had the day off too. They agreed to go to Hyde Park together for a walk, and he suggested a restaurant she didn't know. It sounded wonderful to her, providing they were both alive by then, and he didn't get sent on an emergency mission so his day off would have to be canceled.

That didn't happen. He picked her up at her dormitory at noon on Saturday, and they stopped for fish and chips, which they ate sitting in the park. Then they went for a long walk, admiring the gardens and small pavilions, and rowed a small boat on a lake. He was impressed by how knowledgeable she was about art, particularly the French Impressionists and the artists of the Italian Renaissance, when she talked about it.

"You could teach art history," he said as he rowed her across the lake.

"Hardly. I don't have the education to teach. I know the kind of things governesses teach you. But I know nothing about science, and I'm terrible at math. I can do a perfect waltz, and dance a quadrille without missing a step. My brother Geoff worked at a bank before the war. He went to university. I didn't."

"You probably know more on certain subjects than most people who did."

"My French governess's father taught art history at the Sorbonne. She taught me all about French art. I learned about Italian art from books."

"I know nothing about art," he readily admitted. "I studied Chaucer and British literature at Cambridge. It's not very useful unless you want to teach."

"When did you learn to fly?" She wanted to know more about him too.

"My father was a flying ace in the Great War. He used to take me up in his plane with him from the time I was a young boy. I caught the bug from him. I spent all my time and money on flying planes. I suppose I could be a commercial pilot after the war. I made money giving flying lessons before the war when I finished at Cambridge. But you can't make much money at it. I couldn't have supported a family. I hadn't figured out what I wanted to be when I grew up, when war was declared and I enlisted. That's how I got to be a squadron leader. I've been flying for about fifteen years. Most of my pilots only learned recently. I have a few hot pilots, and I'm lucky to have them, but most of them are wet behind the ears, very green. I flew in air shows for prize money. What I learned saved my life more than a few times since we started flying missions."

"My brother William loved flying too. He probably wasn't as experienced as you, but planes were his passion," she said wistfully. "I still can't believe he's gone." Richard nodded and didn't say anything, but touched her hand, and she was moved by the gesture. He was a gentle person, and a nice man. He was respectful of her way of life, and her limited education, which he respected more than she did. She always felt like the victim of a society that didn't want women to be educated. She was hungry for knowledge, and soaked it up like a sponge.

"One day, I'll take you up in a plane, and we'll go flying together, after the war," he offered. She liked thinking that it was a possibility, although she wasn't counting on it. He wanted to. He had something to look forward to now. It helped soothe the pain of having lost his sister months before. They had that in common, they had each lost a sibling to the war.

Their dinner was perfect. The food was delicious and the atmosphere genteel, and he seemed perfectly at ease there with her. He was every inch a gentleman, by birth and education, but he had no fortune, and no blue blood in his veins. He was certain it would be a problem sooner or later, and she insisted it was nonsense. He knew better, and had been brushed off by the aristocratic parents of women he had gone out with before. He was respectable, but not thought to be worthy of their daughters. Alex wouldn't let him dwell on it, and dismissed his concerns as ridiculous. Besides, they weren't getting married. They were just having dinner, she reminded him.

The day they spent together was just what they had wanted it to be. It was magical for both of them, and a blessed relief from the pains of the last months and the constant stress of the war bearing down on them for the past year since it began. Hitler's war machine was functioning perfectly, although the RAF's victories had recently outnumbered the Luftwaffe's, which meant that more Germans had died than Allies, which was a grim way to look at it.

Richard didn't kiss her when he left her at the dormitory, though he wanted to. He was respectful and polite and good company, and seriously smitten with her. He would be flying missions over Germany every day for the next week, and he told her he'd call her when he had some time off again. They both hoped it would be soon.

Alex floated into the dormitory, and fell asleep thinking about him that night. Geoff called her on Sunday and she didn't tell him about Richard. She thought it was too soon, and nothing major had happened yet. Just two dates.

She went for a walk that afternoon with some of the other women, and when she got back, Captain Potter called her at six o'clock. He gave her the address of a barracks that had been set up for "volunteers," as he put it. And he told her who to report to there. She would be driven to their training center, Experimental Station 6, at Ashton Manor in Hertfordshire.

"You start training tomorrow. Report for duty at 0700 hours. Don't worry about the First Aid Nursing Yeomanry. We'll handle them. We've already taken several of their people into the SOE. Just tell them tonight that you can't work tomorrow. We'll call them in the morning, and release you. Good luck, Miss Wickham," he said, sounding very official, and as she hung up, her hand was shaking. She hoped she had done the right thing, agreeing to work for them. It was too late to change her mind now, and she wouldn't have anyway. Whatever it took, she was going to see it through.

She went upstairs to pack after that, before the other women came back from dinner. Her suitcase was packed by then, and she had slid it under her bed. She couldn't even say goodbye to the friends she'd made there. All she could say was that she'd been offered a place in another dormitory for volunteers. She had no idea whether or not she'd see any of them again. War was a time of constant losses and goodbyes, while pretending you believed you'd see each other again soon.

If Geoff or Richard called her, they wouldn't know where she had gone either. Captain Potter had said she would have a contact number at the SOE, but social contacts were discouraged during training, and she had a month of training ahead of her. She would just have to give them some excuse as to why she couldn't see them. Long hours, too much work, a series of emergencies, and maybe a bout of influenza. She'd think of something. Her life of mystery was about to begin, and she'd have to get used to lying to them, because she couldn't tell them when she went on missions. Geoff and Richard had the same constraints to deal with, but they were flying missions, not spying. Her life was about to become a web of lies, even to her family, and those she loved. If she and Richard continued to see each other, she'd be lying to him too, for a noble cause. She didn't regret it for a minute. Even if it was complicated, it was worth it.

She was about to become a spy for the SOE, with everything that entailed. She had no idea what that was yet. But she was about to find out, starting at seven A.M. the next day. Alex was still shaking with anticipation when she went to bed. She was glad Richard didn't call her that night. She wasn't ready to start lying to him yet. But she knew she would have to soon, and for a long, long time to come. Twenty years, if they both lived that long, and still knew each other then.

Chapter 4

Alex had no idea what she was getting into when she joined the SOE, but she learned rapidly. Everything moved at full speed, from the moment she arrived at the training center where she would spend the next month and dropped off her suitcase. She went to collect the uniforms they would wear during training. They were fatigues. There were eleven other women in her class. They were all given code names and not allowed to divulge their real names to anyone, even each other. Alex became the Cobra. An hour after they arrived, they were in a judo class, learning self-defense, with instructors who spared them no pain, and tossed each of the women on the mats as easily as flipping crepes. They tripped them, nearly strangled them, held them hostage, pitted them against each other and the instructors. Alex felt as though she was bruised from head to foot after two hours of it.

From there they went to a map-making class and were taught how to make precise maps and diagrams. After they diligently copied the maps they were shown, they had to destroy them and re-create them, meticulously, from memory. They did it again and again, and were told that in the next month they would hone their new skills to perfection.

"I can hardly walk after the judo class," the girl next to Alex whispered to her as they left the map class. After that they were taught how to falsify documents and do forgeries. They each made countless mistakes and had to start over again. And their final class of the day was on how to wield the small, lethal commando knife they were to keep on their person at all times from now on. It was small, as light as a feather, and looked like a child's toy, but they were told they could kill a man twice their size with it, once they learned to use it correctly. Two of the girls cut themselves with their knives during the exercises, and by the time they went back to their barracks, they were all mentally and physically drained.

Alex was too tired to eat dinner, and went to bed instead, as did several of the other women. They were woken at two A.M. for another judo class and expected to be instantly alert when attacked by army instructors. They were allowed to go to bed for two hours afterward, and were woken again at six for an exercise regimen, followed by a breakfast of porridge and then taken to a shooting gallery, where they were taught to use weapons, tiny pistols they would carry at all times, rifles, Sten guns, and submachine guns. The expert marksmen who were instructing them said that the Sten gun would be their most useful weapon. It was automatic and came apart, and was extremely lightweight.

They broke for lunch, and then came back to the shooting gallery for additional lessons. They ended the day with another forgery class.

SOE had a department they called Station XIV, which did only forgeries with the precision of Old Masters. All the women in Alex's group felt clumsy as they tried to emulate the delicate work.

They had language instruction that night in both German and French. The instructors tried to trip them up and confuse them, and distract them into slipping into English, which all of them did as they got tired, except Alex who was able to think in both German and French.

In the days that followed they were taught espionage, sabotage, how to handle a grenade, how to kill a man or woman with their commando knives, and how to shoot their weapons accurately. Their memories were challenged constantly.

By the end of the first week, three of the women had dropped out, begging for mercy. They couldn't stand the extreme pressure, the demanding lessons, the challenges, and the mental and physical abuse. The women who remained were determined to stay the course, Alex among them, but every lesson pushed them to their limits and stretched them beyond what they thought possible to endure. They were taught to swim long distances underwater, how to remove a bullet and stitch their own skin. They were taught to transmit by radio and to use couriers. They learned various codes, and how to decode messages. They had to memorize whole pages of text and then reproduce them perfectly, in case they had to destroy a vital document and then re-create it when they returned from a mission. They were taught what to say if arrested. The judo lessons continued and were increasingly brutal. They were taught to shoot to kill with all of the guns they handled and how to land with a parachute.

It was the most terrifying, exhausting, challenging, excruciating month of Alex's life. The women hardly slept, and had to commit everything to memory. They had to strive beyond excellence to perfection. They could make no mistakes. Lives depended on it, theirs and others. They were taught how to conceal their cyanide pill, when to take it, and how. At the end of the month, Alex's brain felt like hamburger meat, her body like she'd been beaten to a pulp daily, but her maps and forgeries were impeccable, she could hit the bull's-eye with any of the guns they'd been taught to use. When she was asked to attack the judo instructor, she broke his nose, and he congratulated her. She had learned everything they taught her, and she had stretched her memory to its limits and could reproduce up to three pages of documents and decode everything they gave her to decipher. She only broke down and cried on the last day when they told her she had passed, which she found incredible. She was sure that they would reject her at the end of the course. She had never worked so hard in her entire life.

Alex had called and left messages for Geoff twice, and Richard once, to say she was working crazy double shifts at odd hours and couldn't see them for a few weeks, but assured them that she was fine. Geoff only called her once at the number she had left him for messages. Richard had called four times to say he was thinking of her and hoped she wasn't exhausted by her long hours, and he looked forward to seeing her when she was back to normal shifts.

At the end of the course, she was sent to a dormitory for lorry drivers, who were actually part of Military Intelligence and also worked as decoders. She was to tell anyone who asked that she only drove lorries now, and had to make deliveries throughout England and Scotland, to cover her absences, which they told her would be frequent, although usually brief. She was given three days off, and all she wanted to do was sleep, but she dutifully called Richard and her brother. Geoff was flying a mission when she called, and Richard called her back two hours later on her new contact number. He was relieved when he heard her voice.

"You must be exhausted, Alex. You've been working double shifts for four weeks and two days." He had kept careful count and sounded ecstatic to finally speak to her.

"I'm okay, just tired." There was no way she could have explained it all to him, even if she'd been allowed to. She had been transformed into a lethal machine to gather information, and destroy anyone who interfered with her. She wore a small pistol and her commando knife in a leather sheath at all times now, and knew how to use them as efficiently as any soldier. She concealed them in her clothing, strapped to her thigh, at her waist, anywhere that she could reach them quickly but they weren't seen. She was waiting for her first assignment, but had three days to recover, unwind, and absorb everything she'd been taught until it became part of her, like breathing or her heartbeat, without effort or thought.

"Do you have time for dinner?" Richard asked hopefully.

"I have time, but I might fall asleep on my plate. I'm not sure I'd be decent company, I strongly doubt it."

"I don't care. You can snore all through the meal. I just want to see you. I'm off tonight. Can you make it?" She just wanted to sleep, without having to fight off a judo instructor, or re-create a forgery while half asleep, but she wanted to see him too.

"Sure, I'd love to." He suggested a small Indian restaurant near her old dormitory, and she told him she'd moved to other housing for lorry drivers. She wasn't driving ambulances anymore. She would be making deliveries around England, Scotland, and Ireland, of materials to build bunkers in the countryside, and gun emplacements on the coast. She said they were driving stones from the debris of bombed-out houses in London to build airstrips elsewhere in England, which was true, although she wasn't doing it. It was her cover story now, and he sounded surprised.

"I thought you liked the ambulance work."

"I did, but they transferred me."

"Typical," he said, and told her the Indian restaurant was casual. She didn't have the energy to put on a dress, and wore trousers and a sweater instead. The SOE wanted her to wear her old Yeomanry uniform for work around London. She'd be in civilian clothes when she went on missions for the SOE. All of her outfits would be carefully chosen for her and packed in a suitcase, depending on the role she was supposed to play. But at home, in England, her Yeomanry volunteer work was her cover. Many of the women she had met during her training and in the dormitory had started, as she had, at the Yeomanry, or in the other volunteer services.

Richard was waiting for her at the restaurant when she got there. He looked as handsome as ever and was thrilled to see her. She could have been wearing her bathrobe and he wouldn't have noticed. He gave her a warm hug when she arrived, and held her hand all through dinner when they weren't eating. It was warm in the restaurant, and without thinking she pushed the sleeves of her sweater up to her elbows, and Richard stared at her arms in horror and touched them gently. She had bruises all the way up her arms from her judo classes and she pulled her sleeves down immediately. The rest of her body looked even worse, but she was relieved he couldn't see it.

"I'm sorry, I was carrying a load of cement blocks last week, and a couple of them fell on me. It looks worse than it is."

"I'm all for women doing war work," he said, frowning, as he held her hand again, "but they can't force you into unsafe conditions that really should be men's work. That's not right, Alex." She smiled at him, happy to see him again, and be in a civilized place, after the abuse of the past four weeks.

"How safe is your job?" she asked him gently. "We all do what we have to. And driving lorries is women's work for now, whatever the load is. I'm fine. Really." He acted as though he believed her but he was worried.

"I missed you, Alex. It felt like a year to me."

"It did to me too," she said, smiling at him. It had seemed like a century. She felt as though she'd been let out of prison, but she knew that everything they had taught her would serve her well, and possibly save her life when she started doing missions behind enemy lines for the SOE.

As soon as they left the restaurant after dinner, he kissed her. There was an urgency now to his feelings, and how he touched her.

"The last month taught me that I don't want to miss a minute with you that we can spend together." And then he hesitated before asking her a question. "Would you ever go away with me somewhere, if we could get a couple of days off at the same time?" She thought about it for a minute and looked at him earnestly.

"I might, but not so soon. Let's get to know each other better, before we do something that risky." She didn't want to get pregnant, and she knew Geoff's warnings when she came to London had been right. Lots of girls away from home for the first time were getting pregnant, and found themselves in dire situations. She didn't want to be one of them.

"I'm in love with you," Richard whispered as he held her in his arms and they stood on the street.

"I love you too," she said gently, and meant it. "But I don't want to do anything foolish that we'll regret."

"If you get pregnant, I'll marry you," he said nobly, and she shook her head.

"If we ever get married, I want it to be because we want to, not because we have to." He nodded and knew she was right. He had been frantic without her for a month, and he wanted more with her than just dinner. But he agreed to wait.

He took her to her new dormitory, which was even uglier than the last one he'd seen, and they stood outside kissing for a long time. "Can I see you in two days?" She knew it meant he was flying the next day but she didn't ask. They both had military secrets to respect.

"I'd like that. It's my last day off," she said, as he walked her up the steps and left her at the door. He wasn't allowed inside. It was a women's dormitory, and men weren't permitted, although she'd heard that girls snuck their boyfriends in sometimes. She didn't want to do that with him. "I'd like you to meet my parents one day, and my brother," she said. It still felt strange to her to realize that now she had only one.

"I will," he promised, and they kissed one last time. She was sound asleep when her head hit the pillow a few minutes later. She slept until the matron came to tell her that her brother was on the phone. She hurried downstairs to talk to him for the first time in a month.

"Where the hell have you been?" He sounded half worried and half angry at her. He didn't like not knowing where she was.

"Driving all over England, I'm on lorry duty now."

"What did you do? Get fired from the ambulances? You're a lousy driver, Alex." He laughed when he said it and sounded relieved. "Are you working today?"

"No, I'm off," she said sleepily, glancing at the bruises on her arms, and remembering how shocked Richard had been when he'd seen them.

"I'll come to see you later. I don't have to be back on the base until four."

They had lunch together at Rules, their favorite and reminiscent of their childhoods. It was only open for lunch now. Afterward, they walked around London between the ruined buildings in her new neighborhood. It felt as though the war would go on forever, and it had only been thirteen months. So many lives had been lost, including their brother's. But Geoff looked better than he had a month before and said he was seeing a new girl, a local who lived near the air base. Her father was a butcher, and he smuggled beef for them when Geoff had dinner at their house. She wanted to tell him about Richard, but it still felt too soon. They had not even known each other for two months, and she had been away for most of it. Things happened quickly in wartime. She had never told any man before that she loved him, but it felt right with Richard. And they were both acutely aware that every time they saw each other could be their last, which intensified everything.

Geoff left her in time to get back to the base, and she lay in bed that night, thinking about Richard, and wanting to be with him. She wondered when she would get her first assignment from the SOE. They had said it could be days or weeks, and in the meantime, they would make an honest woman of her, and have her drive a lorry from time to time, just on assignments around London so she'd be close at hand, if they needed her on short notice. She wouldn't be able to warn Richard when she was leaving, or say where she'd been when she got back. But he wasn't supposed to tell her about the missions he flew either. The war was making liars of them all.

Their dinner the next night was as sweet as all their time together had been so far. Their kisses were getting longer and more heated, and he couldn't keep his hands off her body. She was hungry for him too. She barely managed to tear herself away. She wanted to go to a hotel room with him, like most of the young couples in London, but she wanted it to be right when it happened, and not at some seedy hotel, where they pretended to be married and the desk clerk sneered at them and knew it wasn't true. She wanted their first time to be a precious memory and not feel like a cheap trick. Richard understood and didn't press her about it, although his desire for her was intense, matched by hers.

He had no time off for the rest of the week, and she got a call from the woman designated as her contact at the SOE two days after she saw Richard. She told Alex to come in to the office on Baker Street the next day. Alex knew what that meant. She left the dormitory the next morning in a simple dress and jacket, and was at the SOE office half an hour later. They already had travel papers, a passport, and a suitcase packed for her. They were sending her into Germany to bring back a hundred forms, or as many as she could get, that the Germans used as their passes to travel in the country freely, with military stamps attached. A hundred of them would allow their SOE operatives easy entry and free passage around the country without question. They wanted a hundred but would be pleased with whatever they could get.

"That's it? You want me to bring back a stack of blank passes?" It didn't seem like a difficult mission to Alex. She would have to enter

Germany from Switzerland with her forged documents, as a young German woman returning from Zurich.

"You'll have to talk your way into a police station, or a Gestapo office, and steal them when no one is looking. It may not be as easy as you think," her contact, whom she only knew as Marlene, which wasn't her real name, informed her.

The suitcase they had packed for her was filled with clothes that had been purchased in Germany, right down to her shoes, hat, and underwear. Her coat had a small fur collar. She was supposed to be a secretary in a medical office in Stuttgart, traveling to Berlin to see her sister. She was returning from a medical convention in Switzerland, sent by her employer. She had all the correct papers for it, and enough deutschmarks to look plausible. She was to go to the police station to report a suspicious occurrence and steal the forms while she was there. They had a special pouch for them that she could wear under her dress. She was to be as demure and charming as possible, in perfect German. And as soon as she got the forms they wanted, she was to backtrack into Switzerland, and return to England.

It sounded simple, but had the potential to get complicated, if any part of her story aroused suspicion, or her forged documents and passport were detected. Hopefully they wouldn't be, but she'd been taught that sometimes the easiest missions went awry, in which case Alex would be detained in Germany, possibly sent to jail, a labor camp, or even shot if they suspected her as an enemy agent. Anything was possible once she was in Germany. It had been made clear to her since the beginning that if she got in trouble, she was on her own. They would not get her out. She knew the conditions and had agreed to them. She left London that night, with a forged British passport she was to destroy in the train station bathroom in Zurich when she arrived. She was carrying a small vial of acid in a lipstick to dissolve the pages, and was to dispose of the remains of the passport in the trash. Once she applied the acid, the pages would melt. She was carrying a German passport taped to her body.

Alex sat awake on the train all night, her heart beating so loud she could hear it. They reached Zurich on schedule by morning, the trip took seventeen hours. She had a cup of coffee at the train station, went to the bathroom, destroyed the British passport she'd been using, and buried the traces of it deep in the trash. She changed her clothes then, taking the German passport and travel documents out of the pouch taped to her body, and emerged from the bathroom in time to catch the early morning train to Berlin, with a ticket she purchased for a second class compartment. The trip from Zurich to Berlin took all day, fourteen hours, and from the train station she went straight to the nearest police station she was directed to when she asked. She walked in looking slightly flustered and very young and innocent. She asked to speak to a police officer, and after a brief wait was led into the police sergeant's office. She smiled shyly at him, and just looking at her he nearly melted. He was old and tired and jaded, and had been shouting at his secretary when she arrived. He was just about to leave for his dinner.

"Yes, Fraulein?" He cheered up the moment Alex walked into his office. She told him her story, that a swarthy-looking man had tried to buy her German passport and travel papers, and she thought the police should know about it. She wanted to describe him to the police so he could be caught.

"Ahh, Gypsies!" he said, with a look of immense irritation. He told her that normally it wasn't even worth his while to write a report about it, it happened so frequently, but he seemed anxious to extend her time in his office, and said that for her, because she'd taken the trouble to come to see him, he would write a report, and she was a good German citizen to do her civic duty and expose him as an unsavory person. The sergeant excused himself for a moment to get the correct form, after checking several neat stacks on the windowsill, and as soon as he left the room, Alex walked over and spotted the travel forms with the official stamp on them immediately. She took a thick bunch of them, put them inside her blouse and slipped them into the pouch, buttoned her blouse again, and sat down in a chair to wait for him. He was back five minutes later, with his hair obviously freshly combed and pomaded and reeking of cheap cologne, as he beamed at her and told her what a pleasure it was to meet such a beautiful young woman.

He wrote his report with flourishes, an explanation of the incident, and a description of the man Alex had described to him, and had Alex sign it. She did so while smiling gratefully at the policeman, and told him it was so comforting to know that men like him were protecting the innocent. As she left his office, he gazed at her longingly, shouted at his secretary again before he left for dinner, and Alex hailed a cab and went back to the station. Mission accomplished. Or almost. She still had to get back to Zurich. There was a train leaving an hour later. She bought a ticket, and made one phone call to a number in Zurich before she boarded the train, and said what time the train would be arriving in the code she had been given for the trip. She got on the train then, settled in for half an hour, and it left on time for the fourteen hour trip back to Zurich. It arrived punctually in Zurich. She bought a magazine and some candy, and went to the restroom where she and an older woman collided just inside the doorway. Alex apologized politely and they backed away from each other. The exchange had been made so smoothly it was invisible. The older woman left with Alex's German passport and travel papers, and Alex had acquired a well-used British passport with her photograph in it. There was a ticket to London on the next train in the passport. It was leaving in half an hour. Alex boarded in plenty of time, put her suitcase in the rack, sat down in the compartment, and gave her ticket to the conductor when he asked for it. The train left the station right on time, as Alex's heart pounded, and eventually she calmed down.

When she arrived in London, Alex took a taxi to Baker Street, where Marlene was waiting for her. Alex handed over the travel forms she had taken from the police station, nearly a hundred of them. She stripped off her German clothes, left the suitcase, and put her own clothes on. Precisely two days and a few hours after she had left Baker Street, for Zurich, she had returned, with her first mission completed.

"You were lucky," Marlene said, to remind her that it didn't always happen that way.

"Beginners' luck," Alex said modestly, smiling at her. Marlene didn't return the smile. She was there to do a job, at any hour, not to make friends with the agents.

"We'll be in touch when we need you," was all she said as Alex left. There was a small feeling of victory that she had done the assignment well and it had gone smoothly, and a ripple of fear, thinking about what it might have been like if it hadn't. She could have been dead by then. She shuddered thinking of the fat, greasy policeman in Berlin, reeking of hair pomade and cheap cologne. But she was in it now. There was no turning back, and she didn't want to. She was an agent of British intelligence, and beyond the fear and victory and her own amazement, there was an overwhelming feeling of pride that she had done something for her country at last, something that mattered and would save lives. And she was willing to sacrifice her own life to do it.

Chapter 5

Alex felt dazed for two weeks after her first mission in Germany, as she thought about it and it became clear to her how daring and how fortunate she had been. If any part of the assignment had gone wrong, she could have been in serious trouble. But luckily for her, it had been as smooth as silk. It was daunting to realize what a huge risk she was taking. It seemed an important thing to do, and it was in fact a way to avenge her brother's death, to outsmart the Nazis on their home turf, but she wondered if at first she had decided to do it mostly for the challenge and the excitement. She knew only too well how devastated her parents would be, if anything happened to her. Geoff was flying bombing missions almost every day. And so was Richard, which worried her too. The most effective damage they could do to the Germans, whether on land or in the air, was on their home turf. But if anything went wrong while she was there, she knew that British intelligence would not rescue her. The various officials of the SOE had said it again and again. Trying to save her would put too many other lives in danger.

They sent her on various deliveries driving a lorry several times a week, while she waited to be called for her next mission. She and Richard saw each other whenever he had a free evening and he could get into the city. She was seeing nothing of Geoff. He was having too much fun with the butcher's daughter near the base. She knew he would have killed her if he'd had any idea what she was doing. Alex's seeming innocence and youth kept her above suspicion among the people she knew who didn't work for the SOE, and Richard never questioned her. He had his own worries as commander of a fighter squadron.

One of the things Alex liked best about her new line of work was the variety of women she met, in both her training class and the dormitory where she was billeted. There were a few women who had grown up as she had in a rarefied world of debutante balls, weekend house parties among aristocrats, and governesses who had taught them to do delicate watercolors and embroidery and speak French. And at the same time she was meeting young women who had grown up in much less genteel, and sometimes much rougher, circumstances. But all of them were intelligent, dedicated, amazingly brave, and willing to face the enemy and do all they could to disable them in enemy territory, risking their lives without a second thought. Women were taking on new challenges all over England, working in factories, driving buses and lorries, doing men's jobs, as well as their traditional roles as nurses, teachers, and secretaries.

She liked talking to the girls she lived with, all of whom were officially lorry drivers, and some of whom were still officially part of the First Aid Nursing Yeomanry as she was, although in fact their main job was for the Special Operations Executive, which worked closely with Military Intelligence. In fact, they were a house full of earnest, young, highly trained spies who were truly dangerous women, no matter what walk of life they came from originally. All of their parents would have been horrified by what they knew how to do now. But the SOE had broadened Alex's horizons and her world, and she was no longer constrained by the rules and traditions she had grown up with. When she thought about it, as seldom as possible, she had no idea how she would ever be able to go back to her peaceful country life in Hampshire after the war. Her life had become exciting in ways she could never have imagined, and she felt like a free, independent woman, as she and Richard got to know each other better. The woman he had fallen in love with was not the woman she had been brought up to be, or had been little more than a year before, when the war started. She had blossomed like a flower in summer after years she had thought of as barren and meaningless before. Her life had a purpose now, and nothing could stop her from carrying it out. And Richard didn't try, since he knew nothing about her espionage activities or her real job.

After her mission in Germany, Alex was brought in for a more advanced class as a wireless operator, for which she seemed to have a natural ability. She was also very good at deciphering codes.

She had just broken a particularly tricky code at the Baker Street office, when she was called in to help them and work along with some military decoders, all of them male, and she was sent to deliver a message to the prime minister himself. Her own security clearance with the SOE was high enough to make her eligible for the errand.

She was told to go to the New Public Offices, a government building at the corner of Horse Guards Road and Great George Street, near Parliament Square. She expected to find a normal office building, and to leave the large envelope from her superiors with a secretary outside the prime minister's office. It was an honor to be entrusted with it. She could easily imagine Mr. Churchill in a beautiful wood-paneled office, smoking a cigar while he made important decisions. Instead, when she arrived, she was sent to the basement by a soldier standing guard, and proceeded down many flights of stairs to a teeming underground collection of offices and conference rooms, with officers of high rank from the army, navy, and air force, striding in and out of rooms for meetings. She caught a rapid view of an enormous map room, communication rooms with countless wireless operators sitting in front of complicated panels, and a glimpse of the prime minister himself when someone opened his door and then closed it just as quickly. Alex instantly had the sense that the entire war and the government were being run from this highly efficient overpopulated basement facility, from which, in fact, the prime minister was directing Britain's participation in the war.

After asking for directions several times, Alex was finally directed to a serious-looking woman, older than herself, who took the envelope from her and promised to deliver it. It contained some crucial new information about codes, highly sensitive and related to national security. Alex was only a messenger but it felt like a sacred mission to her to be sent to the hub of the government's war room. The complex basement compound was far below ground so it would be safe during air raids and bombings, and so everyone there could work around the clock without concern. She was fascinated by it and wished she could tell Richard about it when she saw him for dinner that night, but she couldn't, and would never violate the secrets she now knew. And he would never understand why a volunteer with the First Aid Nursing Yeomanry would be sent on an errand like this. She had a hard time believing it herself.

"So what did you do today?" Richard asked, as they settled down at a small corner table at the Indian restaurant they both liked. She noticed that he looked tired, and she sensed that he'd had a hard day.

"We collected debris off the streets, and drove it away, for the air-strips they're building," she said innocently. So many buildings had collapsed in the constant bombings that numerous streets were now impassable and some of the residential areas were a maze of blocked streets, and occasionally they found bodies, as the bulldozers cleared the rubble away. It was a depressing job she had done often, but not that day.

"I wish they'd give you an easier job," he said. "Women were supposed to do clerical work, or work in factories. They seem to have most of you doing men's work now. Some of it is just too much for a woman to handle physically." If he had seen her training with the SOE, he would have been even more in awe, and terrified for her. "I hear they're going to have all civilian women register in a few months, even grandmothers. I think the cutoff will be sixty. It's with an eye to making conscription for women mandatory in the next year, if the war continues." It was obvious to all of them now that it would.

A number of Americans had come to volunteer with the RAF, and many American women had joined the British forces too, in spite of the fact that America had not joined the Allies so far, and President Roosevelt seemed determined to keep the United States out of the war. But they were getting support from individual Americans, as well as Canadians and Australians.

Several of the women Alex had met in the SOE were of other nationalities, French, Indian, Polish, and Alex was enjoying meeting them, and getting to know them. Some of the women in top security work kept to themselves, and no one on the outside would have guessed that they were spies, just as they wouldn't have with Alex, who appeared to be an innocent young woman who had never seen anything more dangerous than a ballroom. She looked like what she was, a well-born young woman, but Richard had already discovered that she was much more than that, her interests and passions were much deeper, and her powers of observation were more acute than many of the men he worked with. The notion that women weren't able to handle the same responsibilities as men was a concept he found absurd. In fact, he found many of the women he knew even smarter than most men. His open-mindedness on the subject endeared him to Alex. He was surprisingly fair and modern in his thinking, unlike her father and brothers who thought that women should stay home, and that even driving an ambulance was too much for them to cope with.

They sat at dinner late that night, sharing their views about Winston Churchill. Richard felt sure he was going to win the war for them, and thought him brilliant. Alex ached to say she had caught a glimpse of him through an open door only that afternoon, but she couldn't. There were no exceptions to the rules, and the high security clearance she had now reflected how trustworthy she was. She also had a permit to carry weapons, which Richard was unaware of.

The air raid sirens began just as they left the restaurant, and they hurried to the nearest shelter and spent two hours among crying children and their tired parents as the bombs fell and destroyed their homes. When they left the shelter, they walked past a small hotel, and Richard cast her a pleading look.

"I don't want to leave you, Alex. Can't we just spend a few hours there together?" She wanted that as much as he did, and was about to say no, and this time something stopped her. What if something happened to either of them? Their life now was about seizing the moment. It might never come again. With her work and his fighter missions, every day they had was a gift. And instead of declining, she nodded. They'd seen the hotel several times, it looked small and clean, and not the kind of tawdry place she wanted to avoid, and where others she knew went routinely.

She followed him into the hotel cautiously, and Richard spoke to the clerk at the desk. He had just come back from the shelter himself, with their handful of guests. He seemed as worn-out as they were.

Richard spoke quietly to the man at the desk, and his rank showed on his uniform. Almost every man in London was in uniform now, but Richard was no mere private with a floozy on his arm for the night.

"Our building suffered damage in the raid tonight. My wife and I need a place to stay until morning," Richard said, appearing upset and apologetic, and the clerk was immediately sympathetic.

"Do you have children?" the clerk asked, noticing how respectable Alex looked. She was wearing a simple black coat and a gray dress, and there was plaster dust in her hair just from walking down the street.

"They're in Hampshire," Richard said creatively and the clerk nodded, as Alex forced herself not to giggle. The clerk handed them a key, and Richard paid him, and they walked up the stairs together.

"That was quick thinking about the children," Alex whispered and he smiled at her.

"The children *are* in Hampshire, they're just not ours," he whispered back, as they found the room and he unlocked the door. It was small and sparsely furnished but clean. There was a white chenille bedspread on the bed, and pink satin curtains, a chair and a desk and a chest of drawers with a mirror that had cracked during one of the bombings. But the building was still standing, and it was their home for what remained of their first night together. There was a sink in the room, and a bathroom down the hall. And without waiting another instant, Richard turned to her, took her in his arms, and kissed her as he carefully removed her clothes. He knew this was her first time and he was gentle with her.

She was standing in her underwear and stocking feet moments later, shaking, as she unbuttoned his shirt, and he took it off, and then his trousers. With the utmost tenderness he lifted her onto the bed, and she moaned as his hands discovered her, their bodies pressed together. Alex had no hesitation now, she had made up her mind, as she did with all things, and once decided she moved forward and never looked back.

"I love you so much, Alex," he said, as she pulled out her hairpins, set them on the night table, and her blond hair tumbled past her shoulders and down her back, as he kissed and caressed every inch of her. He tried to be as gentle as he could when he entered her, but passion swept them both away, as Alex tensed with fear at first, and then relaxed in his arms. It was all over moments later as they lay panting on the bed, and he pulled her tightly against him. "I will love you forever," he promised in a voice raw with emotion, and she knew he meant it. She just hoped that forever wouldn't come too soon for either or both of them. Neither was sure anymore.

"I love you too," she whispered with tears in her eyes, and he was praying she had no regrets and that she wouldn't get pregnant just yet. They hadn't expected to give in to passion that night and he wasn't prepared, and they had decided to risk it this one time. He wanted to have children with her one day, but not now, in a world torn asunder by war. And he wanted their children to be safe when they were born. He never doubted for a minute that he would marry her, if she would have him. He was still concerned that her parents wouldn't accept him as a suitable husband for her. He felt unworthy himself given the difference in their circumstances, but he knew for certain that no one would ever love her more. She believed that too, and she loved him just as much.

She wanted to stay awake all night to savor every instant with him, but finally fell asleep in his arms. She awoke with the early winter sunlight filtering into the room when he opened the blackout curtains, as he gently touched her cheek and she smiled.

"Did I dream last night?" she whispered to him.

"If you did, we had the same dream," he whispered back.

They made love again before she was even fully awake, and he pulled out to make sure there would be no mistake, as he had the night before. He hadn't expected her to give in to him. They took turns tiptoeing to the bathroom, nervous about running into other guests, but there was no one in the halls. When Alex got back, he admired her as she put her clothes on and he watched. It was like a striptease in reverse as she put her garter belt on, and aroused him just as much. He didn't have to be back at the base until that afternoon, and she had no assignment that day, so they were in no hurry. But reluctantly they finally left the room with a last kiss, and returned the key at the desk.

They went out to eat breakfast at a nearby restaurant, and then he took her back to her dormitory. Alex could already sense that everything had changed once they'd made love. She felt as though she truly belonged to him now, and he looked sad when it came time to leave her. Most of the women who lived there had gone to work by then, and they lingered on the stairs, kissing and standing close together, remembering the night before.

"I'm busy tonight, but I'll call you tomorrow," he said and she nodded and looked into his eyes. "Be careful, Alex. If anything happens to you . . ." He couldn't finish the sentence, but it was everyone's fear now for those they loved. A bomb could fall out of the sky at any moment, a building could collapse, his plane could be shot down, or they could send her on a mission into Germany from which she'd never return, which she knew better than he. His appeared to be the more dangerous job, but that was no longer true since she'd gone to work for the SOE.

"I love you," she whispered softly, and then ran up the stairs with a wave, as he turned and walked away. Every time he left her, he felt as though his heart would fly out of his chest. He had never loved anyone as he did her. But it was impossible to envision the future now, there were too many dangers and too many unknowns.

When she walked past the desk, Alex noticed a message for her pinned to the bulletin board. She opened it and saw that it was from Bertram Potter. She called him back immediately.

"I need to see you this afternoon at three," he said without further information, which could mean anything. A mission, a meeting, another class they wanted her to take. She was not to ask questions, just do as she was told.

She dressed carefully, thinking of Richard, wondering what the future had in store for them. She wanted to invite him to spend Christmas in Hampshire with her parents. Geoff had already said he didn't have Christmas off this year, so she would be alone with them, and she wanted Richard to meet them, and see where she'd grown up, at Wickham Manor.

She arrived at the SOE offices on Baker Street a few minutes before three, ready for whatever they assigned her. There was always a thrill of excitement when they called. Every sense was alert, as she waited outside Captain Potter's office, and he called her in immediately.

"We need you as a chaperone on a reconnaissance mission in Germany. We have a recon expert we need to send in. He doesn't speak German and you're going to be his wife. You're flying to Zurich tonight. We have a car waiting for you there. You'll drive to a small town where there's a munitions factory. He'll make the maps. You're just along for the ride, as a cover."

"How's that going to work if he doesn't speak German?" She hadn't worked with a male counterpart yet.

"War veteran. A nasty wound to the throat. He has the appropriate scar. You're his wife and you'll speak for him. You're there to visit relatives in the Ruhr region, which happens to be their main industrial center. We want you both in and out quickly. He'll make the maps, you'll drive, and talk if you get stopped. You'll drive across the Swiss border. The whole thing shouldn't take more than a day or two. You can stay in a hotel if you have to, in the same room obviously." It reminded her of the night she had just spent with Richard, and now she'd be spending a night at a hotel with a strange man as part of her job. "We have clothes for both of you. The other operative should be here in a few minutes. You leave in an hour. No names please, except those on the passports waiting for you in Zurich. You can turn all your British papers in to the agent who gives you the car. And from the moment you walk out of this office, he doesn't talk. Is that clear? We'll give you a map of the area you'll be traveling to. You can study it once you're in the car. It should take you about eight hours to drive to Essen from Zurich. You live in Berlin, you're a schoolteacher, he was a lawyer before the war. He gets veteran's benefits now. He has a limp as well." She didn't know if that was real or not and didn't ask. "Your suitcase has a false bottom, there's a gun with a silencer in it. You may need it. There's a submachine gun in his."

What he told her made it clear that the mission was dangerous. She had her pistol in a hidden pocket in her purse, and when they left the office, she'd have her commando knife strapped to her upper thigh. She had had that in her purse too when Richard undressed her the night before, along with her pistol, which she always carried now.

When she left the captain's office to change clothes, she passed a tall thin man in the hall. He didn't smile at her, and she noticed that he walked with a limp when he entered the office after her and closed the door.

Marlene told her they would be given deutschmarks in Zurich when they got their passports and travel papers. Alex changed into German clothes again. She wore a drab brown coat, with a matching hat, scuffed shoes with thick heels, and a gray shirt and sweater. The cuffs of the coat were frayed, and it was clear that they weren't people with money. Marlene handed her a wedding ring in the right size and Alex slipped it on her finger, and for an instant she wished it was Richard's, and that she'd had it the night before when they checked into the hotel. The SOE had taken all her measurements and had all her sizes. When Alex was finished dressing, she looked like a schoolteacher, had her blond hair pulled back in a severe bun, wore no makeup and put on glasses. She was still beautiful, but much less noticeably so. She looked plain.

Her partner for the mission joined her ten minutes later. They were Heinrich and Ursula Schmitt. Her nickname was Ushi. She had already memorized the details of their biography. He looked as dreary as she did, in baggy trousers, a heavy gray wool coat, and a battered hat. And like hers, his shoes were scuffed. He carried a cane to go with his limp, and there was a radio transmitter in it. He had paper in a hidden pocket for the map.

They left the office carrying their suitcases. Heinrich, or whatever his real name was, nodded to her, and after that, they took a bus to the airport, and caught their flight to Zurich, a nondescript, badly dressed, and not particularly attractive couple. The unflattering hat, severe hairdo, absence of makeup, and glasses had quashed even Alex's usually striking beauty.

The flight was uneventful, and only a few minutes late. Alex noticed that Heinrich had sketched small drawings in a pocket-sized notebook on the flight, and she wondered if in real life he was an artist. The drawings were very good, of several flowers in detail, and a landscape, all in miniature.

They took a bus at the Zurich airport, and got off at the first stop, walked a quarter of a mile to a restaurant, where the agent was waiting for them with their papers and the car. The whole exchange of British documents for German ones took less than a minute. They got the keys to the old tired German car, and a moment later they took off with Alex driving. She and Heinrich hadn't exchanged a word so far and she knew they weren't supposed to.

She turned to him as they drove off and spoke to him in German, asking if everything was all right. He understood the gist of it, and nodded. They drove on into the night, and stopped at a small inn just after midnight. She explained to the innkeeper that she and her husband needed a room. He showed no interest in them. Alex paid for the room and he handed her a key, and Heinrich limped up the stairs to join her in a room that smelled musty with a narrow bed. The sheets were clean but the rest of the room was dirty. She lay down on the bed with her clothes on, and Heinrich pointed to her and shook his head. If the authorities came into the room to check them, they would find it suspicious that she was fully dressed, no matter how dirty the room was. She nodded, and reluctantly put on her nightgown, and Heinrich changed into pajamas. He wasn't an engaging traveling companion, and had a sour look about him. She could see the scar on his neck, supposed to be a war wound, and didn't know if it was real or not, but it was convincing.

She cautiously got into bed next to him, staying as close to the edge as she could without falling out. And her fellow operative did the same and acted as though she wasn't there. He ignored her completely.

She lay awake for the rest of the night, got up and dressed at six in the morning. At seven they went downstairs and had ersatz sausages for breakfast, and watery fake coffee. The Germans were under severe rationing. They left shortly after, for the drive to the industrial area in the Ruhr region as a light snow began to fall. It was freezing. They drove all day, it took longer due to the weather, and they reached their destination at nightfall, but it was too dark for Heinrich to study the area or make his maps. They checked into another hotel, which was as unappealing as the one the previous night, and were lucky to get a double bed this time. The next morning two soldiers stopped them on the road and checked their papers.

Heinrich had all the documents he needed to prove he was a veteran wounded in the war, and no longer on active duty. The soldier who read his papers nodded, and waved them on, as Alex silently let out a breath and a billow of frost in the cold morning air. After that they drove to a spot at the right angle for him to make his maps. There was no one around, and they were some distance from the factories, and no one stopped them, or inquired what they were doing there. Heinrich had almost finished when a soldier appeared out of nowhere and approached them, as Alex appeared casual but caught her breath. He asked to see what Heinrich was doing, and he handed him a sketchpad with gentle rolling hills and a church steeple, everything they saw in front of them, minus the factories. The map he'd been working on was already in his coat pocket. He handed him his veteran's certificate as well.

The soldier studied the sketchpad for a moment, and then nodded and handed it back to Heinrich, and then studied Alex. He was thinking that she would almost be attractive if they weren't so poor and her clothes weren't so shabby. He could see that she was young, but she had the fatigue of an old woman in her eyes. It occurred to him that being married to a mute invalid couldn't be a pleasant life for her, but he said nothing, and waved them on. Alex thanked him, put the car in gear and drove away. She glanced at Heinrich and asked him in German as simply as she could if he was finished, and he nodded. He had everything they needed. He had memorized the rest. She saw him put the meticulous map inside his hollow cane, and they drove in silence the way they had come, and reached the Swiss border by late that night. Two soldiers came out to check their papers, and Alex explained that they were going to see a doctor in Zurich for her husband's throat. They had permission from the Reich to do so, which she showed them as well, since the army doctors had not been able to help him or repair his vocal cords. The two soldiers stepped away from the car and conferred for a minute, and then nodded, and let them through.

They drove to a house on a back road on the way to Zurich, exchanged their documents for British ones, and the agent followed them to the airport on a bicycle, and took the car from them when they got there an hour later. They walked away without looking back. With their papers were two plane tickets from Zurich to London. They boarded without drawing attention to themselves, put their small suitcases in the overhead rack, with their weapons in them, which fortunately they hadn't had to use, although they were prepared to kill any soldiers who stopped them if they had to. Heinrich's cane disappeared, telescoped into an inside pocket of his coat, and when he disembarked from the plane in London, he no longer limped, and after a trip to the restroom, there was no sign of the scar on his throat. Alex quietly took off her glasses and put them in her pocket, and looked instantly prettier without the heavy frames.

In London, they took a bus into the city, keeping their valises close to them. They got off at the stop nearest Baker Street, and walked the rest of the way, still without a word to each other, and Heinrich walking normally in long strides that Alex had to hurry to keep up with. This time, despite the late hour, Captain Potter was waiting for them, and looked expectantly at Heinrich.

"Well?"

The man Alex only knew as Heinrich handed him the cane. "Done. I got what you wanted." Captain Potter's tense face melted into a broad smile. Alex thought the intensity of his work had aged him. He had none of the appearance of youth, or even his forty years. He had the soul of an old man and the world on his shoulders.

"They're waiting for this at the War Office. Thank you both," Potter said, as both agents visibly relaxed. "No problems?"

"Not really. We got checked by soldiers a couple of times, and the border patrol studied me carefully, but Ursula here put them at ease, saying we were going to see a doctor for my throat. And we had the permission slip for it." He turned to Alex then. "Well done." And then he turned back to Bertram Potter. "The car was crap, by the way. I don't know how she got it that far." He smiled and Alex noticed that he had a deep voice and a heavy Scottish brogue. "She was a fine partner, never slipped or broke the rules once, and her German is perfect. I understand it, but my accent is pure Glasgow, not Berlin." He laughed and Alex smiled at the compliment as Captain Potter saluted him and she realized that her partner outranked the captain. Her fellow agent on the trip was a high-ranking officer in Military Intelligence, and Captain Potter seemed impressed by his praise for her and gave her a warm glance, which was rare for him.

She went to change into her own clothes then, and "Heinrich" was gone when she returned. Their mission had been accomplished. Captain Potter left for the War Office, despite the late hour, and Alex left Baker Street alone, thinking about the past two days, realizing again how differently things might have gone. There was always that feeling that they had escaped the lion's jaws by the skin of their teeth. But they had made it.

She took the bus to the dormitory, and there was no message from Richard when she got there. Once again, she had disappeared without warning or explanation, but she wouldn't have to invent a plausible reason when she spoke to him the next day, since he hadn't called. She was sure he was busy too.

He didn't call the next day either, and at the end of the afternoon, she dialed a number he had given her, for information if anything ever happened to him. She felt a little foolish calling, with no real reason for concern, but he hadn't contacted her in three days, which wasn't like him. His missions were shorter than hers and only lasted a few hours.

She hesitantly asked for information about him, and they told her to wait, which she did, for a long time. It was a full five minutes before the voice at the base came back on the line and told her that Captain Montgomery's plane had been shot down during a mission. He hadn't come back with the others, and there had been no message from him so far. She knew that he carried a small transmitter to send messages if he was on the ground in enemy territory.

"Did anyone see . . . was he . . ." she choked on the words, wanting to know if any of the other pilots had seen him shot and killed.

"That's all we know, madam," the voice said formally. "He's missing in action. He may turn up in a few days or weeks, depending on whether he's injured, or has been captured." He was cut and dry.

"Thank you," she said in a whisper, as terror rose in her throat. Richard's plane had gone down, and he was missing in action, but at least no one had seen him get killed. She just prayed that wherever he was, he would find his way out of enemy territory. He had been shot down over Germany, and he was out there somewhere, dead or dying, maybe gravely injured, or alone. Her hand was shaking as she set down the phone. She had survived her mission, and now Richard was lost. It struck her again how their lives could change in an instant, and hers just had.

She went to her room, which she shared with a dozen other women, and lay down on her bed and sobbed as quietly as she could. Her life wouldn't be worth living without him. She had already lost a brother, and all she could do now was pray she wouldn't lose the only man she had ever loved. Or that he wasn't already dead.

Chapter 6

The six weeks between when Richard was shot down and Christmas were the longest of her life. She tried not to call the base too often, and she finally asked Captain Potter to call the War Office and see what he could find out. He reported that they knew no more than they had already told her. For the moment, Richard was missing in action, and presumed dead. But Alex knew others had survived getting shot down over Germany. Perhaps he'd been captured and sent to a prisoner of war camp, or maybe he had died from his injuries. Others had walked across Germany, and crossed the Swiss border on foot.

She had two more missions in Germany in November, and one in France in early December, pursuing information and documents. She was in a daze each time, and wanted to try to find him herself, but she knew she couldn't get him out alone, without papers, even if she did, especially if he was injured. And she knew trying to do that would be a violation of one of the most stringent rules of the SOE. There were no personal missions. Each time she left Germany, it tore her heart out, knowing that she was leaving him there, either dead or alive. She ached to know which it was, but there was not a single message from him in any form.

Her heart felt like a rock as she took the train to Hampshire at Christmas. She had another shock when she got there. She knew her brother Geoffrey wasn't coming home for Christmas, and hadn't been able to get leave, but she wasn't prepared for how severely her parents had aged since Willie's death in August. Her mother looked ravaged and was suddenly an old woman and her father looked even worse. They cried every time they spoke of Willie and insisted on showing Alex the new marble headstone in their cemetery the moment she arrived. If anything, they seemed more depressed than they had been when it first happened. The reality had finally sunk in that William was never coming back. Her father was running the estate and it had become a burden not a joy. His spirit was broken.

She felt the same way now about Richard. She couldn't tell herself fairy stories anymore, that they would hear from him any day, or he would run, crawl, or walk out of Germany across the Swiss border. It appeared that his categorization as "presumed dead" had been the right assumption. It broke her heart to think it, and there was no one she could talk to about it, since no one knew about them. She grieved in silence and mourned him every day. Alex had given up hope by Christmas, and was trying to face his death as bravely as possible. She was even disappointed when she realized she wasn't pregnant. She would have gladly gone through the shame of an illegitimate child, in order to have his baby, but that wasn't to be either.

She never said a word about him to her parents. There was no point now if he was dead.

The only thing that cheered her were the children from London. It was their second Christmas with them, and it had been a hard year for the Wickhams, after losing William. But the children they were housing always brought a smile to her mother's face, and her father had been trying to teach some of the slightly older boys to play cricket. Her mother had made them all Christmas gifts by then, and once again the government had strongly discouraged the children from going home for Christmas, for fear that their parents wouldn't part with them again after the holidays, and it was safer for them in the country. The parents had been urged not to visit them, or as seldom as possible, so as not to torment the children when they didn't bring them home. And most parents couldn't afford to come anyway. Many of them knew that they were orphans now, with parents who had died in the bombings in London, or fathers who had died in the war.

It was a quiet Christmas for Alex and her parents, without her brothers. Alex's own spirits were dragging with no news of Richard, and the almost certainty now that he was dead after a month and a half behind enemy lines. It was unlikely he had survived.

She tried to cheer up her parents while she was there, but it had been an exhausting holiday, attempting to buoy their spirits without success, and who could blame them. They were disappointed not to see Geoffrey, and constantly worried about him. Alex had spent the whole holiday trying to reassure them about Geoff, and looking for interesting topics of conversation to distract them. She was successful at neither.

She felt defeated on New Year's Day, when she left to go back to London, and they looked as sad as they had when she'd arrived. There were some things you couldn't compensate them for, losing their beloved oldest son was one of them. They loved Alex too, but it was different. All their hopes and the future of the family had rested on William. Alex couldn't imagine them being happy again. Or herself, if

Richard was in fact dead. She was trying to accept it, but everything she thought of that had once delighted her made her sad. She dreaded going back to work after the holidays, and doing another mission in Germany. She hated the Germans with a passion now. She knew her work was not meant to be a personal vendetta but it was becoming that way, after William died and Richard was shot down.

She could only get on a slow train back to London, and remembered that she had met him on a train just like it.

The dormitory was deserted when she got there, the women were either asleep after too much reveling the night before, or they were out with friends. None of them were working that day, and she was grateful she wasn't either.

She put away the clothes she had brought back from Hampshire, and hadn't bothered to pack a pretty dress her mother had given her for Christmas. It had been one of hers. Alex had no one to wear it for now, or to go out with. The last thing she wanted to do was celebrate anything with Richard almost certainly dead.

She lay on her bunk staring at the ceiling. Geoff had said he might come by but he hadn't called her, and she wanted to be left alone anyway. For a week, she had done nothing but try to cheer up her parents, now she just wanted to vegetate for a while and not speak to anyone.

It was almost dinnertime, when one of the girls came home, stuck her head in the door, and spoke to Alex.

"Gentleman downstairs to see you," she said. So Geoff had come to see her after all, Alex thought. She hoped he wasn't coming to tell her the butcher's daughter was pregnant and he was getting married, or already had. It would kill their parents if he did. She went down the stairs, feeling beaten, and opened the door to the visiting room. There was only one person in it. A man with a bandage on his head, a cast on his arm, and leaning on a cane. It took a second for it to register who he was, and then she flew into his arms and nearly knocked him over. It was Richard!

"Oh my God! Oh my God . . . you're alive! I thought you were dead. . . ." she said breathlessly, sobbing as she kissed him and he clutched her to him. He had been missing for seven weeks, and she felt like she was dreaming.

"Take it easy, take it easy," he said, as he let himself down gingerly into a chair. "I'm still a little battered." He pulled her down on his lap and she put her arms around him and kissed him.

"Where were you?"

"Skiing in the Alps," he teased her and looked at her as though he couldn't believe he was there either, and this wasn't a dream. "I went down after we bombed some of the factories." In fact, she hadn't been far from him, she realized, on one of her recent missions. "I got banged up pretty badly and hit my head when I landed. A farmer took me in and hid me under his barn. They brought me in at night or I'd have frozen by morning. They even got a doctor from another village. I had a nasty bump on the head, and didn't know where I was for a few days, and eventually it got better. I broke my arm and my ankle and the doctor set them, but they haven't fully healed yet. The farmer got me to the border, where I stayed with friends of theirs until I got stronger. The doctor did a good job and as soon as my ankle was strong enough, I started walking through the foothills and forests toward Switzerland. They gave me enough basic food supplies to keep me going and I drank melted snow. I didn't think I'd make it, but I had to try." She could see what it had cost him. He looked ten years older. "It took me about a month. I called from Switzerland two days ago, and they came and got me yesterday. I'll be in the hospital for a few days getting checked out, my arm hasn't healed yet, but I wanted to see you. I didn't want to call you. I wanted to surprise you." She was laughing and crying all at once and so was he. It was a miracle that he had survived and had walked so far in the condition he was in. No one had stopped him, or helped him. He hadn't seen another human in a month. He had slept in caves, and lived by his wits and sheer endurance. He told her he had refused to die and all he wanted was to come back to her. It had kept him alive, when he wanted to give up. The food the farmer had given him was enough to nourish him, although he had lost a shocking amount of weight. And his face was dark and leathery from the elements. "I want to go back and see them after the war, to thank them," he said, looking deeply moved. And then he lowered his voice to ask her a question. "Are you pregnant?" She shook her head, visibly disappointed.

"When you were shot down, I hoped I was. Before that, I was terrified I might be. But I wasn't."

"We'll fix that at the appropriate moment. But not just yet. We have a war to win first." He smiled at her.

"When do you go back to active duty?" She was worried, she could see the worn look in his eyes and he could hardly stand up. He leaned heavily on the cane. He said the final days had been the hardest.

"As soon as I can fly a plane. Not long, I suspect." His feet had been numb from the cold. They were all pushing hard, and taking chances. It was the nature of the times they lived in. "I'll have a little time off now. I hope they don't send you driving all over England. Maybe you can come and visit me at the hospital while I'm there." She nodded, the question was more if they were going to send her back to Germany on a mission immediately, which was possible on any given day.

"I will whenever I'm not working," she promised. He spent an hour with her, and then he had to go back to the base. They had given him a car and a young airman as a driver so he could come to see her, since he had no other family. They kissed and talked for a long time. She was drinking in the joy of knowing he was alive and hadn't died when he was shot down.

She helped him into the car, and he went back to the base. She promised to visit him the next day, and prayed they wouldn't send her on a mission. But no one from the SOE called her the day after New Year's. She took a bus out to the air base, and spent hours with Richard after they reset his arm. The ankle had healed correctly, as he said. They told him he couldn't fly for a month until he was stronger and had recovered. A number of the pilots he commanded had come to see him, and were thrilled he was alive. He was the hero of the squadron now.

When Alex returned to her dormitory that night, basking in the joy of having Richard back, there was a message for her. She had to report to Baker Street at noon the next day. She didn't know what she'd tell Richard, but she had to think of something. She thought of asking to be relieved of the mission, but didn't want to do that either. She hadn't refused a single assignment since she'd joined them, and didn't think she should. She was with the SOE to help save her country and win the war. She had to go back to work.

Her assignment the next day, when she went to the SOE office, was to go to Paris to gather information. The German high command there had plans to launch a two pronged attack on England, and Military Intelligence wanted to know more about it. She was the perfect candidate to find out. Once they got her into Paris, they wanted her to attend several parties, hobnob with the wives and mistresses of the

German officers, and meet the officers themselves. They knew that she could play the role to perfection. She was the obvious choice. They were putting a wardrobe together for her, and were going to have her stay at an elegant hotel. Paris was full of beautiful women, many eager to collaborate with the Germans, and Alex was going to be one of them.

"When do I leave?" she asked, unhappy to be obliged to leave Richard so soon after he got back. But she had no official role in his life since she wasn't his wife.

"You leave tomorrow. We're going to parachute you in to an operative just outside Paris. He'll take you the rest of the way." She hadn't been parachuted in before and was nervous about it. What if she got hurt? Or stuck in a tree, and shot down by the Germans. With Richard's miraculous safe return, she didn't want to reenact it herself. "Is there a problem?" Captain Potter looked at her, sensing her reluctance.

"No, none," she said, without a quiver in her voice.

At least she could see Richard that night, and explain to him that she would be gone for a few days. She could tell him she was driving up to Scotland, and it would take her time to get back. They wanted her in Paris for three days, and didn't want her to stay too long. And if something went wrong, she could leave Paris sooner. They wanted to gather as much information as they could, without taking too many risks and losing a good agent. She had become a valuable operative for them, in Germany, and now in France. Her language skills had proven to be as useful as they'd hoped.

She took the bus out to see Richard at the hospital on the base that night, and he was happy to see her. His face lit up when she walked into the room. Nearly his whole squadron had dropped by in the past two days, including some new faces who came to pay their respects to the legendary squadron leader. And he was even more of a hero now after his recent escape, and long trek back.

Alex told him casually that she had a long drive to Scotland and back in the next few days.

"What, they don't have enough rocks in Scotland, they need ours too?" he teased her. He was sorry she had to go, but she'd be back soon, and he wasn't worried about her. He would have been if he had known what she was really going to do.

She left in a small military plane from a tiny airport the next day, so as not to draw attention when they arrived. She carried all her clothes in a heavy pack on her back, but had carried more in training, and wore an airman's flying suit and combat boots to make the jump. She had all the arms she needed, an arsenal of small weapons on her person, her commando knife, a Sten gun in her backpack, her cyanide pill in her pocket, and a wardrobe worthy of any high-ranking SS officer's wife or mistress, including a white mink jacket to wear at night. Their clothing sources had gone all out to find it, and had borrowed it from a British colonel's wife, who happened to be French and had bought it in Paris before the war. They had warned her it might not come back, but was for a good cause, so she had agreed to lend it. Alex had tried it on. It fit perfectly and she loved it.

"Can I get paid in mink this time?" she asked when she saw it, and Captain Potter laughed. What she was paid in cash monthly wouldn't have covered any of the wardrobe. They kept the pay of the SOE workers modest, so as not to arouse suspicion with a noticeable influx of funds.

"The person who lent it to us wants it back. So you'd better come back in one piece, with the mink," the captain teased her. He had grown to like and respect her. She was brave and there was nothing she wouldn't do for them.

"I'm going to love being a collaborator. They're so well-dressed," she joked as she preened, still wearing the jacket. Her mother had a black one like it from before the war. But the white one was more stylish.

"Apparently," he said and moved on to the more serious aspects of the mission, and gave her a list of all the information they wanted. They expected it to take several days. And when she was ready, they would get her out, using the same agent outside Paris to help her escape. They were going to pick her up by plane, it was risky on the ground, but they trusted their agents, and flying her in and out was faster, once they cleared the range of the anti-aircraft guns in the area. Alex was well aware of the risks. In some ways, it was more dangerous than what she'd done in Germany so far, but a lot more exciting. She loved the role she had to play and felt like Mata Hari, or a very glamorous modern-day spy.

When the plane lifted off the ground carrying Alex toward France, she was tense as she thought about her mission and how to accomplish it. The weather and visibility were poor, which gave them a certain amount of cover. And it didn't take them long to reach the countryside near Paris. They knew precisely where their agent was expecting them to drop her, and at the exact moment, the co-pilot of the plane slid open the door as they lost altitude as far as they dared, and he told her to jump.

"Shit!" was the last thing she said in English. She hadn't done a parachute jump since her training and it had terrified her then as it did now. She dropped the short distance into a clump of trees, and within minutes her parachute had caught on a tree branch, and she was dangling like a paper doll and being buffeted by the wind. It was how many of their operatives in other places had gotten shot, and Alex knew how important it was to get down quickly.

"Allo?" She heard a whispered voice just below here. "Pompadour?" It was her code name for the mission, after Madame de Pompadour, the courtesan.

"Oui," she responded affirmatively. "I'm caught." They were speaking French, and like her missions in German, there would be no English. Her French documents said she was born in Lyon and had previously lived in Paris, in the sixteenth arrondissement, one of the chicest neighborhoods. She was allegedly a young widow, living in the South of France now.

"I'll come up and get you," he said, but Alex was faster, she slid her commando knife out of her sleeve and removed it from its sheath, shimmied up the tree, holding fast with one arm, like a monkey, and started cutting the cords of the parachute with the razor sharp blade. She was down to the last cord in seconds and looked below her. All she could see was a shadowy form in the darkness.

"Catch me!" she said as she cut the last cord. The operative caught her, and they both fell onto the grass unharmed. "We have to get the parachute," she said quickly, as they both shimmied back up the tree, pulled it down toward them, rolled it into a tight ball, and took it with them. He led her through some bushes moving quickly, and they traveled a considerable distance on foot until she saw a farmhouse. All the lights were out, but she knew there was a Resistance cell based there, and they were meeting there tonight. The local agents were expecting her and knew she would be going to Paris in the morning.

There was a car in the barn waiting for her, which had been stolen for the occasion, and had the license plates changed. Alex would be entering Paris in style.

She followed the operative to the farmhouse, and he led her through a door in the kitchen floor down to a cellar where she would spend the night. He went back upstairs then and moved a rug and table into place over it. He hoped there wouldn't be too many rats down there tonight. He had left her something to eat and a bottle of wine, and heard no sound from below until he went to bed, and he led Alex back up in the morning at the first light of day.

"Thank you for the wine, I slept like a rock." She smiled at him.

"No rats?" He grinned at her.

"Oh God, don't tell me now." He was about her age, slight, in a heavy black sweater and baggy dark blue pants, and he lit a cigarette and put it between his lips and then offered her a cup of coffee, the evil brew that was all they could get in England now too. She declined it. She had gotten out of the flight suit the night before, and left it in the cellar with the parachute. She was carrying a backpack, and still wearing the combat boots with military trousers and a heavy sweater. It was freezing and there was no heat in the farmhouse.

An old woman came out to the kitchen shortly after. He said that she was his grandmother, and that they shared the house with his brother, who had gone to Brittany. He said his parents had died before the war, and only he and his brother and grandmother were left. His grandmother poured herself a cup of the nearly undrinkable coffee and went back to her room shortly after. She took no interest in what they were doing, and had probably seen worse things happening before. This was one of the most important cells of the Resistance outside Paris.

"Can I see the car?" Alex asked him. His code name was Brouillard, Fog, because he was able to disappear so quickly. He led her into the barn then, and slid open the door with a grin. There stood an impeccable, astoundingly beautiful, shiny black Duesenberg in mint condition. "Oh my God, where did you get it?" Alex was stunned.

"We stole it," he said proudly. "In Nice, last week. It belongs to an American. He left it here before the war. I suppose he'll come back for it someday. We borrowed it in the meantime. My brother knew about it. He worked for him one summer. We're going to have one of the boys in the area drive you. He has a clean record. You can't use any of us for that."

"Does he know how to drive it?" It was a spectacular machine, for her triumphant entry into Paris.

"We taught him. He's not so smooth, but he's learning." She laughed at what he said. The plan Military Intelligence had concocted was that she was to make a splashy entrance, dazzle all the men who saw her, find out everything she could from members of the high command, and make a rapid exit before anyone exposed her. It was a daring plan, and Alex liked it. It was going to be very different from her German missions, and hopefully successful. In some ways, the bolder the better. Who would suspect her of trying to hide anything in a car like that?

Brouillard told her she had a suite reserved at an excellent, discreet small hotel. Several of the mistresses of German officers lived there. Le Meurice had been taken over as headquarters by the Germans. The Ritz was only for officers of high rank, and the only civilian who stayed there was Gabrielle Chanel, the designer, a known collaborator. The smaller hotel would suit them. Alex had to get dressed then and Brouillard told her to use his bedroom, upstairs. She took her heavy backpack up with her, and emerged twenty minutes later like Cinderella, transformed. She wore an exquisitely cut navy blue Dior suit which showed off her figure with an elegant dark blue fur hat, high-heeled black shoes with silk stockings, and an alligator bag. She was wearing long navy blue suede gloves, and diamond earrings that weren't real but looked it. The rest of what she had was in the backpack, and Brouillard had managed to find two white alligator suitcases which she packed with her wardrobe, and he put in the trunk of the car.

Alex had done her makeup to perfection, with bright red lipstick, and she looked dazzling, as the young boy Brouillard had enlisted appeared in a black suit, and a chauffeur's cap they'd found in the car. Alex looked like a movie star as they drove the car out of the barn, and she got in, ready for her triumphant arrival in Paris. It was a daring plan, but no one would suspect her of hiding anything. She was having fun as she thanked Brouillard and they took off for Paris, with an occasional bump and grind of the gears, as she told her neophyte chauffeur how to drive it. She would have driven it herself, but that would have aroused suspicions.

They sailed right into Paris through the Porte Dauphine, drove around the Place de la Concorde with the Arc de Triomphe in plain view, and then through the Place Vendôme to her hotel on the rue Cambon, right behind the Ritz and next to Chanel. There were several beautiful, elegant young women in the lobby chatting with each other, and they watched Alex with interest as she checked in. She looked like one of them, but they didn't know her, which intrigued them.

Alex went to Chanel, Dior, and Cartier that afternoon and looked around, while salespeople scurried to serve her, but she bought nothing. The name on her papers was Mme. Florence de Lafayette, and one of their best forgers had done them. They were flawless. And then she went back to the hotel to rest and change. They had forged an invitation to a very grand party that night and she planned to make an entrance. She languished in the bath for half an hour, and put on a white evening gown that fit her like a second skin, with the white mink jacket, and a big diamond ring that was another fake but would fool anyone who saw it on her finger. Florence de Lafayette was easily one of the most beautiful women in the room when she entered the ballroom where the party was being held. It was in honor of Hermann Goering, who was visiting Paris, and considered himself a connoisseur of all fine things, particularly women and art. Every important general was there, mostly with their mistresses, or on the hunt for a new one. "Florence" stood gazing at the scene from the top of a grand staircase that led into the ballroom, and two men approached her almost the moment she walked in. One was a general recently arrived from Berlin, the other was a colonel based in Paris whose name she was familiar with. Both were important men.

The colonel was the first to offer her his arm down the grand staircase. He was a strikingly handsome man in his early forties, very tall, and as blond and blue-eyed as Alex. He never left her side, handed her a glass of champagne, and invited her to dance as soon as the music started. She circled the dance floor gracefully with him as he looked bewitched by her, and she silently thanked her governesses for the endless dancing lessons she had hated, which had finally paid off. The general cut in very quickly. He was portly and much older. Both men spent the evening courting her and vying for her attention as she teased them both and flirted with them shamelessly.

The general invited her to lunch with him the next day at Le Meurice, and said he had a marvelous chef he had stolen from the Ritz.

And the colonel invited her to dinner at La Tour d'Argent the following night and to another party afterward. All eyes were on Alex for most of the night. She looked stunning, and was breathtakingly smooth in her performance, as a woman seeking a new lover from among the high command. Her intentions were plain, the outcome, whom she would choose, not yet sure. At one o'clock, she smiled enticingly at the colonel, whispered that she would see him the next day, and disappeared back to her hotel in the stolen Duesenberg with the farm boy at the wheel. The plan was unfolding just as she and her superiors wanted. Already that night, she had gleaned some interesting information, and made notes in code, which she put in the lining of the suitcase, where her Sten gun was too, for emergencies. She had her tiny pistol inside one thigh, and her commando knife attached to the other. These were dangerous men she was playing with, and she knew it. They could turn on her in an instant, and might before the charade was over.

Lunch with the general the next day at Le Meurice was elegant and informative. She titillated him with funny stories and teased him, while pretending not to care about anything serious. He bragged about some of their plans for Paris, and how soon they would be in London, after they crushed the English. He tried to kiss her and she wouldn't let him. When she got back to her own hotel, her room was filled with flowers from both her suitors, and a third one she hadn't noticed. When the colonel arrived to pick her up for dinner, she was wearing a very daring silver gown with almost no back and he looked incredibly handsome in his uniform, he bowed and clicked his heels as he kissed Alex's hand, and handed her a box from Van Cleef & Arpels with a diamond bracelet in it. This was serious business. He was playing for high stakes, and so was she. He was far more discreet than the general and not quite so liberal with information, and he made it clear to her by the end of the evening that he would be honored if she would decide to become his companion on a regular basis, and of course the SS would provide her with an apartment. He said they had commandeered several truly beautiful ones, and she could choose among them. He complimented her on the Duesenberg and said that she was obviously a woman with exquisite taste who deserved only the finest things. She told him how bored she had been in Paris after her husband died, and she had been living in Cap d'Antibes more recently, and felt that the time was ripe to come back to Paris. She didn't give him an answer about the apartment, but she was exquisitely seductive, and he was completely under her spell, and wise enough not to be crude about it. He didn't force her hand or rush her, which the general would have.

They talked more seriously about the war at the end of the evening, and she shared with him that she had read all of Adolf Hitler's writings, which was true because she thought him a madman, but she didn't say that, and she praised Gabrielle Chanel's impeccable talent, taste, and courage, to let him know that she approved of collaborators. He got the message clearly, and kissed her lightly on the lips when he dropped her off at her hotel. More than that would have panicked her, but so far it was all manageable, and she was having fun, taunting and teasing them, and gathering more information than they realized. While they protected their major secrets, which British Military Intelligence knew from breaking their codes, she was pulling miles and miles of smaller secrets from them, like a clown pulling silk scarves from his sleeve, or taking coins from someone's ear. She knew she was playing a dangerous game, but it was addictive.

She got more flowers the next day, and she didn't know what to do about the diamond bracelet. She would insult the colonel profoundly if she refused to accept it, particularly if she wanted him to think she was open to being his mistress, but she could hardly keep it and return to England with spoils of war of that value. She herself was the trophy the colonel wanted, as did the general, but he was a less ardent and convincing suitor. Alex actually enjoyed the colonel's company, and their intelligent conversations. She felt like a courtesan in the days of Louis XIV, playing with palace intrigues.

The plum she had come for fell into her lap that night, when the colonel decided that treating her as his established mistress would convince her to accept his offer, and he shared some of the more intimate details of his job with her, including the bombings he knew were planned for Europe in the coming months, and that they were planning to plunder France before they left it, which was why Hermann Goering was there. He had already shipped several trainloads of France's greatest art treasures to Berlin, and he was here for more. They were going to empty the Louvre eventually and give its contents to Hitler, although he was less of an art enthusiast than Goering. The Führer wanted power and control over all of Europe. Goering wanted their art. It was a lethal combination and made Alex's blood boil to hear it. France was already in their clutches, and they wanted to strip her to the bone. It took all her self-control not to react, and simply listen, and he trusted her enough to brag to her about future bombing missions. He respected her discretion and intelligence, and in real life, he wasn't wrong. But this wasn't real to her, it was a game.

Alex was wearing a black satin gown that night, held by a tiny string of rhinestones to her neck, and he warned her that with a single tiny tug on the string, he could leave her standing naked in the nightclub where they were dancing, and had been talking for hours, while drinking champagne. She drank far less than he did.

"Why would you want to have me stand naked here?" she said innocently, as he looked as though he might grab her, he could no longer resist her tantalizing charms and teasing.

"Because I would like to see you naked, my dear. And I don't want to wait much longer." He was normally not a patient man and was used to taking what he wanted. She was making him work for it.

"You won't have to," she said softly.

"Tonight?" He looked as though he were going to eat her alive as his eyes lit up, and she could sense how dangerous he could be. She was playing with fire and she knew it, and she already had all the information the SOE wanted, and more. Now she was just taunting the lion to see how far she could go. And he was a dangerous predator.

"It's not the right time," she said shyly, and he nodded.

"I understand. I've acquired a very beautiful boat in the South of France, in Cannes. Would you like to join me on it? We could pick your apartment when we come back. I have just the right one in mind. It's a smaller Versailles, with its own ballroom. It would suit you. Should we go to my boat in a few days?" he said, running a finger slowly up her arm, and barely brushing past her breast as he gazed into her eyes.

"I'd like that very much," she whispered.

"We'll fly to Nice on Friday, and spend a few days on the boat."

"How did you get it?" She couldn't resist asking him, looking young and innocent.

"Ah . . . we have our ways, you know. . . . Its owners had to go away, and left everything behind. I'm very fond of the sea. The boat was given to me. It's quite marvelous, with a crew of twenty-three." She could perfectly imagine how he had gotten it, and the thought of it turned her stomach. There was no doubt in her mind now. It was time to go. She had all she needed, and the game was too dangerous. It was time for Cinderella to leave the ball.

They went on talking for a while longer, and she smiled at him and said she was tired. She said she had fittings at Dior the next morning. Many of the women of the officers of the high command bought their gowns there.

"Next time I will come with you, and I will pick what I would like to see you wear." She nodded as though she was touched and pleased. And he kissed her lightly on the lips when he left her. She had also gleaned from him that night that he had a wife and five children in Munich, which didn't seem to slow him down in Paris. They were a special breed of men, conquerors to their cores, of women and priceless objects and art. They had to possess it all. "I can't wait until the boat on Friday," he said, barely able to contain himself as she drifted into the hotel with a smile and a wave.

As soon as she got to her room, she started packing her gowns and the white mink jacket. She had had everything she needed, her wardrobe had been perfect, and she wore it well. She left out one chic black suit to wear as she left the hotel the next day, allegedly for her fittings at Dior. After she packed, she wrote down all the information again, in code, and put it in the suitcase Brouillard had gotten her with the tricky lining, which suited her purposes.

She settled her hotel bill the next morning at nine o'clock, before anyone was up, and the lobby was empty. She left a handsome tip for the maid, and got in the car ten minutes later with all her belongings and the farm boy at the wheel. She asked the concierge not to let anyone know she had left until that night and slipped him an enormous tip. He said he understood, and she was sure he didn't. He had no idea who he was dealing with.

She arrived at Brouillard's house before ten in the morning in her fancy suit, and he told the boy to put the car in the barn. She gave Brouillard a coded message to send, which meant to pick her up that night, and she smiled at him.

"Time to go."

"It went well?" She had been in Paris for three days.

"Yes, but I don't want to push my luck." The ruse had worked, but you had to know when to stop.

She put her belongings in the backpack, and the coded information in a pouch on her body, and had the boy put the empty alligator luggage in the Duesenberg. She changed into her flight suit and combat boots, and waited in the cellar all day. Brouillard had gone to another farm to send the coded message and came back with the response which she decoded and nodded at him.

"Nine o'clock pickup."

"We'll be ready," he assured her. Four or five of his operatives would have to shine torches to guide the plane in, and she'd be ready to run for it from the tree line. The mission wasn't over until she was back in London, and they weren't there yet, by any means. She handed him the box from Van Cleef then with a piece of notepaper from the hotel.

"Do you have a courier who can get this back to Le Meurice tomorrow after I'm gone, without causing your man any trouble? I'm returning something to a colonel there."

"We'll manage it," he said, looking unconcerned. She wasn't sure if it was bravado or real, but she handed it to him. The note said simply,

"It turns out that I'm just a small town girl after all. I'm going back to the provinces, where I belong. Thank you for a wonderful time! Florence." It was the elegant ladylike thing to do, no matter that he was a German and an SS officer, and they were enemies. She wasn't going to steal a diamond bracelet to prove a point, and God only knew who it belonged to and how he had gotten it. She addressed the package to Colonel Klaus von Meissen, and knew she would remember him. She could have been a highly paid mistress if she chose. The thought made her smile. It was a story to tell her grandchildren one day.

It was a long day waiting in the cellar, and finally at eight-thirty that night, they went out to the clearing in the trees where the plane would come in. They had their torches ready for when they heard the plane. Four of his friends had come, and Alex had her heavy backpack on. It was cold that night and they were all shivering, and she suddenly wondered if Klaus knew yet that she was gone. They were supposed to have dinner that night, and she had begged off lunch with the general. It had been an extraordinarily odd few days compared to her real life, and in sharp contrast to the agonies of war that she saw every day.

They heard the plane coming, as Brouillard's collaborators lit their torches, and just as they did, powerful arms reached out and grabbed Alex and pulled her backward with a hand over her mouth, and Brouillard saw it happen. A German soldier had snuck up on them and had been watching from the bushes. Alex struggled for an instant, and would have grabbed him, but the backpack was in her way. The young soldier pulled his gun from his holster as the plane approached. With no warning that anything was wrong, and with a flick of her wrist, Alex slipped her commando knife out of her sleeve and unsheathed it, and without hesitating, she plunged it backward into the German's stomach. He gave a gasp, dropped his gun, looking wild-eyed. Brouillard realized what had happened, and what she'd done, as the soldier fell to the ground dead.

"I'm really sorry," she said to Brouillard, cleaning the blade on the grass, and sheathing it again, as she slipped it in her sleeve. "Now what are you going to do?" She hated to leave him with a German corpse to dispose of, as a souvenir of her visit.

"Don't worry, one Boche more or less. We'll take care of it. They won't find him. He'll just disappear." The plane landed as he said it, and she had to run. "You're quite a woman." He smiled at her. "Can you do that in an evening gown and high heels?"

"I've never tried, but I'm sure I could. Thank you. Take care of yourself. Are you going to keep the car?"

"For a while." She laughed in answer, waved, and ran for the plane, before other soldiers discovered them with their torches. They turned them off as an airman pulled her in, and she fell onto the floor of the plane as he closed the door. They were already racing through the clearing and lifted off a minute later. There was no sound of gunfire. The young soldier had been alone. The plane gained altitude and headed toward London, in the cold French night and a sky full of stars. It had been a heady experience and a strange few days. It was the first time any man had given her a diamond bracelet, and the first time she had killed anyone. And in her current line of work, possibly not the last. The soldier had been young, but he was her enemy, and she felt no guilt at all.

Chapter 7

Richard got a pass from the hospital, and he and Alex had dinner two days after she got back from Paris, and he asked her what she'd been doing since he last saw her.

"The usual," she said, smiling at him. Captain Potter had been very pleased with the results of the Paris trip. "Just driving rocks around."

"Why is it that I sometimes get the feeling you do a lot more than that, and don't tell me?" But so did he. They all had to be secretive.

"Oh, sure," she countered with a grin, "like spending a few days in Paris, having fittings at Dior and ordering new clothes, going to parties, wearing ball gowns, dancing with handsome officers, getting diamond bracelets from my admirers." She had summed up the Paris mission perfectly, and he laughed when she said it.

"All right, all right. I wasn't suggesting anything that extreme. I just think they ought to use your talents better than they do. We need lorry drivers, but you're capable of so much more than that."

"I'm glad you think so. At least I'm not stuck in Hampshire, knitting. I'll take driving rocks over that any day."

"There must be something in between."

"Maybe so," she said, and they moved on to other subjects. He was being released from the hospital earlier than they thought originally. He was healthy and young, in spite of his long trek, and he had arranged to borrow a small apartment from a friend so they could spend another night together. The opportunities to do so were few and far between. One of them was always working, and he flew night missions most of the time. She had her unaccountable absences to cover for. She wondered at times if he was suspicious, but he didn't seem to be.

The air strikes Colonel Klaus van Meissen had boasted to her about when she was in Paris turned out to be real. Thanks to her, they were forewarned, so much better prepared for them. Her superiors at the SOE were amazed by how much information she'd come back with. The air strikes continued while London took a beating, and the RAF retaliated. There were constant bombing missions, and Alex knew Geoff went on many of them. He seemed stressed and tired whenever she saw him. The war was wearing everyone down. It had gone on for eighteen months when she got a call at the dormitory from her mother, and luckily she wasn't away on a mission. Her mother could barely speak she was so hysterical, and it took Alex fully five minutes to understand that the War Office had sent someone to tell them that Geoff had been killed on one of their bombing raids over Germany.

The news hit Alex like a bomb too. Both of her brothers were dead now. And she and Geoff had always been so close. William had been more standoffish and responsible, the perfect big brother. Geoff had been her best friend and partner in crime when they were younger.

She couldn't imagine life without him. She requested an immediate leave from the SOE, and told Captain Potter about her brother. He was deeply sympathetic and very kind to her, as she sat and cried in his office. He had grown very fond of her. So far, she had been an exceptional agent and she had earned his respect.

"You know, you have the opportunity to opt out now, honorably," he said quietly. "As the last surviving child in your family, you don't need to do dangerous missions for the SOE anymore. It would be a tremendous hardship for your parents if something should happen to you too. Maybe you need to think about that, and decide what you want to do. I know your parents aren't aware that you're working for intelligence now. But you know it. Maybe you need to work in a factory or something more suitable than going on sabotage missions in enemy territory where your life is at stake. Think about it, Alex." She had confessed to Captain Potter about killing the German soldier when she left France in January, and he had been calm and understanding about it. He said that the first time you took someone's life, it was a shock. But he pointed out that if she hadn't, he would have shot five people in the Resistance cell that was helping her, and he would have shot her. She had had no other choice except to use her commando knife on him. "And even if you'd left him unconscious and still alive, he would have reported them to the authorities as soon as you left."

"I know. I knew it was the only thing to do. I just wanted you to know I did it. It was a strange feeling. I thought I should feel guilty, but I didn't."

"That's why you're a good agent. You know what you have to do, and you do it, whatever it takes. We've all done something like it at some point. It goes with the kind of work we do. Sometimes we have to kill people to save ourselves or others. It's part of the nature of war. And then we have to make our peace with it and leave it behind us." He wasn't unfeeling about it, but he was matter-of-fact and reasonable, which set the tone for her too. He was her role model, and she knew she didn't want to give up SOE work now because Geoff had died. The Germans had killed both her brothers, and she also knew that what Captain Potter said about her parents was true. It would kill them if something happened to her too. And she couldn't tell them and ask their advice, or even Richard's. She could tell no one about her work in espionage. It was one of the conditions of her job. She had sworn to twenty years of silence about her wartime experience and the SOE.

She took a two-week leave to be with her parents in Hampshire, left a message for Richard, and left that afternoon, feeling dazed. Once she was home, she no longer felt like an espionage agent. In the setting where they grew up, she was a girl who had lost both her brothers.

Her parents were even more devastated now than they had been at Christmas, mourning only William. They had lost two sons, and looked destroyed. They had another funeral without a body or a casket to bury. The whole county came to the simple service they arranged for their second son, and Alex did all she could to help her mother. She wondered if the twenty children from London were too much for her now, but Alex also thought they cheered her up. She tried to talk to her father about all of it a few days after the funeral, when they were out walking together.

"Do you want me to come home, Papa?" she offered bravely.

"And what would you do here?" he said, smiling sadly at his daughter, his last remaining child. This wasn't how he had expected his family to turn out, with both of their sons gone, and Alex living in London. It was a high price of war for them all. "You've led a bigger life now. Could you really come back here and sit knitting with your mother night after night? There are no able bodied young men left in the county. They're all at war. You'd be alone with us, and you'd be unhappy, Alex. We miss you terribly, but it would be selfish of us to expect you to come home." Her eyes filled with tears at the thought of how generous he was, and he was right. She would have hated coming home now. Maybe after the war, but even then it would be hard. And for now there was nothing to come home to except her parents. It wasn't a life for a girl her age, and her father knew it too. She was twenty-four years old, and Hampshire would be a tomb for her. Her childhood home was all about loss now, not action, where she knew she was truly making a difference for the war effort.

She decided to broach another subject with him then, she wasn't sure if the timing was right, but she had been putting it off for months.

"There's someone I'd like you to meet sometime, Papa. A friend in London. Maybe he could come down and visit sometime." It was the first time she had mentioned Richard to them.

"A young man?" He searched her eyes and she nodded. "Is he important to you?"

"Yes, he is."

"Then we should meet him. What do you know about him?" It was a good question, and her father wanted to know. He thought Alex was inexperienced in the ways of the world and about men. Geoff had thought so too.

"He loves to fly planes and has since he was a little boy." She smiled at her father. "He's gentle and kind and intelligent. He went to boarding school in Scotland, and Cambridge after. He's afraid you won't like him because his background isn't quite as . . ." she searched for the right word, "social as ours. He thinks that because I made my debut at Queen Charlotte's Ball, and was presented at court, you won't think he's good enough for me. His father was a gentleman farmer, but I think it was quite a small farm."

"Do *you* care if he's less aristocratic than we are?"

"No, I don't," she said. "I love him. He's good to me, and he would take good care of me."

"Do you want to marry him?" Her father looked surprised. He didn't think she was that serious about anyone. They'd heard nothing about him.

"Not now, during the war. We both want the war to be over before we think about it. Everything is too insecure now. It colors everything."

"Yes, it does," he agreed with her, thinking of his sons. Their family was altered forever without them. "That's wise of you. This war is going to change everything after it's over. The last one did too. The Great War shook up the whole social order of the British aristocracy, and destroyed the economy. But this war has thrown people together who would never have met before. There's very little left of the old ways, and maybe there will be nothing at all left of it once the war is over. People used to marry within their acquaintanceship, they married the people they grew up with, they stayed in their counties, and married the sons and daughters of their parents' friends. Now so many of the young men will be gone after the war, and you meet many more different kinds of people than you would have if the war had never happened. The son of a gentleman farmer doesn't sound so bad to me now. Twenty years ago, I wouldn't have liked it.

But now? What's left? Nothing of the old order and the old rules. I'd like to meet your young man. Tell him he's welcome here whenever you come home, if he can get leave." Edward was intelligent about it and knew there was no fighting change, and he wanted her to be happy.

"Thank you, Papa," she said, grateful for his open mind. "Do you think Mama will feel that way too? I know she wanted me to get married when I came out, and she'd like me to have a title. But I never met anyone I fell in love with. And I don't care about a title."

"And you're really in love with this young man?" He still looked startled since it was the first he'd heard of it.

"I am," she said quietly.

"Then we should meet him soon. He'll think we're savages if I don't meet the man my daughter is in love with. What command is he with? He's RAF, I assume, if he likes to fly."

"He's the commander of a fighter squadron in the RAF."

Her father shook his head. "Tell him to try to stay alive till the end of the war. We've had enough heartbreak in this family, we don't need more. And I think your mother will understand too. She would have loved to see you married to an earl or a duke. But a good man is all you need. You don't need a title," he looked at the land around him, "and one day all this will be yours. You'll inherit everything," he said sadly, because it meant that both of his sons were gone, but he loved her too. "Does he like the land?"

"I think so, Papa. I'm not sure. He likes the skies and everything in them."

"Maybe he'll come to love the land too," he said hopefully as they walked back to the house, quiet and lost in thought. He was thinking of William and Geoff and how different things might be if they were alive.

It was a peaceful visit although a sad one, and they were sorry to see her go back to London after two weeks. She hadn't solved her dilemma about the SOE, if it was too unkind to her parents to continue working for them and risking her life. But she could be killed in a bombing raid in her dormitory in London too. No one and no location was entirely safe anymore.

She was still wrestling with her conscience about what she should do about the SOE when she got a call from Captain Potter himself, at her dormitory. She was in her room at the time and she came downstairs to talk to him on the phone in the hall.

"Have you made a decision yet?"

"I haven't," she said. "I want to keep on with it. But you're right too, if something happens to me, it might kill my parents. Losing my second brother just now has been very hard on them, on all of us," she admitted.

"I'm going to make it even harder for you, I'm afraid," he said. He felt bad for her but he needed her. Alex had become one of their best operatives and they had a dicey situation on their hands. "Whatever you choose in the end, I need you for a big mission in a few days. Could you come in and talk to me about it tomorrow?" He wouldn't discuss it on the phone and she didn't expect him to.

She met with him the next day in his office, and he told her what it was about. They wanted reconnaissance information on a munitions factory in Germany. He knew how precise she was, and how diligent. She didn't need a partner but if something went wrong, she could easily be trapped in Germany, and killed or sent to a prison camp, the former being more likely. It was a cruel thing to ask her to do on the heels of her brother's death. Bertram Potter was willing to respect whatever she wanted to do. But the war wouldn't wait. She had never turned down a mission, and he needed her more than ever. This assignment would require split-second precision, or she wouldn't get out. They wanted her to transmit some critical information and then they were going to blow up the munitions factory immediately. They were going to airlift her in, as they had in France. And this was no genteel mission. This was hardcore, and she knew it as he described it to her. But he had no one else right for the job. He trusted her completely.

"Can I think about it tonight?" she asked him.

"Yes, and I'll respect whatever you decide. If you don't want to do it, I won't push you, and we'll get someone else, though maybe not someone as good." She never failed. He smiled at her. She had turned into someone he could rely on. He hoped she'd agree to do the job. "Maybe you can retire after this one."

"I probably won't want to," she said seriously. "This kind of work becomes an addiction. I think I might already be hooked." But this wasn't going to be the kind of fun she had in Paris, toying with the enemy, enjoying every minute of it, and going to parties in glamorous gowns. This would be using her wits from the moment she hit the ground. She told Captain Potter she would call him in the morning. She wanted to sleep on it.

She was supposed to have dinner with Richard that night and she was relieved when he had to cancel. Two of his pilots were sick and he was going to fly a mission himself that he hadn't planned to. She wanted time to think.

She was awake most of the night and called Captain Potter in the morning.

"I'll do it," she said simply. "When do I leave?"

"In two days, on Friday. I need you to come in and be briefed all day tomorrow. We're getting our directions directly from the prime minister and the War Office." It was a very big deal and she had to tell Richard that she couldn't see him for the next few days. She said she was going back to Scotland.

All she really knew was that she was going to parachute into Germany and they estimated that she'd be there for five days, and then she had to get out. It was the kind of mission people often didn't return from. She knew she had to, for her parents' sake, if nothing else. And she didn't feel she could turn Captain Potter, or her country, down. She had to do this, even if she retired afterward.

She spent all of the next day in briefings, and particularly studied the list of requests from the War Office. She saw a memo from the prime minister himself. This was no small mission. It was huge. And it was an honor that they wanted her to do it.

She had dinner with Richard the night before she left. She was leaving early the next morning and she told him she couldn't go to a hotel with him, but she would when she got back, and she wanted to plan a trip to Hampshire with him when they both had leave. He was touched that she had spoken to her parents about him, and thought it was a good sign. She had said that her father was aware that the world was changing and didn't hold it against Richard that he didn't have a title, which was something of a relief.

"Will you be all right going to Scotland tomorrow?" he asked her gently. "You seem tense." He always noticed her every little mood and nuance and paid close attention to it.

"I probably am," she said casually. "You know how the roads are. They're a mess all the way up there and back."

"I wish I thought it was just the roads you're worried about. But whatever it is, just take care of yourself. Your parents and I need you." She nodded and said very little that night. She couldn't. She had too much on her mind. She had forged papers, would be switching between three passports, travel documents that were also forgeries, maps to learn, signals to send and decode, sabotage if possible. It was a massive assignment, and a very delicate one.

She hit the ground running, literally, when she parachuted in the next day. Everything went smoothly, and she met her first contact in the place she was meant to, and got the documents she needed. She was going to be spending all five days in the vicinity of the munitions factory and she didn't want to be recognized, or become a familiar face either, which would be dangerous for her then and in future.

She slept with her Sten gun under her pillow at the hotel, and carried her pistol in her pocket at all times. She had her commando knife on her, and was on the alert day and night. She slept little, and sent encoded messages through couriers a local agent sent her. This was a highly coordinated combined effort, and by the fourth day, she had gathered all the information they needed in the war room. She was to be airlifted out the next day.

That night a bomb exploded at the munitions factory, placed there by a random group trying to sabotage the factory, and all hell broke loose. She contacted London through a local operative and asked what they wanted her to do. They told her to leave anyway. They had all their own sabotage mechanisms in place, and felt that their operation could go forward. They didn't care that someone else had planted a bomb too. But it had drawn countless German troops to the area and heightened vigilance.

She went to the meeting place for the plane that was due to pick her up. She was precisely on time, and heard the engines purring in the distance, and when the plane got close enough to land, an anti-aircraft gun behind her ripped through it, the plane crashed, and the pilot and gunner were killed. She disappeared into the brush and headed for some distant hills before going back to her contact. The Germans didn't find her, but she had no idea how to get out and back to England now. She had valid though forged German travel documents so she could move around Germany, but she was going to need to make an exchange for a British passport to get back into England. And she couldn't walk home. It was too dangerous to go back to the local operatives after the explosion. The Germans would be covering every inch of the area for the saboteurs who had done it.

She hid in the hills and waited until the munitions factory exploded on schedule the next day. It was blown to smithereens, and the result of Alex's work was complete, but escaping didn't seem possible for the moment. She was stuck hiding in the forest. She retreated into the hills for four days after the explosion, and took refuge in a cave with some supplies she had with her, which sustained her. She sat up the entire time listening and trying to stay awake and be alert. And then she made her way back into town and contacted one of their operatives using a drop and a code. He was stunned that she was still there. They arranged for a plane to pick her up that night, and that time it worked without a problem. The Germans were searching the area, and she had to hide right up until the time she left at ten o'clock that night. Alex had been gone for nine days instead of five, and they had been tense ones. But she had cleverly avoided being captured by the Germans.

She reported to the SOE office on Baker Street when she got back to London, and Captain Potter was waiting for her to congratulate her on an extraordinarily successful mission. She had had a lot of time to think while hiding in the hills, about what she wanted to do.

"Are you going to retire now?" he asked quietly. He hoped she wouldn't. Her calm sangfroid under pressure was of great value to the SOE.

"No," she said with a sigh. "I suppose I'm in forever. What do spies do when they get old?" She was beginning to wonder.

"They keep spying until they can't remember who's on what team anymore. Some operatives stay in forever. I probably will," he said, smiling at her, grateful that she was staying. She had accomplished her mission with infinite precision.

"Maybe I will too. Anyway, I'm going to bed now. At least I didn't kill anyone this time." But they both knew something like it would happen again one day. It was the nature of their work, along with ingenuity and courage. And she had plenty of both.

"So how was Scotland?" Richard asked her when she saw him for dinner the next day. She looked more rested after a good night's sleep. There was no visible sign of what she'd been through for nine days.

"Oh you know, pretty tiring, the usual . . . the same."

"I will do you the honor of not asking you anything more about it," he smiled at her, "and spare you the embarrassment of lying to the man you love."

She didn't try to convince him otherwise. She just let it go. She was too tired to convince anyone of anything. All she wanted to do was sleep. She had spent the afternoon in the War Office, telling them what had happened in minute detail, and everyone was pleased with the end result and how they had achieved it. The munitions factory had been utterly destroyed in the second explosion, the mission she had been in charge of that was nearly bungled. The prime minister's secretary made due note of the identity of the agent who had parachuted into Germany and stayed there until all her goals had been accomplished.

"Can I talk you into going to bed with me tonight?" Richard asked her after dinner, but she looked exhausted.

"Can we put it off just a bit? I'm too tired to move," she said, smiling at him.

"I think you've gone off me," he teased her.

"I promise I haven't. I'm just tired."

"That's what you get for driving rocks all over Great Britain."

"I suppose so," she said, and melted into his arms when he kissed her.

Chapter 8

Richard and Alex finally managed a trip to Hampshire that summer, in August. It was the first anniversary of William's death, so the family spent some quiet time in the cemetery and Richard joined them. There was a marker there for Geoff now too. But the rest of the weekend was easy and pleasant. Alex showed Richard all her favorite spots where she had played with her brothers, every tree she had climbed, or almost, the tree house they had built together when Willie was fifteen, Geoff thirteen, and she was eleven.

He spent time with her parents, and took a long walk with her father. Edward didn't ask him what his intentions were, he already knew from Alex, but he wanted to get a sense of the man she wanted to marry one day, and he liked him. Richard was polite, well brought up, and well educated. He didn't come from an important family or have a great deal of money, but he was a gentleman and a kind person and he loved Alex. Her parents could see it. Her mother was still a little disappointed that Alex didn't care about marrying within the aristocracy, but Alex said it meant nothing to her. And most of the men she had known growing up were dead now.

She was happy with Richard, and they insisted they wouldn't get engaged until after the war. They didn't want to jinx themselves by making plans before it was all over. The war had been going on in Europe for almost two years.

The Americans came into the war in December of that year, 1941, after the Japanese attacked Pearl Harbor in Hawaii. Their joining the war gave the Allies fresh energy, and they needed it.

Alex and Richard spent Christmas with her parents in Hampshire, which was different now with neither of her brothers present, but Richard added a new male element, and he was wonderful with the children from London.

Alex was surprised by how much they had grown in the last two years. Some of the older ones were teenagers now. Richard thanked her parents profusely for letting him join them, and they went back to London on New Year's Day as Alex always did.

In the spring, Alex hardly saw him.

A thousand bombers were sent to bomb Cologne in May, another thousand to bomb Essen in June, and a little later in the month, another thousand bombed Bremen and the Focke-Wulf aircraft factory. The bombings continued all through 1942, and in 1943, the British concentrated on destroying the German industrial base. While Richard was fighting them from the air, Alex was in and out of Germany frequently for the SOE. In November 1943, the Allies began a four-month bombing campaign to destroy Berlin.

In March of the following year, 1944, Alex parachuted into Germany to help a handful of RAF officers escape the German Stalag Luft III prisoner of war camp, a hundred miles southeast of Berlin, and successfully made it across the border with three of them. With the help of several operatives, she got them back to England. Seventy-six prisoners had escaped the camp, of which fifty were murdered, twenty-three were captured and put back in prison, and three made it to freedom and came back. The camp had been thought to be escape-proof. Alex had only been able to save three of them.

Two months later she was a frequent visitor to the war room and had become a familiar face as plans for D-Day, the invasion of Normandy, got under way. She supplied all the information she could, was parachuted into France twice, and successfully got back to England. When the actual battle began on June 6, Richard's squadron was involved from the air, while the U.S. Marines and the army landed on the beaches.

Alex no longer made excuses to Richard for her frequent disappearances. He was used to them by then. Even the king and queen hadn't been to Scotland as often as Alex claimed she had been. All he cared about was that she was safe and came back quickly each time after she'd disappeared. They both had parts of their jobs that they couldn't discuss with each other, but their goals were the same, to win the war, and have it end.

By the time the invasion of Normandy began on D-Day, Alex was twenty-eight, Richard was thirty-six, and they had been in love for almost four years. Her parents were used to him by then, and enjoyed his company. Even Victoria had stopped regretting the fact that Alex was not going to marry a peer of the realm, and have a title. She was perfectly content to have Alex become Richard's wife one day, if they both survived the war.

For the next year after Normandy, most of Alex's missions were in France and no longer Germany. She met with Resistance cells in the countryside, and became proficient with explosives. She had frequently been obliged to defend herself by then, when caught in tight situations, and her commando knife had proven to be more useful than her pistol, which had its purposes too. She never discussed the weaponry she used with Richard, although on one occasion, in an amorous moment, he slipped his hand under her skirt into her garter belt and removed it holding her pistol. He didn't question her about it. He knew better, but the nature of the dangers she faced and the risks he suspected she took worried him constantly. When he found the pistol in her garter belt, he handed it to her with a bemused expression.

"I assume you use this to help with your driving. Do you shoot other lorry drivers if they get in your way?" he asked with a raised eyebrow.

"Something like that." She smiled at him and offered no further explanation.

"Pretty little weapon, though. It's so small. Does it really work?"

"Would you like me to show you?" she said wryly.

"Actually no, I wouldn't." He had come across her commando knife once and hadn't said anything about it. He had never seen the submachine gun she concealed in her belongings, which would have truly shocked him. She had recently gotten a new one with a silencer, the latest model Sten gun, which was extremely useful. When they were fooling around on the lawn one day during a visit to her parents in Hampshire, she flipped him on his back with a judo move that knocked the wind out of him, and left him breathless on the grass for several minutes as he looked up at her in amazement. "You're a dangerous woman, Alex Wickham."

"I try not to be," she said demurely.

"Did they teach you that when you were driving ambulances, or when you got your license for the lorries?" He was curious about what she did, but didn't press her. He knew better than to pry.

"A little of both." He had sensed for several years that there were things about her he didn't want to know, and couldn't. Just as there were things about his missions that he couldn't share with her. It didn't matter. They knew enough about each other, and their love deepened year by year. They trusted each other completely.

In the final days of the war, both of them were constantly running from one assignment to the next. Alex was working closely with Military Intelligence, while still receiving assignments from the SOE, and Richard's squadron was in the air more than it was on the ground.

Eleven months after the invasion of Normandy, it was finally over, on May 8, 1945. Both she and Richard had been instrumental in the final days of the war, and a week after Germany surrendered, Richard's commanding officer informed him that he was to be awarded the Distinguished Flying Cross. Alex was enormously proud of him, and expected no recognition herself. What she had done for the past five years, she had done for love of country, and to speed up the end of the war. It had been a long time coming, after almost six years of war in Europe. She would get no acknowledgment for her clandestine activities as a spy, unlike Richard, who was a war hero.

Her mother was busy then locating the parents who hadn't visited the children for several years. A few had, but not many, either following government recommendations, or because they couldn't afford it or it was too difficult. And many had died, which they knew. Victoria had stayed in touch with the parents for the most part, but at the end of the war, eleven of the twenty children were orphans, and only nine had families and homes to return to.

Victoria had a lengthy discussion with Edward about it, and they consulted Alex too. They wanted to continue to offer a home to the eleven children who had virtually grown up there and no longer had families. Alex agreed. It seemed like the right thing to do, and the children were thrilled. The youngest would turn eighteen in seven years, and Victoria felt taking care of them would occupy her since both of her sons were gone, and she doubted that Alex would move back from London, even now. She was happy that Richard and Alex visited as frequently as they could.

The nine children whose parents were still alive went back to London within two weeks of peace being declared, and everyone cried when they left. They promised to write and visit often. The Wickhams had been wonderful to them. The children called their benefactors Aunt Victoria and Uncle Ed.

In the final days after the war ended, Alex met with Bertram Potter, and they shared a sandwich in his office. He had papers on his desk stacked up nearly to the ceiling.

"What happens now?" she asked him. After five years of working together, he was still her boss but they were also friends.

"I suppose they'll shut us down eventually," he said. "We've served our purpose. The war is over."

"There are no peacetime spies?" she said, smiling at him.

"There are, but that's all run by the military. We were separate and independent, even though we cooperated with them. We had fun, didn't we?" He looked nostalgic about it.

"Sometimes," she admitted, "at other times I was scared to death." Alex had done things she had never thought herself capable of, but working for the SOE had always seemed like the right thing to do. She had only questioned it briefly after Geoff's death, for her parents' sake, but had stayed in anyway. She was willing to die for her country.

"What are you going to do now? Go back to Hampshire?" Bertram asked her.

"I thought I'd go for the summer, to help my mother. She's decided to keep eleven of the children. They're all orphans. The other nine just went home. It won't feel like home to them after six years. Anyway, after the summer, I suppose I'll look for a job, hopefully in London. Hampshire is too quiet for me. It always was. And you?" She knew he had no wife or children. His whole life was his work, and the people he knew there.

"It will take me about a year to get through the paperwork, and get everything in order before we can officially close our doors." He looked around his office, and Alex could easily believe it would take him a year to get through it all, maybe two. "You can always help me with the clerical work if you want to. There's enough to keep a dozen people busy."

"I might." She looked as though the idea appealed to her, she liked working for him, and Bertram clearly liked the idea too. "I'll call you in September when I'm ready to come back. I want to get Richard to stay in Hampshire for a while too."

"What's he going to do without a squadron of fighter pilots to command? He's got flying in his blood. He won't give that up easily."

"It's a good question. He hasn't found the answer yet himself. Flying lessons aren't really enough to keep him busy. And nearly everyone knows how to fly now, at least those who want to. The others hope to never hear the sound of planes again. It will remind them of the war."

Two weeks later, while she was cooking lamb chops for dinner in the apartment they occasionally borrowed from a friend, she turned around to see Richard behind her, perched on one knee on the floor, with a determined expression.

"Are you all right?" She had no idea what he was doing, and then it dawned on her. He had a purposeful expression on his face. "Now? While I'm cooking?"

"Yes, now. I've waited long enough. I've waited nearly five years for this moment." She stopped what she was doing, took off her apron, and turned off the stove. "Alexandra Victoria Edwina Wickham, will you do me the honor of marrying me and becoming my wife?" She hadn't expected it to affect her that way, but her eyes filled with tears immediately, and she nodded, and answered.

"Yes, I will," she said solemnly, and then he surprised her even more. He reached for her hand and slipped a small diamond engagement ring on her finger. It was beautiful and she stared at it in disbelief. "Oh my God, when did you do that?"

"Yesterday," he said proudly. "I went to Asprey. It's an antique." It fit perfectly, and he stood up then and kissed her. She thought of something after he did. "Did you ask my father?"

"Three or four years ago. I told him we wouldn't get engaged until after the war." Richard looked very pleased with himself and the lamb chops were forgotten.

He was still living at the base, and she in the dormitory, and she knew she had to move out soon. They used their friend's apartment when they wanted to spend a night together and didn't want to go to a hotel. The apartment felt more like a home. The couple who'd been living there were getting divorced and weren't using it for now. She had met someone while he was stationed elsewhere.

Alex warmed up the lamb chops again, and they sat down to dinner at the table in the kitchen. The apartment was really too small for them, but they loved being able to spend occasional nights together. That would have never been possible for Alex before the war. But after six years of freedom, air raids, and sabotage missions, no one paid any attention to what others did, and most of the old rules had fallen by the wayside. They couldn't live together without being married, but they could spend nights together as long as they were discreet and no one knew.

"When do you want to get married?" she asked him, as they ate dinner.

"Soon. Yesterday. Four years ago," he said, smiling at her. "Do you want to get married here?"

"Let's do it in Hampshire with my parents. In July?"

"Perfect. I should be out of the RAF by then. And then I have to find a job. I have some ideas."

"I need to get a dress," she said dreamily, and he smiled at her. He was glad that they'd waited. Now they could plan their future together, without worrying about who would be dead the next day, or if she'd be widowed in the first month of their marriage.

They called her parents that night and told them the news. They were delighted. They would have the wedding at the church, and a reception at the house for friends in the neighborhood. Richard thought a few of his RAF friends would come too. He wanted one of them to be his best man. Alex wanted her parents as her witnesses, and her father would walk her down the aisle.

She wanted to find a dress before she left for Hampshire, and her mother offered hers from thirty-four years before, which meant more to her. Victoria had come down the grand staircase in her parents' home in 1911. They had moved into Edward's family home after that, with his mother still living in the dower house at the time. It was unoccupied now. They'd been saving it for Alex one day, but eventually the entire estate would be hers, with her brothers gone.

Richard still owned his father's farm, but rented it to a tenant farmer and hadn't been there in years. The farmer was very responsible and Richard liked deriving a small income from it, although he didn't want to live there. And like Alex, it was his now, as the only survivor. Alex would own her father's entire estate one day. The war had decimated their families and killed all their siblings. It had happened to so many.

Alex left for Hampshire two weeks later. She had emptied what she had at the dormitory and was taking it on the train to Hampshire with her, in two suitcases. Richard was going to join her there in a week. They were to be married at the end of July and Richard said he had people to see in London in the meantime, about their future. He was being slightly mysterious about it, and Alex let him. She knew he would tell her when he was ready.

For their honeymoon, they were going to the South of France. They had talked about going to Venice, but Italy was still in turmoil, although Venice had come through the war relatively unscathed. They had only been attacked once when a hundred planes had bombed the harbor and destroyed all the German ships there, but the city had been untouched. In other areas, many of the roads had been bombed, and there was rubble everywhere. Parts of Italy were in ruins. They were going to Cannes on the Riviera instead, to lie on a beach for a week, and soak up the sun together and then go back to Hampshire for the rest of the summer. Alex had assured him that he'd earned this, after six years of flying fighter planes and commanding a squadron.

She felt like a princess when she got home. Her mother fussed over her, and had gotten their best guest room ready for her and Richard. Her childhood room was too small for them. And in the guest room they would be in the opposite wing from her parents.

She and her mother spent the next two weeks getting ready for the wedding. They chose the flowers at the nursery, set the menu, and hired a caterer for the lunch. They invited fifty friends from neighboring homes and farms, and a few good friends from London. With rationing still in effect, they couldn't have a big wedding or serve more people. But they were happy with close friends. They had both lost so many. And her mother altered the wedding dress for Alex. It fit perfectly.

Victoria hired a small local band so there would be dancing. At last they were having a celebration. There was something joyful to share with their friends, not a tragedy. The war was over, and at last, Alex was getting married. She only wished her brothers could have been there.

Chapter 9

The wedding her parents gave for them was exactly what Richard and Alex wanted. Small, elegant, intimate, but more informal than most weddings of the past. It was a beautiful sunny day for an outdoor reception in her parents' garden. The music in the church was what they had selected. Victoria had arranged the flowers herself, and Alex carried an exquisite trailing bouquet of tiny white orchids and lily of the valley, which grew in the greenhouse of her parents' estate.

The food was delicious. Some things were still difficult to get, but there was enough and it was beautifully prepared and served, and the dance music was wonderfully romantic. Richard danced with Victoria, and Alex with her father, and he could see how happy she was. Their eleven foster children had been Alex's only attendants, all dressed in white. Victoria made their clothes, and they were proud to be part of the ceremony. They had preceded her into the church and looked adorable. At the end of the day, when the last guest had left, after enjoying quantities of champagne, malt whiskey, and the excellent food, and dancing until nearly midnight, the bride and groom went to their room, which Victoria had decorated with white orchids.

The next day, after breakfast, the couple boarded a train, which would ultimately get them to Nice in the South of France for their honeymoon. Richard had reserved a suite for them at the Carlton, with a balcony and a view of the Mediterranean. The elegant hotel on the Croisette had been used as a military hospital during the war, and was being restored to its original use now, and already open as a hotel. For the next week, they ate in intimate restaurants, walked along the Croisette, swam in the sea, and lay on the beach and reveled in finally being a couple in peacetime. Alex had carefully locked all her weapons of war in a trunk and moved them to the attic in Hampshire before their wedding. It was the past now.

Their honeymoon was everything Alex had dreamed of and always wanted, and they returned to Hampshire suntanned and relaxed. Alex wore a simple gold ring with her engagement ring, and Victoria and Edward were happy to see them.

A few days after they got back, at dinner with Alex's parents, Richard shared his plans for the future. He had been to the Foreign Office before he came to Hampshire for the wedding. He had tried to think about what he would be good at, and would provide an interesting life for them. Neither of them wanted to settle down in Hampshire, at least not yet, and he couldn't imagine himself as a banker, or even a teacher. The only training he'd had was as a pilot, and he couldn't see himself supporting a family on what he'd made giving lessons before the war. He didn't want to be a commercial pilot and be away from Alex all the time. The thought of flying commercially made him feel like a bus driver.

"This may sound crazy to you," he said cautiously, "but I thought the diplomatic corps could be interesting. We'd be assigned to a foreign country for four years, and then move on somewhere else. And at the end of it, I would have a respected position in the Foreign Office." He looked at Alex after he suggested the idea, and she was smiling. He had said it with considerable trepidation. What they had described to him sounded very exotic, and with Alex's gift for languages she would be the perfect diplomat's wife, and he had a feeling she would entertain beautifully, after what he had seen of the way Alex had grown up. She had the background and the training. "What do you think?" He looked at his wife as he said it. "Would you mind living all over the world for a number of years, before we settle down in England?"

"We were hoping you'd want to move back to Hampshire," Edward said, sounding disappointed. "It's a wonderful place to raise children."

"I'm sure we'll end up here eventually," Richard said politely, "but it would also be an extraordinary experience for children to grow up in different countries and cultures before that, and for us too."

"I love the idea," Alex said when she spoke up. "We'd never be bored and we'd meet so many interesting people." It was the perfect counterpoint to her past five years as a spy, which she had some qualms about giving up. Life was going to seem very quiet, even dull, without her harrowing missions. Richard was thrilled that she liked his idea, and hadn't run screaming from the room. She was the ideal partner for an adventure of that kind. She had a thirst for new experiences, people, places, and languages.

"They said I would spend six or nine months at the Foreign Office, getting trained, and then we'd be given our first assignment. It could be someplace quite unusual." Alex's parents were startled, it had never occurred to them that they would want to be jaunting around the world, changing homes and countries every four years. But Victoria had to admit it suited them, and she thought it was very enterprising of Richard to have thought of it. Alex was full of admiration for him too, and she couldn't think of anything better or that she'd like more.

"You're brilliant!" she said to him when they were alone in their bedroom a little while later.

"Would it be too difficult bringing up children in different countries and moving every four years?" It had been his only hesitation, and they both wanted children.

"I don't think so," Alex said, thinking about it. "It would broaden their life experience immensely. And we'd have so much help provided by the embassies. We'd get very spoiled." She smiled at him. It was the perfect plan.

"If you agree, I'll start at the Foreign Office in September, and they'll send us to our first post next spring. We could start a baby now, if you want, and then it would be born before we leave," he said with a twinkle in his eyes. He was eager to have children.

"I think that would be hard, taking a very young baby to some exotic place. Let's settle in first and get to know the country, and then have children." It sounded like a much better plan to her, rather than taking a newborn to some far off country that might be primitive, or even hostile. "I love the idea of being in the diplomatic corps, though. My darling, you're a genius!" She put her arms around his neck and kissed him, and a little while later, they found their way to the bed, and made love. They had the time and opportunity now, a summer when neither of them had to work, and they were married. Alex had never been happier, and Richard was thrilled that she liked his plan for their future. The problem was solved.

It was mid-August when Alex was opening the mail that had been forwarded to her from her dormitory. She'd received an official-looking letter, and her eyes widened in surprise as she read it. Her parents had just come in from a walk, Richard was about to go fishing, and Alex had promised to go and play with the children.

"I'm to receive two medals," she said in amazement as she looked up at them with the letter still in her hand. The George Medal and the OBE. They were civil medals and not military, because the SOE was not officially part of Military Intelligence.

"What for?" her mother asked.

"My war work," she said, smiling at Richard.

"For driving a lorry?" Her father looked skeptical.

"Well, not exactly. I did a bit more than that." Richard was smiling at her, remembering the pistol and the commando knife he had discovered, and he had suspected for several years that she was doing more than she admitted for the war effort, probably a lot more, although he couldn't even begin to guess the extent of it, or the training she had received to do it.

"How much more than that?" her mother questioned her. They weren't awarding her two medals for a minor contribution.

"Oh, not a lot," Alex said vaguely, unable to say more, even now. "Richard is the war hero, I'm not." She was well aware of her promise not to reveal her espionage activities for twenty years. It had been a solemn vow.

"You must have done something if they're giving you a medal." Her father was perplexed but she couldn't tell them or anyone of the reconnaissance and sabotage missions she'd carried out, and the frequent assignments behind enemy lines assisting Resistance groups in occupied Europe and in Germany. Bertram had reminded her of her sworn promise recently. She remembered it well.

"I translated a lot of documents for the Yeomanry," Alex said as Richard watched her intently and sensed there was much more to the story than she could tell them or ever would. He remembered her frequent absences, supposedly delivering rocks to other parts of Great Britain. He suspected the truth might have amazed them but he didn't insist. Her parents were baffled and afterward she looked at Richard gratefully.

"Thank you for not pressing me," she said to him.

"I understand, and I'm proud of you," he said in a tender voice. Without knowing the details, he suspected that there was a great deal more to his wife than any of them would ever know. He could only guess, and wondered if she had worked for Military Intelligence for the entire war. And if so, she would never be able to tell them. "All those times you disappeared, Alex, that was part of it, wasn't it?" She nodded but couldn't say more. "I thought so," he said quietly.

She still had her weapons locked in the attic. They hadn't asked her to return them. She wanted to keep them, if they'd let her. Captain Potter hadn't told her to give them back, so she hadn't.

"I'm just grateful you weren't killed," Richard said with feeling. And so was she, about both of them. Richard was only sorry that she couldn't tell them more. "I thought you were up to some mischief, I just hoped it wasn't too serious," he said, relieved. "I don't know what medals they're giving you," he said solemnly, "but I'm sure you deserve them, Alex, and you earned them." She nodded and was grateful that he respected her silence and didn't push her about it.

"I hope I did," she said with a serious look.

"I'm going fishing," he said then, letting it go. He kissed her and they walked out of the house together so she could play with the children as she'd promised.

"What do you suppose she did to get those medals?" Victoria asked Edward as they sat in the library together, after the two young people went out.

"Maybe we wouldn't want to know," he said wisely. "There were a lot of secret activities during the war."

"I hope she didn't do anything dangerous," Victoria said, but at least she had come through it and the war was over.

On his way to go fishing Richard was thinking about how little they knew Alex. She was a brave woman, he had always sensed that about her.

And as Victoria glanced out the window, she saw Alex playing tag with the children in the garden, like any other young woman her age. She wondered what they couldn't guess about her, and decided it was best they didn't know.

Chapter 10

The small ceremony in September awarding Alex the two medals she was being given was a modest event in the offices of the SOE with Bertram Potter presiding, and a minor official from the War Office present. Bertram made a short speech, and his respect for Alex and affection for her shone through. The War Office representative pinned the medals on her, and shook her hand. No one else was there to see it and she was sorry Richard and her parents couldn't be there. Marlene served port and cookies afterward, which Betram had purchased himself to make the occasion more festive.

He spoke of Alex's courage and passion for her country, her determination to accomplish every mission, no matter how dangerous or challenging. He said that she had never refused or balked at a single assignment, and had gone behind enemy lines again and again in frightening conditions, without a moment's hesitation. He said she had been one of their best operatives, and richly deserved the medals and the appreciation of her country. He spoke of her loyalty, her bravery and willingness to do everything in her power and beyond to help win the war. Alex was deeply touched by what he said.

Bertram acknowledged that there were too many unsung and unknown heroes like her, who had acted in secret, followed every order, risked their lives, and in too many cases lost them to the enemy. It had been a costly war for the entire country.

Alex had already agreed to come in to the office twice a week to help Bertram organize his mountain of papers, so there was no need to say goodbye to him. And she was sad to hear that there was already talk of closing the office. There was no reason for the SOE to exist once the war was over, and there were no further assignments anticipated. Their operatives had already been disbanded. From now on, MI5 would be overseeing any intelligence missions domestically, and MI6 would handle anything international. SOE had become obsolete in peacetime, which made everyone who had worked for them sad to know that it would soon disappear into the annals of history. It made putting Bertram's files into the archives in good order that much more important, and Alex was happy to help him do it.

After the ceremony, which Richard couldn't attend, he took her to dinner at Rules, where they hadn't been since the war. It was their favorite restaurant. They had just found a small apartment in Kensington, and rented it furnished for six months, since they knew they would be leaving for Richard's first assignment in the spring. They still didn't know where it would be. The country was struggling to get on its feet, with massive rebuilding and restoration projects to face. In many areas, the city had been gutted, as had others in Europe. Germany was in shambles, and Italy not much better. France had suffered less damage by capitulating so quickly to the enemy. Their art treasures had been plundered and stolen in vast quantities by the occupying army, and members of the SS high command who had come to Paris strictly for that purpose. It was known now that the French had been clever about hiding many of their treasures underground, and the Resistance had been instrumental in helping them dig tunnels and caves, where their most valuable art was stored. But much had been lost and taken into enemy territory, and would be difficult to trace and even harder to retrieve. French museum officials were determined to do it, and many artifacts were already being brought back from the tunnels and returned to the Louvre.

Alex remembered Colonel von Meissen referring to Goering's many trips to France to bring trainloads of France's art treasures back to Germany. It was all too real now that the war was over and the enormous losses they had suffered were being revealed. Alex wondered if the colonel was still alive and had survived the war. She wondered too if he had just thought her a shy, unwilling young woman, or if he had realized that he had been duped. She knew she had gotten out just in time, but it had been one of her more entertaining missions, the only one of its kind, and a successful one. She had gotten all the information the War Office wanted.

By October, Richard had settled into his job at the Foreign Office, preparing him for his role in post-war diplomacy. He was carefully monitoring world news, while trying to guess where he would be sent for his first assignment, and he remained open to all possibilities. He and Alex would discuss world politics late into the night. Europe was still in turmoil, with every country severely marked by the war. Food was still scarce in England, crops limited, and the economy suffering with so much to rebuild. Asia had its own troubles. Richard didn't think he'd be sent there. Russia had taken over eastern Germany, slicing right through Berlin. A post in the Eastern Bloc countries would be challenging. They too were ravaged by the war and destitute, with people starving. And there were problems throughout the British Empire.

There had been trouble in India since the viceroy at the time war was declared, the unlikeable and unpopular Lord Linlithgow, had declared war on behalf of India without consulting India's nationalist politicians. As a result, their left wing congressmen opposed the war, and the most vocal among them, Jawaharlal Nehru, was sent to prison for three years, and had only recently been released. Imperial India was being torn apart by constant battles between the Hindus and the Muslims, with demands to split the country, frequent bloodshed, and a risk of civil war. Two million Indians had served in the British armed forces, most of whom would return to India now, to add to the dissent and confusion. It appeared to be an insoluble problem, and while they were focused on the war in Europe, the British had lost power and control elsewhere in the empire. British India's days appeared to be numbered, which Richard was studying intently.

It was February of 1946 when the Foreign Office finally informed Richard of his assignment, as deputy counselor to the viceroy, a respectable position, which would provide him a front row seat to the changes that would be inevitable in the coming months, and a valuable training ground for him. There had been a mutiny of the Royal Indian Air Force a month before. And a few weeks previously there had been demonstrations in Calcutta, in which many of the participants had been killed, and then further strikes to protest their deaths within a day. They had just been notified in the Foreign Office of a mutiny of the Royal Indian Navy as well, and of another strike in Bombay where two hundred had been killed.

"These are troubled times in imperial India, Montgomery. You won't have an easy task. We believe that Indian independence will be inevitable, and we'd like that to happen with as little bloodshed as possible, which may not be feasible. Partition may be inevitable too. Nehru will be an important player in the future. Krishna Menon is a troublemaker of the worst sort, and Mahatma Gandhi is their spiritual leader. There are extraordinary economic opportunities there, Karachi and Bangalore are booming, while they're starving in other areas. You'll be briefed on all of it of course now that we know where you're going," the Foreign Office official said, smiling at him.

"Living conditions are exceptionally good, just as always, with many servants. We have a quite pleasant house for you there, and there are a multitude of social events in the British and international communities. It has always been a post that our people have enjoyed. I'm sure you will too. And lots of other women to keep your wife amused. You leave in four weeks, by ship. It's a long journey, but passenger ships are being returned to service by the navy, and refitted for peacetime use. It will be an adventure, Montgomery. Best of luck to you. Your briefing sessions start in three days.

"Viscount Wavell is the viceroy, he's a good chap. I've worked with him myself, very fair. He's the right man for you to start your career with. Four years in India, particularly at this time, will teach you a great deal. I'm sure you'll make ambassador on the next round. Four years go faster than one realizes. It's enough time to settle in and really get to know the country, but not so long that you won't want to move on to the next post." Richard nodded, trying to absorb everything he had been told.

What stuck out in his mind was that they were leaving in four weeks, and he wanted to tell Alex so she could start getting ready. He knew she wanted to spend time with her parents in Hampshire before they left. He had a lot to do, and wanted to advise his tenant on his own farm that he would be in India for the next four years. It sounded like a lifetime right now. But his tenant was solid and reliable so that was one less worry for him. Richard smiled as he wondered how many children they would have by the time they moved on to their next post. And aside from the political issues which would keep him busy, it would be a comfortable life for them, far more so than in their tiny flat in London, or even life on her parents' estate. After the war, it was nearly impossible to get help. No one wanted to be a servant anymore. They all preferred to work in factories and offices, and so many of the young men hadn't returned from the war.

He was waiting for Alex when she got home from her work with Bertram that night. She had stayed later than usual, struggling to create an archival system for him. He was a brilliant leader, but not adept at creating records, or keeping files updated, and they had a lot of catching up to do, since they knew the players and the assignments so well.

The minute Alex saw the excitement in Richard's eyes, she knew that there was news. He told her as soon as she took off her hat and coat, before she even had time to sit down.

"We're leaving in four weeks," he blurted out like a schoolboy with something important to report. "We're going to India. I'll be deputy counselor to the viceroy, which isn't an important post. But I have a lot to learn." She could see how happy he was, as he threw his arms around her and lifted her off the ground.

"That's very exciting!" She was happy too. India sounded fascinating, she had been reading about it extensively. "I wonder if they'll get independence while we're there."

"It sounds like it, although that's not going to be a simple change, with the Hindus and the Muslims. The Muslims want partition and their own state. There will almost surely be bloodshed over that. But we'll be safe in New Delhi. They said we have a very pleasant house. So we're off and running. Your pilot husband has a real job, and we have some exciting years ahead of us. Thank you for being such a good sport," he said and then kissed her. "Let's go out to dinner to celebrate." They went to a neighborhood pub they frequented and had bangers and mash. The sausages were still a bit thin, but they were tasty.

Alex was already thinking of everything she had to do in the coming weeks, and what she wanted to pack. What she didn't need, she was going to leave with her parents. She knew she'd need evening clothes in India, for the social life they'd lead there, and she wanted to be properly dressed and make Richard proud of her. Her evening gowns from her London Season eleven years before looked tired and outdated now. She hadn't bought any new ones since. Her mother had said she would give Alex some of hers. She had to give Bertram notice that she was leaving, so he could hire someone else to help with the files. Marlene was overwhelmed. They still called her by her code name, although her real name was Vivian Spence.

When Alex told Bertram the news the next day, he looked crestfallen. He had known that they were waiting for Richard's foreign assignment, but he had hoped it wouldn't be so soon.

"In four weeks?" He was visibly dismayed.

"I hate to do it, but I really need to leave in two. I have to pack and get everything organized, and I want to spend time with my parents. It's a long way for them to come, and I'm not sure how often they'll get out there to see us. It's going to be hard for them when we leave."

She was dreading it for them, now that she was their only child. But she had to follow Richard, as his wife, and they hadn't complained. It would be painful for them, though. She was even more grateful now that they had the foster children to distract them.

"We'll have to work more quickly then, and do all we can in the next two weeks," Bertram said with an air of determination mixed with panic. There was so much left to do. And he had just been given notice that the SOE office would close in June, only four months away. He didn't see how they could finish by then, but they would have to. The SOE was history, it was over.

Alex was working earnestly at her desk in the tiny office she'd been assigned, and she was diligently closing file after file, and packing them chronologically into boxes as she finished. It was all to be delivered to the archives of the War Office when SOE closed.

Bertram walked into her office with a serious expression as she put another folder into a box that was already half full. It would be easy for anyone to understand her system if they ever wanted to exhume the files from the archives, and she was making a careful inventory for a master list, with the names of every operative, and each assignment had a file number they could cross-reference.

"I hate to interrupt you, but could you come into my office for a minute?" Bertram asked her.

"Of course," she said, stopping what she was doing. "Is something wrong? Did I forget something?"

"Not at all. There's someone here to see you." She followed him into his office, and a tall lean man with gray hair was standing at the window, looking out, and turned to smile at them as they walked in. Bertram introduced them. His name was Lyle Bridges, he was very distinguished looking, and had eyes that took everything in. Alex could sense that he was scrutinizing her as she sat down across the desk from Bertram, and Lyle Bridges sat down in the chair next to her. He got right to the point, and the purpose of his visit.

"I've heard a great deal about you, Mrs. Montgomery, and Captain Potter has allowed me to read your file. It's very impressive. I wish you'd been working for us for all these years, in Military Intelligence, but you did indirectly. Thanks to operatives like you, we won the war." She smiled at what he said. "The country needs more people like you. Sometimes I think women are our best agents. They're more practical than men, and sometimes more fearless. They don't talk about it, they just go in and do the job. I understand that you'll be going to India soon," he said.

"My husband has joined the diplomatic corps," she said cautiously. "India will be our first assignment. We're very excited about it."

"It's an interesting time there, with independence in the offing, and possibly partition. You won't have a dull moment." He smiled at her. She still had no idea why Bertram had introduced them, or what Lyle Bridges wanted with her. The war was over, and so was her job with the SOE, and they were leaving in four weeks. She had understood that he'd been with Military Intelligence during the war, but all of that was over now. It was history, for her anyway. "You must be wondering why I wanted to meet you. The war is over, for most people. But we are the watchdogs who never sleep. MI5 keeps track of national security domestically, and MI6 is the foreign branch. We have operatives all over the world, even in peacetime. And your going to India now is a very interesting situation, for you and for us, and an opportunity for you to continue to serve your king and your country, and to protect our fellow countrymen from threats of any kind, sometimes even before they happen.

"I've seen and read about the kind of dedication you brought to your work for the SOE, and you caught the attention of some of my colleagues during sessions you attended in the war room, particularly before D-Day. Nothing goes unnoticed there." He smiled at her, and his eyes were needle sharp, watching her reaction to what he said. "If you joined us, we wouldn't expect you to take an active role, as you did in the war. But you have an opportunity to gather information from the people you meet, the things you hear or observe. India is far from London, sometimes people have a tendency to be more outspoken in the colonies, even if India is about to not be one, and become an independent nation, which makes it even more important to keep a finger on its pulse. You will meet many of the Indian officials who interest us, as the result of your husband's job with the viceroy. We would like to ask you if you would be our eyes and ears in India, and simply report to us what you see and who you meet, what you hear, who attends the dinner parties you go to, or who you invite to your home. You might even receive some direction from us on that. Lunch with the wife of an important official could give you a wealth of information. We're interested in all of it," he admitted.

"And how would I share the information with you?"

"We'll give you a small radio transmitter, disguised as a first aid kit, and you can send us messages in code. There's no risk to your transmitting, there's no danger now of someone intercepting it and shooting you, as there was during the war behind enemy lines. It's just an information flow between you and MI6, and a way for you to continue serving your country, if you agree to do it. There is no risk. But your security clearance would remain the same as it is now, in case you come across sensitive information. You haven't been deactivated in our files yet, so there would be nothing additional to do. You could contact us once a week if there's nothing going on, or after every social event, to give us a list of who you met. It's very low key compared to what you've been doing for the last five years. And it would take very little of your time. I imagine your husband will keep you busy with all the events you have to attend as part of his job. That's why your current situation will be so interesting to us." She nodded, and didn't say anything as she thought about it.

"Would I be able to tell my husband?" she asked. She didn't want to keep secrets from him again, as she had to about the SOE and couldn't even tell him now. An open flow of information and honest exchange between them seemed important.

"I'm afraid not," Bridges answered. "Just to be on the safe side. We consider it top secret, in case you come across something important to national security. It's best, in fact obligatory, that he doesn't know." Alex nodded again. "Will you give it some thought?"

"I will," she said quietly. What he wanted from her was clear. Even if the stakes and consequences weren't as severe, he wanted her to continue being a spy, and she wasn't sure she wanted to do that. For the past eight months, she had considered that chapter of her life closed. And now they wanted her to open it again, and lie to Richard. What they wanted didn't sound difficult, but it put her in an awkward situation. She *did* like the idea of having something more important to do than just having lunch with other women and going to parties with Richard at night. As long as they didn't have children yet, she had time on her hands.

"You would be paid by MI6 this time. Not a fortune. We pay a very average sum into a bank account each month. Too much money would draw attention, so we keep it to an amount you don't have to explain, as we did before."

It was all swirling around in her head as the man from MI6 shook hands with them and left, and she looked at Bertram across his desk.

"Did you contact them, or did they initiate it?" she asked, curious about it.

"I got a call from MI6 yesterday. This was entirely their idea. They must have seen Richard's file in the Foreign Office. They see everything."

"What do you think I should do?" She was troubled.

"I think you should do it," he said without hesitating. "You're not the sort of woman to just spend your life dressing up and putting on makeup, and chatting with other women. You need something more important to do. And this isn't just about you, Alex. You love your country, so do I. People like us need to find a way to serve. What else is there? Where would England be without us?" He smiled at her.

"It can't be that important telling them who I meet at parties."

"You never know. They wouldn't ask you if it wasn't, and India is a hotbed of intrigue and political conflict right now. It could turn into a real mess if they don't handle it right, particularly with partition. The Muslims want a piece of India to make their own country, Pakistan. India is mostly Hindu, and they want the Muslims out too." Alex had been reading about it for months. "There could be a full-scale religious war there, the likes of which we've never seen."

"What are you going to do?" She had wondered about it but hadn't asked him recently.

"I'm going back to MI5, to keep the country safe at home," he smiled, "while you junket around the world and have a dozen servants to dress you and serve you breakfast in bed. It won't be a bad life," he said affectionately. Life in the colonies had always been luxurious and pleasant.

"There's more to India than that, a lot more," she said. "I want to visit the shrines, and try to understand the religious issues better between the Hindus, the Muslims, and the Sikhs." She sounded naïve but well-meaning to him as she said it.

"That alone is a life's work. It's a magical place. I served in the army there years ago. But there's a cruel side to it too. Be careful of that."

"Do you think I'd be in danger if I take the job?" she asked him candidly, trusting him to be honest with her.

"No, I don't. This is the tame side of spying, what they're proposing to you. You'd be an information source for MI6, nothing more. They have thousands of them all over the world. They don't expect you to solve their problems out there. The issues are too big for that. They just want names and places and what people say. It might be fun." She thought so too. She just wasn't sure if she wanted to be a spy again. She had enjoyed not working since peace was declared, but she did want to find something to do in India, or she knew she'd be bored. "Think about it tonight," he suggested and she sighed.

"I hate lying to Richard."

Bertram laughed at that. "Most women do, about far less worthy things than national security. And you wouldn't be lying to him. He's not going to ask you if you're still a spy. It would never occur to him." That was true. He might have suspected something about her wartime activities but he had never asked and wouldn't. If he did suspect, he knew she couldn't tell him. "Sleep on it tonight. MI6 is very anxious to have you. They said as much when they called me. They'll wait."

Alex went home after that, her thoughts filled with the conversation with the representative from MI6 that afternoon, and Richard noticed that she seemed distracted. She said she had a headache from going through dusty files all day.

"Well, that's almost over." He smiled at her. "You'll be a lady of leisure with an army of servants to wait on you soon." He was proud to be able to provide that for her through his job.

"That sounds sinfully indolent," she said, looking embarrassed. "I'll have to do something to keep busy."

"Have babies," he said, smiling tenderly at her again. "It would be easier for you there, with so much help." She nodded. She liked the idea too, once they settled in, which was their plan. She wondered if spies had children. She supposed they did. She felt less guilty as she thought about it now. Her love for her country hadn't diminished with the end of the war. And working for MI6 would be a way to be useful, with no great risk to her, as Bertram said. There were no dangers to the job. And what harm would it do if she told them who she saw at dinner parties and what they said? It was so little to do for her country. She had almost made up her mind when she fell asleep that night.

She awoke the next morning to a beautiful day. Richard talked about the political situation in India over breakfast, and she found all of it fascinating now.

By the time she got to the SOE office, she had made up her mind, and no longer felt guilty about it. Richard was serving their country in his own way. She had hers, even if it was more clandestine. Her conscience was clear.

She walked into Bertram's office as soon as she arrived.

"I'm going to do it," she said in one breath, and he looked up with a smile.

"Good girl. I knew you would. It's very little effort, with some possible benefit to national security, and no risk to you." That was her conclusion too.

She called Lyle Bridges from her office a few minutes later, and he sounded pleased. "Welcome to MI6, Mrs. Montgomery. You should have been one of ours all along. I don't know how we missed you. We should have snatched you from SOE at the start of the war. We'll need a day to brief you. You don't need training from us. I read your training scheme. You won't need any of that now, but it's good to know. I assume you still have your 'accessories.'" He meant her weapons and she understood.

"Yes, I do."

"Keep them. They're always good to have. We'll give you the transmitter when you come in to be briefed." They set a date for her to come to their offices before she left for Hampshire for her last two weeks in England. She walked back in to see Bertram to tell him.

"Brava, my dear. Once a spy always a spy," he said and laughed. "There's no reason for you not to do this," he said more seriously. "And MI6 is a good branch. The best."

"Thank you for the advice," she said, and she was walking out of his office when he spoke again.

"Call me Bertie," he said softly and she looked at him and smiled. He wasn't her boss anymore. They were colleagues, and there was a nice feeling to it, like graduating, or growing up.

"Thank you, Bertie," she said and walked back to her office. She sat down at her desk, still smiling. She was a spy again. It felt much better than she thought it would. It gave special meaning to her life. And Bertie was right. Richard didn't need to know.

Chapter 11

Alex's two weeks in Hampshire with her parents flew by, and Richard joined her for the last few days. He had finished all his briefings by then. She had done hers with MI6 in a single day, before she left for Hampshire, but no one knew except Bertie. She had a last lunch with him before she went, and he promised to stay in touch. She was going to miss him and his wise advice.

Edward and Victoria came to see them off on the boat when they sailed from Southampton. The Foreign Office had booked passage for them in first class on the SS *Aronda,* a ship of the British India Steam Navigation Company. It was five years old, there were forty-five passengers in first class, a hundred and ten in second, and two thousand two hundred and seventy-eight "unberthed deck passengers." It was a very comfortable ship though not as luxurious as some of the European or even British ships. The food was known to be excellent and first-class passengers dressed fashionably and formally in the evening. The ship carried cargo as well, and the journey would take four weeks, which seemed long, but they had both brought a stack of books and articles to read, for work and pleasure, mostly about India. There was so much to learn, and Alex wanted to know all she could when she got there. There were going to be social events to attend on the boat in the evening too. Alex had brought several trunks with her, mostly of summer clothes to wear in the crushing heat. They had no plans to return to England in the next few years. Her parents had said they would try to come in about a year, and Alex hoped they would. They might even have a grandchild by then, in which case she was sure they would come.

Their final parting was as painful as Alex had feared it would be. Victoria was sobbing, and Edward had tears in his eyes when he hugged Alex, who could barely speak. Richard felt acutely guilty for taking her away from them, but the opportunities in the diplomatic corps were limitless and too tempting, and Alex had wanted to go too. She just hated to leave her parents now that her brothers were gone. She was their last surviving child, which they all still found unimaginable. And the pain of loss seemed so fresh.

The boat horn sounded and her parents got off and waved from the dock for as long as Alex could see them, and then she turned to Richard standing at the railing next to her in the brisk March breeze.

"Are you all right?" he asked her, worried, as he put his arms around her. "I'm sorry, Alex." He felt as though he had stolen her from them.

"Don't be. We're going to have a wonderful life in India," she said generously, wiping the last tears off her cheeks with the handkerchief her mother had given her. It smelled of her perfume.

They went to explore the ship after that, and reserved a table in the dining saloon. The sea was choppy as they left Southampton, and the sky was gray. It was a suitable way to leave England, but it smoothed out after that, and that night Alex wore a simple black evening gown of her mother's, and Richard played billiards afterward. It felt like a honeymoon to them.

They lay on deck chairs and read most days, with blankets covering them and deck stewards in attendance, serving them bouillon and biscuits, for those who were seasick, although not many passengers were. It had been a smooth voyage so far. They had dinner in the dining saloon every night, and played shuffleboard in the daytime. They chatted with other couples making the trip, and felt like old friends by the time they docked in India four weeks later.

Alex could hardly sleep the night before, waiting for the mysteries of India to unfold, and Richard was eager to get to work, and meet the viceroy and the counselor, his direct superior, the man that he would be working for.

Two Anglo-Indian assistants came to meet them at the dock in Calcutta, with a car provided by Government House, and another vehicle for their luggage. As Richard watched their trunks come off, Alex looked around at the people, the women in gem colored saris, with their heads covered and bindis on their foreheads. There were beggars in the streets near the dock, and children with missing limbs who tore at her heart. And threaded among them there were colorful carts, pedicabs, a palace in the distance, the smell of flowers and spices heavy in the air. It was everything she had thought it would be. The roads were choked with people as they drove away from the dock and she stared out the window at the sights as they went past. She hardly spoke to Richard, she was so intrigued by everything around them, and he was watching intently too.

They were driven from the dock to the train then for the nine hundred mile journey to New Delhi where they would live. The first-class compartment was comfortable and luxurious. They had a thirty-hour journey ahead of them.

The trip to New Delhi was long and tedious, and when they finally arrived they were driven to the Lodhi Estate area, near the Lodhi Gardens. It was the most recent residential area built during the British raj, where government officials lived. They entered a gate, and drove down a narrow driveway past a riot of colorful flowers, and a garden and lawn that were perfectly tended. There were big trees shading the house, which looked like a small Victorian palace, and was referred to as a "bungalow." Half a dozen servants were standing outside, all dressed in white, waiting to greet them as they arrived. It was even more beautiful than anything Alex had imagined. Young boys came running from the back of the house to help the drivers with the luggage, and an Indian man in western dress came forward and bowed deeply.

"I am Sanjay, your butler, sir. My wife, Isha, and I are at your service." He bowed again to Alex, and a graceful-looking woman came to stand next to him. He introduced her to their new employers, as she bowed too.

Alex's trunks were being carried into the house at a rapid rate, as a flock of young men and women appeared. There were at least a dozen of them, and four men tending the immaculate garden. Richard and Alex walked into the house then, and the beauty of it took her breath away. The ceilings were at least fifteen feet high in two large reception rooms and a dining room, each with a wide balcony. The fragrance of exotic flowers was heavy in the air in the house, and enormous fans were circling lazily on the ceiling, moving very little air, but the rooms were relatively cool. A handsome staircase off to the side led up to the bedrooms. There were two huge bedrooms on the second floor, with dressing rooms for each of them, and on the floor above were half a dozen guest rooms. Isha explained that the servants were housed in a separate building. She offered to show Alex the kitchen then, and Alex followed her down the back stairs to the main floor, and through a narrow passage to an enormous room where half a dozen people were working and a male cook was giving them orders in Hindi, a language Alex had not tried to master yet. The most common choices here were Hindi, Urdu, or Punjabi. And there were numerous other dialects around the country.

The chef was dressed in white Indian dress and bowed low to Alex and spoke to her in rapid Hindi, assuring her of his deepest respect and dedication, as translated by Isha.

"Please tell him thank you." Alex was not used to speaking through an interpreter but here she had no other choice, and Richard was planning to use interpreters too.

"How many people work here, in the house?" Alex asked Isha.

"Only fourteen in the house, ma'am, but many of them have children or family who come to help in the day." Alex had counted at least twenty people rushing around so far. And she suspected that all of them were poorly paid, but they looked happy and cheerful, and grateful to be there. There wasn't a sour, unhappy face in the lot, they were all clean and tidy, and the house was immaculate.

Their bedroom was decorated in pale blue satin, with curtains to match the bedspread and furniture, enormous windows looking out over the balconies, and shutters for when the days were too hot. It was already warm, and it was only April, she could imagine how hot it might get in August. Alex had read that men always complained about their dinner jackets and tailcoats and the heavy winter uniforms they had to wear for state occasions and formal functions, particularly in the case of visiting royalty, which until now had happened often, and perhaps would occur less once they achieved independence, which was becoming more and more likely. Independence was bound to affect how people lived in India, if it was no longer a colony of the British Empire. They would be following Indian traditions then, and not British, as had been the case for the past two hundred years.

When Alex went back upstairs, she found Richard on their bedroom balcony, admiring their surroundings. Everything around them felt exotic, and it was easy to see, even at a glance, why people loved living here. Nearly twenty domestics and a beautiful house for the deputy counselor of the viceroy seemed extraordinary. But it was what they had heard about before.

"I should go to the office and introduce myself," Richard said to her.

"The house is so beautiful," she whispered as she stood next to him, and he put an arm around her. "And so many servants I won't know what to do with them." Isha had explained that there were two laundresses, one for her and one for Richard, a duster, three cleaners in the house, the cook and his two assistants, and sometimes many more when they entertained, two footmen to serve at table for only her and her husband, and a woman whose grandmother had been trained as a ladies' maid in London to help Alex dress if she wished it, and Isha and Sanjay. And that did not include the four gardeners and a chauffeur, and extra people who were added for special occasions. In all, there were nineteen people to wait on them, and Alex could easily understand why people who had lived in India for most of their lives, or a long period of time, had trouble adjusting when they came back to England. That kind of opulence and service hadn't existed in England for half a century.

The cook had prepared a light meal for them by then, and Isha led them to the dining room where Sanjay was waiting, and introduced them to the two footmen, Avi and Ram.

Two places were set at the table with embroidered linens, silver, and crystal, and a moment later, Avi and Ram served them a light Indian meal, under the stern supervision of Sanjay, worthy of any English butler. He had already explained to Richard that he had worked in the viceroy's palace as a young boy. Richard could only imagine what that looked like, if the deputy had a house like this with nineteen servants.

Richard left quickly after lunch to meet the viceroy and the first counselor, and Alex went upstairs to find three women and her lady's maid unpacking her trunks with Isha. Alex wanted to do it herself but was afraid to offend them, so after studying the closets, she told them where she wanted things put away, and she instructed them to leave the final locked valise for her to deal with. Richard wasn't aware that she had brought them, but she had her weapons in there. She hadn't carried them in nearly a year, but given her new assignment with MI6, she had brought them. The very small radio transmitter they had given her was in the same case. She found a locked cupboard with the key in the lock in her closet. After she closed the closet door behind her, so no one could observe her, she put her weapons away there, locked the door, and put the key in her pocket. She didn't want anyone coming across her Sten gun, especially Richard.

Richard came home that evening, as pleased with his two superiors as Alex was with the lovely house they had been assigned. Richard had expressed to them how comfortable and luxurious their living quarters were, and Counselor Aubrey Watson-Smith said with a broad grin that theirs was even bigger, and his wife had become totally spoiled. He said she hadn't stopped having babies since they got there and would have a rude awakening when they went back to England, and she had to take care of four children herself, which made Richard smile. And, he said, she was expecting another.

"We're hoping to do the same," he said in an undervoice. Alex had said she wanted to wait until they got settled, but Richard couldn't see that it would take long, given how they would be living.

He'd had a serious meeting with the viceroy, whom Richard found very impressive, and he liked Aubrey, his immediate superior, who invited him to join the local cricket team made up of the British men who worked there. There was to be a formal dinner at the viceroy's palace the following week, and he and Alex were expected to be there, and would meet everyone then. Their life in India had begun.

For the next three months, their social life was a constant round of parties and formal dinners. If anything, the social gatherings were even more formal than those in London, from what Richard knew of it. People in England had lost most of their servants after the war and couldn't replace them. The style now for extremely formal living had begun to relax ever so slightly, even among the upper classes, whereas in India nothing had changed. Those who lived there wanted to show that they were more British than the British, so everything was lavishly, beautifully done, and extremely formal and elegant. They had an army of servants to help them maintain a lifestyle that was faltering or had disappeared everywhere else. Alex felt like her mother in the old days, as she dressed in an evening gown every night and Sanjay laid out Richard's dinner jacket and black tie, since Sanjay doubled as butler and valet.

"I've never had a valet in my life," Richard said, when he came into Alex's dressing room as she put her lipstick on. She was wearing an exquisite pale pink evening gown, and looked like a young queen.

"And you probably never will have a valet again," she teased him, "nor I a lady's maid. I feel like a character in a nineteenth-century novel. It's fun, though, isn't it?" He smiled, pleased that she was enjoying their exotic new life so much. And she liked the women she had met so far. She had met Samantha Watson-Smith, the counselor's wife, and liked her, but she was eight months pregnant, and said she was going into hiding soon. She could hardly move, and was terrified she was having twins. She said she was twice the size she'd been with the last one. She had four boys and was hoping for a girl.

The formal dinner and reception at the viceroy's palace was spectacular, and very British. The next day Alex dutifully sent a list of all the guests she remembered meeting with a brief synopsis of their conversations. She did that every morning, after the social events of the night before. She used her radio transmitter as soon as Richard left for work.

In May, Jawaharlal Nehru was elected the leader of the Congress Party, which she reported to her superiors at MI6 immediately, although they would know that themselves from other sources. Alex reported it when she met him at the next state dinner at the Viceroy's House in June and she had a chance to chat with him. Nehru spoke to her of the end of British rule, and the importance of independence for India. He also mentioned partition. He felt strongly that the Muslims in India should be moved to what would become the dominion of Pakistan, and the four million Hindus in Pakistan should return to India, a massive and complicated undertaking. She transmitted what he said verbatim to her contact at MI6, whom she knew only by a code number and not a name. Meeting Nehru was the most important encounter she had had so far. She waited until she received confirmation that they had gotten her message, which she sent in code, and then she put the transmitter away in her locked closet. The ritual never took long and her transmissions were all benign. There was none of the urgency of the war in what she had to relay to them. It was as easy as Lyle Bridges had said it would be, and took almost no time at all. Her messages to MI6 were simple.

Everything about their life in India was easy and exceedingly pleasant, until August when violence between Hindus and Muslims left at least four thousand dead in a Calcutta bloodbath, which Alex reported to MI6 immediately, along with everything she heard about it. They were far from the violence in New Delhi, nine hundred miles from Calcutta.

She had been visiting Samantha Watson-Smith and her new babies, twin boys as she had feared, when she heard the news. Samantha commented that Aubrey was afraid that there would be more violence in the near future. The Hindu population was afraid of extreme violence if the British agreed to an independent India and pulled out too quickly. The twins were three months old by then, and as she handed them to two Indian amahs, she said to Alex that they really had to stop. They had six boys now, and she would never be able to cope with them if Aubrey ever got transferred back to England. Alex laughed when she said it. It seemed to be the opinion of most of the women she met there, who enjoyed a lifestyle they couldn't have had anywhere else. And even in India, that life was about to disappear, or would eventually, with the end of British rule.

"I can see how one would get incredibly spoiled here," Alex admitted. She had described it in detail to her mother, who said she wished she had some of that at home. She was managing all eleven of the foster children with only one girl to help her now, since the other one had gone to London to find better-paid work.

Two weeks after the violence in Calcutta, an interim government was formed, and Nehru became vice president, which set off more violence two days later between Hindus and Muslims in Bombay.

In the fall, there was an atmosphere of unrest throughout the country, and skirmishes between Hindus and Muslims were constantly occurring. Alex and Richard talked about it at night, and whatever information she gleaned, or insights into the problems, she passed on to MI6 rapidly, in a steady stream of daily commentary about the problems in India, all relating to the eventual independence of India, and possible partition from Pakistan.

On several occasions, Richard expressed concern that there would be violence in New Delhi, and without saying anything to him, Alex began wearing her commando knife again, and carrying her tiny pistol in her purse. She wasn't frightened of the violence herself, but the reports of the riots were concerning, with Hindus and Sikhs wielding sabers and swords, and massive bloodshed in the streets. The Sikhs were neither Muslim nor Hindu, but a separate religion entirely. They were monotheistic, believing in one God, originated in the Punjab region, and broke from Hinduism due to their rejection of the caste system.

But in their British circles all was peaceful. Viscount Wavell's Christmas party was the most extraordinary event Alex had ever attended, with elephants lining the drive to the viceroy's palace, and caged Bengal tigers decorating the front lawn. She described all of it in her letters to her mother, and sent lists and reports of everyone she met and spoke with to MI6 on her radio transmitter. Everyone she talked to with some knowledge of the subject felt certain that there would be more bloodshed between the Hindus and Muslims, and more strikes and riots, before India achieved independence, and Richard felt sure they were right.

As the year ended, the only disappointment they had experienced since coming to India eight months before was that Alex had been trying unsuccessfully to conceive a baby almost since they arrived, and so far it hadn't happened. Richard was less concerned about it than she was. Alex was afraid that something might be wrong. She visited a doctor Samantha Watson-Smith recommended, a kind old Englishman who had delivered all of Samantha's babies, and he told Alex to relax, that coming to India was a big change, and when he heard something of her war experiences, he told her that her body needed time to adjust to peacetime and her new environment. She had lived through six years of stress and trauma during the war, and the loss of two brothers. Now she was living in a foreign culture with the drumroll of violence in the background. It was hardly the right atmosphere to conceive a baby, which didn't explain why Samantha had been pregnant non-stop almost since she'd arrived, but she had nothing else on her mind. She was a sweet woman, but parties, and wearing pretty clothes and seducing her husband, and then giving birth, were her only concerns. Alex was far more involved and interested in local politics, while appearing not to be, and following the news closely was of greater interest to her. She liked talking to the men at the parties they went to, not to flirt with them, as most of the women did, but to hear what they had to say and then report it to Military Intelligence at home.

But whatever the reason, Alex was still not pregnant at the end of the year. She shared her concerns with her mother, who said the same thing as the doctor and told her to relax, which was Richard's theory too.

The clashes between Hindus and Muslims continued, and erupted in March in Punjab. And just before that, in February, Viscount Wavell stepped down as viceroy, and was replaced by Viscount Mountbatten of Burma, great-grandson of Queen Victoria, uncle of Prince Philip, and protégé of Winston Churchill. He was greatly favored and much admired, and it was hoped that he would help make the transition to Indian independence smoother, and put an end to the violence that was spreading across the country. He had a warm relationship with many of the princes of India. He also had an absolutely dazzling wife, Edwina, who charmed everyone, became a close friend of Vice President Nehru, and was frequently seen with him. Viscount Mountbatten seemed to be off to a good start from the moment he arrived. People adored them both and were in awe of them.

It made a great change for Richard, as he had enjoyed working for Viscount Wavell, and Viscount Mountbatten made stronger social demands on all of them. He and the spectacularly beautiful and charming Edwina entertained constantly, and Richard and Alex were expected to be there. Although Richard found it tiresome after a while, Alex found it very useful, and met scores of new people, and influential men in politics, which she reported to MI6 diligently. They rarely asked her for additional information. She supplied so much of it, about people and politics and key players, that they got a very clear picture of the state of India on the ground.

When she arrived, Alex had wanted to spend some time visiting the shrines of India, but with the increasing unrest, Richard had asked her not to, and she spent most of her time with social pursuits, meeting people, going out at night with Richard, and writing coded reports to MI6. Her lady's maid had seen her pistol and commando knife on her dressing table one morning while she was dressing, and had pointed to them and told Alex she was very wise. Alex put a finger to her lips, urging her not to tell, and the woman nodded immediately. She understood, but Indians were worried these days about what independence would cost them, and how many lives would be lost in the process.

The great moment finally came after years of negotiation and months of violence and riots. India won her independence and became the Dominion of India, free of British rule, on the fourteenth of August 1947, fifteen months after Richard and Alex had come to India, and on the fifteenth of August, Pakistan became independent of India, and became a dominion. India was largely Hindu, and Pakistan Muslim. The exchange of many millions between the two countries had not happened and would be virtually impossible to implement.

Jawaharlal Nehru was made the first prime minister of the Dominion of India, and stood on the ramparts of the Red Fort, on the day of independence, and unfurled the Indian tricolor flag to mark the end of British colonial rule, and Lord Mountbatten moved out of Viceroy's House, all of which Alex reported to MI6. It was the end of two hundred years of British history and the beginning of India's freedom as an independent country. And Viscount Mountbatten, no longer viceroy, at the request of the new Indian leaders, became governor-general of the Union of India.

Mohammed Ali Jinnah became the governor-general of Pakistan, and Liaquat Ali Khan became the prime minister.

For the next three months, there were massacres and migrations of Hindus and Muslims between India and Pakistan. The violence was unspeakably brutal, with murders, arson, mass abductions, and rapes. Seventy-five thousand women were raped and most of them disfigured or dismembered in the process. Villages were burned to the ground. Old women and infants and children were savagely murdered and hacked into bits. Pregnant women were viciously killed and babies set on fire and killed. The violence was unthinkable and unimaginable to civilized people, with extreme atrocities. It was in fact a religious war no one could stop.

As the months wore on, fifteen million people, mostly Muslims, had been forced from their homes, and close to two million were dead.

As viceroy, Viscount Mountbatten had agreed to India's independence ten months before it had been provisionally scheduled to happen, and people wondered if the violence would have been less extreme if the British had stayed in power longer, and made the transition more slowly, all of which Alex reported to MI6.

In September, a month after independence had been declared and the partition of Pakistan had taken place, Prime Minister Nehru asked for four million Hindus to be removed from Pakistan and sent to India, and an equal four million Muslims in India to relocate to Pakistan. Both countries were in an uproar and at the end of October war broke out between India and Pakistan. Alex wore both her pistol and her commando knife all the time now whenever she went out. Although most of the violence was in Punjab, India was becoming a dangerous place. She kept her Sten gun where she could reach it quickly, in case she ever needed to defend herself or their home. So far, they weren't in danger in New Delhi, and they were far from most of the violence, but that could always change. Her parents were worried about her, and she always assured them that they were safe.

Also a month after independence was declared, the Watson-Smiths were transferred and Richard became counselor, no longer deputy, an important promotion for him.

The turmoil in India continued into 1948. In January, the country was shaken when their spiritual leader Mahatma Gandhi was assassinated. For the rest of the year various princely states seceded from India to join Pakistan, or the reverse. The Indo-Pakistani war continued insolubly. In June, Viscount Mountbatten gave up his position as governor-general of the Union of India, after less than a year in office. The position of viceroy had disappeared with independence, and the position of governor-general was taken over by an Indian, while Jawaharlal Nehru staunchly remained prime minister, with a firm grip on the country.

Richard's position in India was more delicate after Viscount Mountbatten left, and Richard quietly remained below the radar, making himself available for British subjects still living in India, and attempting to pour oil on troubled waters wherever possible. But life in India wasn't nearly as pleasant as it had been when they arrived. They still had the same luxuries and remained in the same house, but Alex had her small weapons on her at all times, and Richard caught a glimpse of them one day while she was getting dressed.

"How long have you been wearing those?" he asked her, surprised to see them again. He thought she'd put them away after the war.

"For a while," she said quietly. "Old habits die hard. I wore them night and day for five years." But he knew she had stopped carrying them before they came to India.

"Are you afraid here?" He was concerned and trusted her judgment and evaluation of the situation.

"Not really," she said thoughtfully. "But I like to be cautious. Things can get heated in religious wars." The fighting was geographically far from them, but they no longer had the status in India that they once had, now that colonial rule was over.

A year later, Nehru changed that, or altered it somewhat, declaring that despite becoming a republic, they could remain part of the British Commonwealth. The Indians and Pakistanis had agreed to a ceasefire in January, and signed a peace treaty in July. And in November, the man who had assassinated Mahatma Gandhi was executed. India was finally returning to some semblance of order more than two years after they'd won independence. Richard and Alex enjoyed a peaceful Christmas, and the best Christmas present of all was that three days before Christmas, the doctor confirmed what she suspected. Alex was pregnant at last.

Chapter 12

Alex was surprised by how ill she felt in the early months of her pregnancy. It was worse than she'd expected and she went out less than she had in the more than three years they'd been there. They had come to India at a historic time, and it had been a roller coaster ride being there, but all of that was eclipsed now by the joy she felt over the baby she was carrying, and Richard's delight. Her own joy was dampened somewhat by the misery of feeling ill from the moment she woke up, until she fell asleep at night. She went out with Richard in the evening whenever possible, but the rest of the time she stayed in bed, and Isha tried every Indian remedy she knew for the nausea of pregnancy and so far nothing had worked. Alex felt sick all the time.

The baby was due in July 1950, and they were to be transferred before then. Their four years in India were almost over, and Alex was worried about having to move to another assignment, and another country, shortly before the baby came. They had no idea yet where they would be going. Richard had had feedback from the Foreign Office in London that his superiors were pleased with him, and had promised him a good post on the next round. He and Alex both loved India and the people, and they had been heartbroken over the violence that had cost so many lives.

Alex began to feel better in January, and only days after the intense nausea had begun to wane, she received a letter from her mother that devastated her. Her father had died the day after Christmas, and Victoria sounded shattered. He was only sixty-three years old, had had a heart attack and died instantly. Alex was convinced that his sons' deaths had shortened his life. She was crushed over the loss. Alex was in the living room waiting for Richard when he came home.

"Are you all right?" She was so pale that he was worried, although he was used to it by now. She had been deathly sick since November, although she had concealed it from him at first, until she was sure she was pregnant. And now she was sheet white again.

"My father . . ." she said and couldn't finish the sentence. He'd been dead for nearly a month by then, and she hadn't known it. While they were celebrating Christmas, and rejoicing over the baby they were going to have, her mother had buried her father in the family cemetery, all alone, with none of her children present to support her. "I have to go home to be with her," Alex said, stunned by her father's death, and worried about her mother.

"You can't," Richard said fervently. "You're not well enough."

"I don't have malaria." She smiled weakly at him. "I'm pregnant."

"You'll lose the baby," and they had waited so long for it to happen. They had been trying for three years.

"No, I won't. Women have been taking ships while they're pregnant for centuries." But it would be a long journey, and would take weeks to get there. "Maybe I could fly."

"Ask the doctor. That might be worse, with the altitude." He didn't want her to make the trip at all.

"Flying would be faster. I want to spend a few weeks with my mother. I have to, Richard. She's all alone. She sounds overwhelmed by everything she has to handle now." It was the first time that Alex truly regretted their having left England. Before, they had each other. Now her mother was alone at sixty-one, and hadn't expected to be widowed. Going home to be with her for a while seemed like the least Alex could do. She was the only child Victoria had left.

She went to the doctor the next day and explained the situation to him. He didn't love the idea of her traveling so far, but the first trimester was over, and he thought flying might be less traumatic for her than a long journey by ship.

Richard reluctantly made the arrangements for her. She would fly BOAC and change planes several times. The whole journey would take nearly forty hours, and would be exhausting, but she would have more time with her mother that way, rather than wasting weeks going by boat, and she was determined to go. Richard had gotten her a seat on the plane for the next day. They lay together that night, while he held her and she cried for her father, and he feared she would lose the baby from the long trip.

"Just take care of yourself, please. I'll be worried sick about you."

"Don't be. I'll be fine." She got up, finished packing, and appeared in their bedroom carrying her Sten gun, and he gave a start when he saw it.

"What are you doing with that?" He sat up straight in bed.

"It's my old friend." She grinned at him. "I thought you should have it while I'm gone. You never know when you'll need it."

"I'm married to a mercenary. You're the only woman I know who travels with weapons, and your own submachine gun."

She grinned at him again. "Where do you want me to put this?" It was another reminder to Richard that whatever Alex said, she had done more during the war than drive rocks from England to Scotland to build airstrips. She didn't need a gun for that.

"Where's that been for the past four years?"

"Locked in my closet." She was carrying a box of the bullets too, and he shook his head.

"Leave it where it was, just give me the key." She left to put it away and handed him the key when she came to bed, and he shook his head again as he looked at her. "Sometimes I think I don't know you. You're always stronger than I think. I was in the same war you were, and I don't run around with a submachine gun, or a pistol and that nasty little knife of yours."

"I relied on them for five years. You were in a plane," she said simply, and he leaned over and kissed her.

"I'd hate to see you use them, you're probably a better shot than I am."

"I doubt it." She wondered what he would think if he knew she was working for MI6. He wouldn't like it. She had radioed them that day, and explained the situation, that she was returning to England for a few weeks, after the death of her father, and would make contact with them when she was there. She would have nothing to report in the meantime. Things had been quiet lately anyway, and she had gone out very little, feeling so ill.

* * *

Richard took her to the airport the next day, for the first leg of her trip. He kissed her and held her for a long time before he let her go, and she waved as she walked to the plane. She was sad, but strong, and anxious to see her mother. He watched her until she boarded, and then watched as the plane took off. He prayed that she and the baby would come back to him safely. He didn't want anything to happen to either of them. And as his driver took him to the office, he smiled at the memory of her, looking like a young girl in their bedroom the night before, holding her old gun. She was a remarkable woman, and he was just sorry she had to go home alone. But he couldn't leave India right now, he was too busy.

The flight to London seemed interminable although she slept a lot. Alex had been traveling for forty hours when she arrived in London.

She took a bus from the airport to the train station, and caught the train to Hampshire. Her mother had no idea she was coming. Alex got a cab at the train station and walked into the house carrying her suitcase, just as her mother was leaving for the market with a basket over her arm. She screamed when she saw Alex and looked like she was going to faint.

"What are you doing here? You're in New Delhi, and you're pregnant."

"I'm pregnant," she smiled at her mother and hugged her, "but I'm here now. I came to see you." And with that, her mother burst into tears, and they walked into the library and sat down. She told Alex all the details of how it had happened. He'd had a sudden terrible pain in his chest, and then he just collapsed and he was gone. Alex held her mother's hand and had an arm around her. Her mother was stunned and grateful she had come.

"I don't think Papa ever recovered from losing Willie and Geoff. It was too much for him. He had such high hopes for both of them," Alex said sadly. He had had far fewer expectations for his daughter, except about who she married. But in the end, he had liked Richard and by the time they married, he was very fond of him.

"I think you're right. How are things in India?" her mother asked her.

"Better. The country is settling down. It was a mess for a while. I think they did it all too soon. We're almost through there. Richard is waiting for our next assignment."

"I wish they'd send you home for a while," Victoria said wistfully.

"They won't." She didn't want to mislead her mother, and give her false hope. "They don't send us home between assignments. But at least I'm here now."

"Are you exhausted? You must have flown for days!"

"Forty hours. And I'm a bit tired, but I slept on the planes. Do you want me to go to the market with you?"

"I'll go. I won't be long. You have a bath and a cup of tea, and I'll be back as fast as I can." She looked better just seeing Alex.

"How are the children?" Alex asked, and her mother looked wistful about them too.

"There are only three left. The others are working at jobs in London. One of them is in Liverpool, and one in Manchester. One of them is at university in Edinburgh. They're lovely kids. They all came home for Christmas." Alex smiled. It had been a wonderful thing to do. Her parents had never had any regrets about them. "I'll be back quickly," Victoria said and picked up her market basket, and walked out the front door. Alex wanted to visit her father's grave with her mother, but she wasn't ready for it yet.

Alex walked to the phone as soon as her mother left. She sent a telegram to Richard that she had arrived safely, and was in Hampshire. And then she called her contact at MI6 for when she was in country. She reported where she was and how to reach her, and said she'd call again before she went back to New Delhi. And then she called Bertie at MI5. He was happy to hear from her, and sorry to hear about her father. He said he was fine, and enjoying the work. She brought him up to speed on India in a nutshell and none of it surprised him.

She thought about calling Samantha Watson-Smith when she hung up. They'd been back in England for a year, living in a tiny flat outside London with no help, and she was hating every minute of it. They were hoping for a plush assignment where they'd be comfortable. They had exchanged a few letters since they'd left, but she was so busy with the boys, she rarely had time to write.

Alex went upstairs to her old room then, and decided to stay there, since she was alone this time. She had bathed and changed into a black sweater and skirt and black stockings by the time her mother came back. She was wearing black out of respect for her father.

She went to help her mother with the groceries when she heard her come in. It felt good being there to lend a hand.

"How are you feeling, by the way?" her mother asked her.

"Better now. I was sick as a dog for the first few months."

"I was sick with you. I never was with the boys." She smiled at Alex.

"It's due in July. We'll have transferred by then."

"I hope to someplace decent with a good hospital," her mother said, and made lunch for both of them.

Alex went to bed early that night, exhausted from the trip, but she was happy to be home, and she knew it made a big difference to her mother. She still couldn't believe her father was gone. She wished he had lived long enough to know about the baby. He was too young to die, but so were her brothers. And now she had a new life inside her. She was thinking about how strange life was, with its losses and gifts, and then she fell asleep.

It was snowing when she woke up, and after breakfast, she and her mother went out to where her father was buried. There was no headstone yet. They stood there for a long time, holding hands, with the snow falling on their hair and shoulders, and walked back to the house for a cup of hot tea. Alex built a fire for them in the library and it felt strange to be home, but warm and comfortable too. They had been living in India for so long, and their life was so different there.

They played cards that night, and took the children to the cinema on the weekend. Several of the neighbors dropped by to check on Victoria, and they were surprised, and pleased for her, to see that Alex was home.

Alex stayed with her for three weeks, which gave them time to discuss who would manage the estate now, since Victoria didn't feel equal to it and Alex was so far away. The man who'd been helping Edward was willing to do it, and he was going to stay in touch with Alex on bigger decisions. And then she had to go back. It was even harder to leave than it had been the first time. She hadn't been home in four years. Her parents had promised to come out to India, but never had. And she knew her mother would never come alone, so she didn't know when she'd see her again. She didn't want to go years without seeing her, especially now, with her father gone and her mother alone.

"I want you to come and see your grandchild," she said in a husky voice as she was leaving.

"I will. I promise. And your letters are wonderful," Victoria said, as tears spilled onto her cheeks. Alex wouldn't let her come to the airport. It would have been too hard for both of them, and she wouldn't have her husband to go home with now. It would be a long, lonely train ride back to Hampshire.

"I'll send you pictures of the baby. If it's a boy, we'll name him after Papa." Hearing it only made Victoria cry more, and finally Alex tore herself away, and got into the car waiting to take her to the train station to get to London, and from there to the airport by bus. Her long journey back had begun.

Her mother stood in the doorway waving to her, until the car was out of sight, and then she sat down in the kitchen and cried. She wondered if she would ever see her daughter again, or the baby she was carrying. Wherever they went now on Richard's next assignment, it would still be so far away.

Alex thought about her mother all the way to London, considering the same things. She felt so guilty leaving her, but she had to get back to Richard. Her home was with him now, and they would have to move soon. She was glad she had come to see her mother. The trip seemed even longer on the way back.

She had sent Richard a telegram with her arrival time in Delhi. She didn't know if he'd come to the airport, but she hoped he would. You could see the small swell of the baby now. She was four months pregnant. She had gone to see her old doctor in Hampshire, and he said everything seemed fine, and the baby was the right size.

Alex slept on the last flight until the plane landed in Delhi, and walked down the steps with her hand luggage. Her mother had knitted a little sweater and cap for the baby and she'd brought them with her in her valise.

She was dazed from the long trip as she walked toward the terminal. She saw Richard as soon as she stepped into it, and he came toward her and held her close in his powerful arms.

"Oh my God, I missed you so much," he said as he held her for a long time and then they walked out of the airport together. His car and driver were waiting, and he handed Raghav Alex's suitcase, and got into the car next to her.

"Did you shoot anyone with my gun?" she whispered and he laughed.

"I never touched it. You're a menace. How's your mother?" he asked.

"Sad." He nodded. How else could she be? "I felt terrible leaving her. She's going to be so lonely now. I hope she comes to see the baby, wherever we are." He looked troubled when she said it, and Alex had the feeling something was wrong. He looked happy to see her, but as though something else was bothering him. She didn't ask him until they were alone in their bedroom when they got home. Isha had brought her a tray with some soup and little things to tempt her to eat, and Alex thanked her warmly. "What's wrong?" she asked him immediately.

"Nothing, really. I got my new assignment. I was hoping for a change from here. Europe maybe, now that the country is recovering." She would have liked that too, especially now with her mother alone.

"What did we get?" She wondered if they were being sent to the wilds of Africa, or someplace primitive.

"Pakistan." His disappointment showed on his face, and in his eyes. "We've been here for a long time, and it isn't much of a change. They feel that I know the situation so well here by now, having been here for the transition, that they want to move me over to the other side. It's really the flip side of the same coin, and things won't be as comfortable for you in Pakistan as they are here. They say they're giving us a nice house in Karachi. I'm sorry, Alex. They promised me a plum job next time. They made me deputy high commissioner this time, which is a step up."

"A very nice step up." She smiled at him. It was like being ambassador somewhere else. Inside the British Commonwealth, they had high commissioners, not ambassadors. "When do we go?"

"May." It was in three months. She'd be seven months pregnant by then. "Do you mind having the baby there?"

"It's as good as anywhere else." It didn't worry her.

"The embassy has its own doctor, at least he's British. So you won't have some guy speaking Urdu or Bengali delivering the baby." She laughed at the thought.

"I don't think the baby will care," she said and he laughed.

"You're a trouper. I'm sorry I didn't get a more glamorous assignment."

"I don't need glamour," she said and kissed him. "I just need you."

"I'm a lucky man," he said and meant it. "Even if you do carry a lot of weapons around." They both laughed at that.

They were sad to leave the friends they had made in New Delhi, but a number of them had already left. The diplomatic community was always a group of ever-changing faces, which also made life interesting. Alex had come to love it and Richard did too.

Alex was particularly sad to leave Isha and Sanjay when they left New Delhi. They had been loyal and gentle and kind. She promised to stay in touch with them, and to send them pictures of the baby.

They had already sent most of their things to Karachi and Alex was pleasantly surprised when she saw the house there. It wasn't as pretty and luxurious as the house in New Delhi, or as lavishly staffed, but it was large and pleasant and peaceful, and there were enough people working there to keep them well served. Alex picked a room for the nursery almost as soon as they arrived. She ventured into the marketplace the following week with her driver, to buy a cradle. She found a pretty one that was hand carved.

Richard liked the high commissioner he was working for, Sir Laurence Grafftey-Smith, who had been there since the partition and Pakistan's independence. He would be leaving in a year.

The social life in Karachi was much quieter than in New Delhi, which suited Alex for the moment. Once she got their new house in order, she was too tired to go out. She went to a few cocktail parties with Richard, and one official dinner, and by then she was eight months pregnant, and felt like a beached whale in the heat. The baby was big now and she was exhausted.

She met the local British doctor, and he thought the baby was large, but she'd had no problems except nausea in the beginning. There was a maternity clinic the wives of European diplomats used, and she was planning to give birth there. All the nurses were English or French.

Their house in Karachi had a wide porch that got a nice breeze at night. She was lying there with Richard a week before her due date, when her water broke. They called the doctor, and he sent them to the clinic and said he'd come later. Labor hadn't started yet, and traditionally first babies took a long time. Richard drove her there himself. He had already checked to see where it was. The clinic was spotless when they walked in. They examined Alex and said nothing had started and let Richard sit with her for a while. For the first time, she wished she were at home in England, with her mother. She suddenly felt far from home, and scared. She had braved the enemy a hundred times, and been in situations most men would have been afraid to face, but now, about to have a baby, she didn't feel equal to the task. He could see the fear in her eyes.

"Did you bring your gun?" he whispered to her, and she laughed. He had a way of lightening the moment, and making everything seem okay, even when it wasn't.

"My pistol's in my purse," she whispered back.

"You can always shoot the doctor if you don't like him."

"I wish I were home with my mum," she said sadly, as a tear crept down her cheek. She suddenly looked young and afraid.

"I wish they'd let me stay with you," he said, worried, but they'd already asked and been refused. There was a waiting room for fathers, or he could go home and come back later, after the baby was born, which most men did. The nurses said they would call him when the baby came, but he had promised Alex he wouldn't leave.

She dozed for a while after that, and woke up around midnight when the pains started. They came hard and fast, and Richard could tell things were moving quickly, when the doctor arrived and he left the room. He assured Richard it wouldn't be long.

"The nurses tell me your baby's in a hurry." He smiled and closed the door, and Richard thought he heard Alex shout in pain after that. He paced the halls for an hour waiting for news. They had taken Alex to the delivery room a few minutes after the doctor arrived. Finally Richard sat down in the waiting room in despair. All the nurses would say was that they would notify him as soon as the baby was born.

She'd been in the delivery room for two hours when the doctor came to find him in the waiting room with a broad smile.

"You have a handsome son, Mr. Montgomery. Your wife did very well. You have a big boy, nine pounds." Richard almost winced when he said it. It sounded painful to him.

"When can I see Alex?"

"She'll be back in her room in a little while." He didn't tell Richard that he had just finished stitching her up. She was badly torn by a baby that size, and labor had been difficult and fast. A nurse brought the baby to show him then. He had a round face and Alex's blond hair. He looked like a chubby duck with pale peach fuzz on his head, and Richard's heart melted the minute he saw him. He was wrapped in a blue blanket, and they took him to the nursery as soon as his father had seen him. The doctor had left by then.

It was another two hours before Alex came back to the room. She was groggy from the ether they had given her when they stitched her up, and a shot afterward for the pain. When Richard walked into her room, she looked like she'd been hit by a truck, with dark circles under her eyes.

"Are you okay?" he asked as he bent to kiss her.

"I think so." She didn't want to tell him how bad it had been, but he could see it. They hadn't given her anything for the pain, until the stitches, and it was much worse than she'd been told it would be. Samantha always said it was like shelling peas, which was a bold-faced lie, she knew now. Her mother had hinted it might be hard the first time, but didn't want to scare her.

"He's so beautiful, and so are you." Richard kissed her, and sat next to her bed, holding her hand until she went back to sleep. As she lay there, the sun came up, and streamed into the room, and it felt like a blessing, as he watched his sleeping wife. They had a son. And he knew as he sat there that it was the most precious moment of his life.

Chapter 13

They named the baby Edward William Geoffrey Montgomery as she had promised her mother they would. Richard took a picture of Alex holding him, to send to her. They let Alex leave the clinic after a week. She was nursing him, and he was a hungry baby. He looked three months old when he was only a week old.

Richard was settling into the job, and getting to know the city. They were still dealing with religious issues, the fallout of partition, and the exchange of four million Muslims for four million Hindus, an immense undertaking which was nearly impossible to accomplish and still wasn't fully complete. Those they moved had nowhere to go.

Alex was happy to see him when he came home at night. She was on her feet again in a few weeks, enjoying the baby, and she had cut back her social life radically from what it had been in New Delhi. But she realized that she had to get back to it soon so she could report to MI6. The social life in Karachi wasn't as intense. She was enjoying being home with the baby and didn't feel like going out.

She started joining Richard for diplomatic social events again in October. She was very impressed when she met the prime minister, Liaquat Ali Khan. He was one of the great leaders of Pakistan, a champion of independent rule. He was a statesman, lawyer, and political theorist. He had been the finance minister of India's interim government, the first defense minister of Pakistan and the prime minister, and also served as the minister of Commonwealth and Kashmir affairs. Alex admired him and found him to be a fascinating person when she talked to him. She sent a report about their meeting to MI6, with high praise for the prime minister, who was much loved in Pakistan.

The rest of the year slipped by without event.

The new high commissioner, Sir Gilbert Laithwaite, Richard's new boss, arrived after the first of the year. He was British-Irish, born in Dublin, and a war hero from World War I. He had been in India for more than thirty years, on various commissions with the India office, as principal private secretary to the viceroy. He had also been deputy undersecretary of state for India and had just returned from a tour of duty as ambassador to Ireland. Now he was high commissioner to Pakistan. Richard liked him from the moment he met him, and knew that he had a lot to learn from him. It would make his appointment to Pakistan that much more worthwhile. It had been uneventful so far, which in some ways was a relief after India.

In February a failed coup d'état caught everyone's attention. After a relatively peaceful year, the country was badly shaken on October 16, 1951, by the assassination of Prime Minister Liaquat Ali Khan, whom Alex had met and been so impressed by. It was viewed as a tragedy and he was called the Martyr of the Nation. Khan was shot twice in the chest and his assassin was killed on the spot, and said to be a professional killer for hire. The country mourned their prime minister's death intensely. Richard and the high commissioner met with Pakistani leaders several times.

The relatively peaceful year before that had given Alex and Richard time to enjoy their son, who had turned a year old that July, and started walking a few weeks after that. He was a happy, bouncy toddler, and Richard spent every moment he could with him and Alex when he wasn't working. Alex was trying to convince her mother to come and see him, without success so far. She didn't want to travel on her own, although she missed Alex terribly and wanted to see her grandson. But not enough to leave home. And she hadn't been well. She had become increasingly retiring since her husband's death, and didn't even venture to London, let alone Pakistan.

Little Edward was fifteen months old the week after the prime minister's death when he came down with a flu of some kind and a high fever. Alex wasn't sure what it was, but they took him to the hospital the same night. He was delirious when they got there, and Richard and Alex were frantic. They were told by the doctor who examined him that he had cholera, which was common in both Pakistan and India at the time. He was unconscious half an hour after they got him to the hospital, and nothing brought down the fever as they sat with him through the night and Alex and the nurses bathed him with cool cloths. He was deep in a coma by morning, with Alex and Richard sitting next to his bed and holding him. Little Edward died at noon.

Alex held him in her arms after he died, and the doctor assured them that nothing could have been done for him. They were inconsolable, and held a funeral for him two days later. He was cremated after that, and Alex kept the little urn with his ashes next to her bed. She lay there day and night with her eyes closed, thinking of him, running the film of his short life through her head. And the last terrible night when they could do nothing to save him. She felt as though she had died herself.

Alex called a friend of her mother's in Hampshire, and asked her to go and tell Victoria in person what had happened. She didn't want her mother reading it in a telegram when she was alone.

Victoria called Alex in Karachi as soon as she'd heard, and tried to offer what consolation she could, having lost two sons herself. She felt terrible that she hadn't come to see him, but she hadn't been well herself. She had started having heart problems after Alex's father died, and was afraid of the long trip. And now she had lost a grandson she had never met.

Alex talked to her mother for a long time, and cried the whole time on the phone. A week later, Richard found her in their son's room when he got home, packing the baby's things. She hadn't touched any of it until then. But he wasn't coming back. Richard stood with her and they both cried as they folded all his clothes and put them with his toys in a big box. She wanted to save them, but couldn't stand seeing them every day. And she gently closed the door to his room after everything was packed. She didn't go in for months. It was too painful. Whenever Richard came home from work, she looked as though she'd been crying. She went out with him to important social events, but anything she could avoid, she did. She couldn't imagine being happy again. The death of King George VI provided some distraction, although everything seemed remote and unimportant to her now.

A month later, five months after Edward's death, Alex was shocked when she discovered that she was pregnant. They wanted another baby sometime in the future, but not so soon. She was still mourning Edward and knew she always would. She didn't feel ready to open her heart to another baby just yet. But fate had made the decision for her.

She wasn't sick this time, but her spirit wasn't in it. She acted as though nothing was happening, and never spoke of the baby or the pregnancy. She didn't want to fall in love with another child and have the fates steal it away.

"Do you want to go home to have the baby this time?" Richard asked her gently, and she shook her head. She was still sending coded messages to MI6, and she went out with Richard occasionally, but she had been depressed ever since Edward died, and Richard didn't know what to do. He had spoken to the doctor about it, and he said that she'd feel better after the new baby came, but Richard wasn't so sure. In all the years he'd known her, he had never seen her like this. He was wondering if he should take her home and leave her with her mother for a while. Alex barely spoke to him. The baby was due in October 1952, almost exactly a year after Edward's death. She was still depressed.

They went through the motions of sharing a normal life with each other, but Richard knew Alex wasn't there. She hadn't been for a year.

He took her to New Delhi for a party the high commissioner was giving. He thought it would do her good to see her old friends, and New Delhi was livelier than Karachi. The party was lovely and Alex looked beautiful, but he could tell that she didn't care about any of it. Something in her had died with little Edward, and Richard couldn't find a way to bring her back. He could feel the baby kick at night when they lay close together, and Alex never said a word. She never put his hand on her belly, or smiled when the baby kicked, as she had the first time. She seemed to be disconnected from everything in her life now, even Richard.

Alex had been in a fog all year. He wondered if she'd ever be the same. He got her to help him entertain, reluctantly, and he almost had to drag her out of bed to do it. Two weeks from her due date, she had still done nothing for the new baby. They were totally unprepared. They had put away Edward's cradle with his things, and they didn't even have a basket or a crib for the baby to sleep in. She had given Edward's crib away to someone who needed it.

She was putting something away in the nursery when her water broke, and she panicked, and suddenly there was a lake around her feet.

She looked at Richard with terror in her eyes, as though she was going to bolt and run.

"I'm not ready . . . I can't . . . I can't do that again," she whispered to him.

"It's going to be all right." The delivery had been fine the last time. Edward's death had nothing to do with the delivery.

When Richard called the doctor at home, his wife said he was out but would be back soon. He went to tell Alex, and she was lying on their bed, staring into space.

"We should go to the clinic," he said quietly, "the doctor is out, but his wife said he'll be back soon." He was worried about her.

"I don't care. I'm not going to that place again." Richard looked frightened by what she said, and the vehemence with which she said it. He could see how panicked she was.

"Well, you can't have the baby at home," he said reasonably, but there was nothing reasonable about Alex. She was a cornered animal, and she looked like she was ready to attack him, or run.

"Yes, I can have it at home. Everyone does here."

"Everyone we know goes to the same clinic we went to before."

"I hated it. I won't. And Pakistani women don't go there. They have their babies at home." He didn't want to remind her that Pakistan and India had among the highest infant and maternal mortality rates in the world.

"I won't let you do that. It's not safe for you or the baby to have it here." He could see from the expression on her face that the pains had started, and he didn't want to waste time arguing with her, but he wasn't sure how to get her out of the house if she refused to go. "I have some say in this too."

"No, you don't. It's my body, and I'll do what I want."

"It's our baby, Alex. Please don't take a chance with this. I wouldn't know what to do if something goes wrong, for you or the baby."

"I don't want to go back to where he was born," she said, sobbing. "It's too soon, I'll expect to see him there. I'm not ready for this baby, I can't do it again," and between sobs, she was writhing in pain. "What if this baby dies too?"

"It won't," he said, his eyes pleading with her even more than his words.

"You don't know that. It could get sick, just like Edward did." He had died in a matter of hours and there was nothing they could do.

"Please, Richard . . . I want it to be different . . . I don't want this baby to die too." All the pain and anguish and terror of the past year were pouring out of her like a tidal wave and she was finally reaching out to him, but he couldn't let her have it at home. What if everything went wrong? Then this baby would die too.

She hadn't been ready for this baby, and now he knew it, but the baby was coming anyway. They hadn't even tried to get pregnant this time. It happened with no effort on their part.

"What if I stay with you this time?" he asked, feeling desperate. They were losing time, and the clinic was twenty minutes away.

"They won't let you," she said through clenched teeth. "They refused last time."

"I'll refuse to leave you. I swear." As he said it, he scooped her up in his arms, and she didn't fight him. She was in too much pain. It was happening even faster than the last time. He ran down the stairs carrying her, as one of their servants came running to help him. "Get Amil," he said, asking for the driver, who came immediately. He'd been in the kitchen talking to the others. "We're going to the clinic," he told him, and ran toward the car with Alex. One of the maids rushed toward him and handed him a stack of towels. But by then Alex had stopped arguing with him, and Richard wasn't sure they'd make it to the hospital before the baby was born. It had been less than an hour since her water had broken. "Drive quickly," he told the driver, who took him at his word, as Alex lay against him in the backseat, and smiled up at him.

"I'm sorry I've been so difficult. I've been so broken."

"I know," he said gently, as another pain tore through her and she clutched his arm.

"I think I'm having the baby," she said, as he stared at her in panic.

"Now?"

"Soon." But just from the look in her eyes, he could see that she was back. Heartbroken over Edward, but sane again. She hadn't been in months. And he'd been at his wits' end.

She didn't make a sound for the rest of the drive to the clinic, but she had his arm in a vise-like grip. And the moment they got to the clinic, Amil opened the door, Richard scooped her up, and rushed inside carrying her.

"My wife is about to deliver," he said to the nurse at the desk, and she rushed toward them, pressed a buzzer, and led them to an exam room at a dead run, as four nurses came flying out to help them. He lay Alex gently down on the exam table, as two nurses took off her clothes as quickly as they could. "You may leave now," the oldest of the nurses said in an imperious tone.

"I'm not going to. Just so we have that clear. My wife had a traumatic experience. I'm not leaving her for a minute." He looked fiercely at the head nurse.

"Her baby was very big. I was at the delivery."

"He died a year ago. I'm not leaving her alone." The nurse was shocked and didn't say another word. It was obvious that Richard wasn't going anywhere. And Alex was lying naked on the exam table and let out a hideous scream, as two of the nurses rushed to see what was going on, and the third covered her with a thin drape, and put her feet in stirrups. But as soon as the pain had passed, Alex looked at him and smiled.

"Thank you. I can do this if you're here," she said softly.

"I'm not going anywhere." Another pain seized her then, and she started pushing with a look of anguish on her face.

"Stop," one of the nurses commanded her. "The doctor isn't here yet." Alex paid no attention to her and went on pushing as she held Richard's hand. She let out another scream, and there was a wail between her legs, as one of the nurses checked under the drape, and lifted up the baby with the cord between its legs so they couldn't see what it was, but Richard didn't care, just so it was healthy. It was the most beautiful sight he had ever seen, and Alex lay back smiling, exhausted from the effort but looking victorious at what she'd done.

"It's a girl!" one of the nurses said, as the doctor walked in.

"What's going on here? And what are *you* doing here?" he asked Richard with a frown.

"Watching my daughter be born," Richard said with a broad grin. And the shock of the baby coming had finally shaken Alex out of her depressed and nearly catatonic state. She was crying as she saw the baby. She looked nothing like Edward. She had dark hair and dark eyes like Richard, which was a relief. If she had looked just like Edward, it would have been too hard, and too much of a déjà vu. Everything had been different this time, and it was a girl.

"May I examine your wife now?" he said to Richard, indicating that he should leave.

"You may, but I'm not going anywhere." The doctor turned to examine Alex and she was worn-out but happy. Richard was deeply moved by what he'd seen. "What are we calling her?" he asked Alex when they were alone, and she looked thoughtful.

"How does Sophie sound to you?"

"I like it," he said as he bent to kiss his wife. "You were spectacular, by the way. You deserve a medal for this too." She laughed at what he said, and for an instant there was a sad look in her eyes, and he understood and kissed her again, and spoke softly to her. "He was beautiful too. But this is the little angel we were meant to have." She nodded and squeezed his hand as a tear slid down her cheek. One of the nurses walked into the room and handed the baby to her, all cleaned up and in a pink blanket. She was the most beautiful sight they had ever seen. The doctor had left the room, and the nurses left them alone with Sophie, who peered at them as though she had seen them before. And, as Alex looked into her daughter's eyes, for the first time in a year she felt alive and at peace.

Chapter 14

When they left Pakistan for their next assignment in April of 1954, Sophie was eighteen months old, running everywhere, and full of life. All the servants and everyone who saw her loved her. Their time in Pakistan had been difficult for Alex, losing her father and little Edward, and her depression afterward. But Pakistan had been less turbulent than their years in India, although less interesting too. Their life in New Delhi had been more exciting and more fun. One of the highlights of their time in Pakistan was the spectacular party they'd given for the coronation of Queen Elizabeth II ten months earlier. It had been a glorious occasion and people were still talking about the party nearly a year later. They had gone all out to honor the young queen and no one would ever forget the party at the embassy, with a ball in white tie and tails for the men, and the women in exquisite evening gowns and magnificent jewels.

This time, they were happy to be going to Morocco, somewhere so different from anyplace they knew. After eight years in India and Pakistan, which were so closely related, they were ready for something new. Alex had promised to visit her mother with Sophie as soon as she could. The last of the foster children had left for university while they were in Pakistan, so Victoria was entirely alone. Morocco was close enough to England that Alex hoped her mother would finally visit them. Victoria had never been to India or Pakistan in all the years they were there, and Alex had only been home to see her when her father died. They wrote to each other a great deal but that wasn't the same as visiting would have been.

This time, after eight years in the diplomatic corps, Richard was going to Morocco as the ambassador, which was a huge step up for him, and Alex was very proud.

She had advised MI6 of their transfer to Morocco, and they had expressed considerable interest in what was going on there.

Once again, they were going to an assignment in a country that wanted its independence. In this case from France and Spain. Morocco had been divided into a French and a Spanish protectorate since 1912. There had been considerable dissent and unrest in Morocco for the past two years, before Richard and Alex got there. In December of 1952, a Tunisian labor leader had been murdered, and riots had broken out in Casablanca. The French government's response had been to ban the new Moroccan Communist Party and the Istiqlal, or Independence Party, which was conservative and royalist. A year after the banning of the two political parties by the French, they had aggravated the situation further by exiling Morocco's much loved and deeply respected Sultan Mohammed V. They had sent him to Madagascar, and replaced him with the very unpopular Mohammed Ben Arafa. The sultan was considered a religious leader, and the Moroccans objected strenuously to his exile. By the time Richard arrived in Rabat, the capital, as ambassador, Moroccan citizens were demanding the sultan's return, and responding with violence to France's reluctance to bring him out of exile. They now wanted independence as well.

Everything about Alex and Richard's arrival in Morocco was exciting. The embassy was an exquisite building with the Moorish architecture that Alex found exotic and appealing. The British ambassador's residence was a maze-like palace that she found fascinating, and she couldn't wait to entertain there. The diplomatic community was warm and welcoming, and Richard loved his very efficient staff. At the same time, they were living in a warm coastal city with a festive atmosphere that the French regularly flocked to as a vacation spot.

The ambassador's palace, like almost every house and villa in the city, was surrounded by beautiful gardens with lush flowers in a riot of colors. Some of the architecture dated back to the seventh century, and had originally been built by Spanish Muslims who had been expelled from Spain, hence its Moorish influence. The French had come much later in 1912.

Alex loved everything about the city. The medina in the older part of the city, in the center of town, was a conglomeration of shops and small inviting restaurants and cafés that Alex couldn't wait to explore, along with the nearby city of Salé, which had originally been built by the Romans. There were Roman ruins in many areas, and two major Roman roads. The city was rich with history. Everyone spoke French, which was an advantage for Alex, and she had already decided to study Arabic, and add it to her repertoire of languages. She was pleased that Sophie would learn French here once she started talking.

Alex had bought miles of sari fabric before she left India, and wanted to find a local dressmaker to turn it into harem pants, and flowing dresses to wear when they gave dinner parties. She felt as though she could be more daring in her dress here than she had been in Pakistan. Both were Muslim countries, but Pakistan was more conservative and traditional. Everything from the music to the history of the architecture delighted her about Morocco. Richard was going to be busy watching the evolution of their demands for independence from France, and their efforts to regain control over the areas still ruled by the Spanish.

The first order of business as far as the Moroccans were concerned was the return of Sultan Mohammed V from Madagascar. He had been there for a year when the Montgomerys arrived, and moved into the British ambassador's palace.

Morocco provided precisely the kind of exotic experience Alex had hoped to have when Richard joined the diplomatic corps. She enjoyed it even more than India, where the situation had been so dire at various times, and there had been so much bloodshed at the end of British rule, although Alex had loved India too. Once again, they had an army of servants to attend to them, and a flock of lovely young women to help care for Sophie.

In the first months of their residency, Alex visited all the historical sites and told Richard about them, since he had no time to explore them with her. She had visited the Roman ruins, the city of Salé, and the areas where the Phoenicians and Carthaginians had lived on the banks of the Bou Regreg River, right next to where the Romans had built Salé. She already knew the medina intimately after their first month there, and had found treasures in the shops. She had sent her mother a beautiful antique hand-embroidered caftan to wear around the house, and found fun blouses for herself with little bells on them, and wonderful Moorish leather slippers with bells on them as well.

Alex was busy moving the furniture around and freshening up the ambassador's palace. She filled it with flowers every day. Richard commented that he had never seen her so happy, and they discussed the political situation when they met at night. Richard felt certain that ultimately Morocco would win its independence, without the bloodbath that had occurred in India and Pakistan. The situation was much more manageable here. It was a wonderful place to bring up Sophie in balmy weather most of the year. She was enjoying playing in their gardens, and had begun to say her first words in French by that summer. Alex's lessons in Arabic were proceeding well. As usual, Richard was vastly impressed by Alex's ability to jump in and adjust to a new culture and environment almost immediately. She had fallen in love with the country, and was perfectly suited to the demands of a diplomatic life.

Richard broached the subject of another baby with her shortly after they got there. Rabat seemed like an ideal place for them to have another child, and Sophie was such an easy happy little girl that another baby appealed to Richard more than ever. Alex was thirty-eight by then, and less enthusiastic about having another child. She was enjoying Sophie, and felt too old to try again. Richard said that was ridiculous. She looked ten years younger than she was, but she didn't feel it. She had suffered so painfully over Edward's death that she didn't want to risk having another child where something might go wrong. Sophie felt like enough to her and was a gift. Her parents adored her.

They went to numerous social events, entertained frequently at the residence, and rapidly became the most popular hosts in Rabat. Alex liked the wife of the French ambassador, who had been in the Resistance during the war, and they had much in common.

Six months after they'd arrived, Alex could hold her own in Arabic.

She wasn't fluent yet, but she was working on it, and took lessons every day. Sophie was chattering in French by then, as well as English.

They had been there for a year, when the French government finally brought Sultan Mohammed V back from exile, and reinstated him. Richard had discreetly been part of the negotiations to convince the French to do so. Just before the sultan's triumphant return, Alex received a coded message from MI6, requesting that she meet with a high up member of the Communist Party, at a café in the medina. They wanted his assurance that there would not be riots if the sultan returned. They had set up the meeting through their operatives in country, and wanted her to see him face-to-face. It was the first time they had asked her to meet with anyone since she had started working for them nine years before. She felt she couldn't turn them down. She just hoped that no one would see her with a strange man at a café in the medina. The coded message said that she was to carry a blue book and wear a red sweater, go to a specific café and sit down, and he would find her.

The meeting was set for the following day, and she had to change some appointments, her Arabic lesson and a haircut, to do it. The next day, she was at the designated place on time. As she walked through the medina to the café, it suddenly reminded her of her clandestine meetings in Germany to receive stolen papers or forged passports, while working for the SOE.

A nondescript man sat down across from her two minutes later, and she guessed that he'd watched her arrive. They exchanged their agreed upon code greeting so she knew it was him, and she asked him what MI6 wanted to know. He assured her there wouldn't be any trouble. The riots two years before had been about the murder of a

Tunisian labor leader. They had no objections to the sultan, and thought his return to power would be a good thing, and help the country get independence from the French.

She thanked him and he left a few minutes later. She ordered a mint tea, and afterward wandered through several shops, looking unconcerned, didn't buy anything, and then left. It had been an easy mission to accomplish, and she sent her coded report of the meeting to MI6 as soon as she got home. They confirmed that they received it.

She ran into the French ambassador's wife at the hairdresser later that afternoon. She gave Alex an odd look and then asked her in an undervoice if she had met a man in a café at the medina that morning. She had seen her, and Alex laughed.

"Hardly, I stopped for a cup of tea, and he tried to sell me a watch or something, probably stolen. I told him I wasn't interested, and he left." She brushed it off and her French friend looked relieved.

"You shouldn't go to the cafés there alone. There are some very odd people around, and women sometimes get kidnapped in Morocco and sold into the sex trade. Be careful, my dear. We don't want to lose you." They both laughed then, but it was good to know that she'd been seen. If Richard had asked, she wouldn't have known what to say. She hadn't had reason to lie to him in years.

The sultan returned to Rabat three days later, and once back, he successfully negotiated independence, with French-Moroccan cooperation and interdependence. He instituted reforms that transformed Morocco into a constitutional monarchy with a democratic form of government.

In February of 1956, Morocco was granted home rule, to a certain degree. And on March 2, full independence was achieved with the French-Moroccan agreement. Mohammed V took an active role in modernizing the country's government and he remained leery of both the Independence Party and the Communists. Alex had much to report to MI6 in their first two years there. And as always, she culled great information from dinner parties and the people she met and entertained.

A month after the French-Moroccan agreement, Spain also recognized Moroccan independence, and over the next two years, Morocco eventually regained control over a number of the Spanish-ruled areas. Tangier was reintegrated later in 1956, and the sultan became king the following year, with lavish celebrations, which Richard and Alex attended.

Once again, they were in residence for an era of great changes in Morocco, all of them considered positive, and effected peacefully.

Richard felt he had accomplished a great deal there, and had been successful at assisting with the delicate negotiations for independence. He had done well, and they had spent a wonderful four years there when they left Rabat in 1958. They had made friends they would never forget, both among the other diplomats and the Moroccans.

Alex was able to spend a month in Hampshire with her mother and Sophie, at the end of Richard's ambassadorship in Morocco, before they went to their new post in Hong Kong. Her mother seemed even more frail than before, which saddened Alex.

Alex had every intention of learning to speak Mandarin or Cantonese while she was in Hong Kong. Mandarin was the most common dialect spoken in China, although Cantonese was spoken in Hong Kong. Sophie was five and a half when they left Rabat, and totally bilingual in French and English. Alex's Arabic was fluent by then. They had bought many treasures while they were there, and interesting objects she'd found in the medina. She'd never been asked to have another meeting for MI6, but she wondered if she would be again someday, depending on where Richard was posted. He was excited about Hong Kong, and so was she, but nothing had prepared her for the vibrant, bustling overcrowded city they encountered from the moment they landed at Hong Kong's international airport, Kai Tak.

The war years had been brutal for the residents of Hong Kong, during the Japanese occupation. Those who could had fled and those who lived through it had experienced harsh treatment by the Japanese, and malnutrition to the point of near starvation. The Communists winning the civil war and taking control of mainland China four years later had caused an influx into Hong Kong of displaced immigrants fleeing Communist rule. This added masses of available cheap labor. In the thirteen years since the end of the war, the population of Hong Kong had quadrupled to over two million. Business was booming, and the British colony had flourished. Money, business, and large investments had moved from Shanghai to Hong Kong. Those who had fled before the Japanese occupation returned after the war. Skyscrapers had sprung up. Money was plentiful. The textile industry had taken hold, as well as several others. It was a center for business under British rule, although only a stone's throw from Communist mainland China. Hong Kong was an extremely valuable trade center, and did business with the new government in Beijing. The government was committed to making Hong Kong a center of business, trade, and manufacturing. It provided a trade bridge between Communist China and the rest of the world.

There had been riots two years before Richard and Alex arrived, due to low wages, long working hours, and overcrowded conditions among the poorer population, but by 1958, when Richard was assigned to Hong Kong as high commissioner, all was peaceful, and business of every sort was thriving. Hong Kong was against Communist policies, and defined capitalism at its best.

Those in power were mostly British, or European, with a strong Scottish influence among the old established firms. In true British style, club life was extremely important to the men doing business in Hong Kong. The Hong Kong Club was the most venerable and prestigious, and the Royal Hong Kong Yacht Club was almost as important. Richard had automatic membership at both. As high commissioner of Hong Kong, he would be working closely with the British governor of Hong Kong, Sir Robert Brown Black, during his stay there.

In some ways, Hong Kong was more British than Britain itself, as happened sometimes in the colonies, and there was a close trade relationship with the Chinese as well. Unlike the Old Guard in England, made up of aristocrats with rapidly diminishing funds, but who still frowned on "trade" and "commerce" no matter how desperate their financial situation, in Hong Kong, money and business were king, and vast quantities of money changed hands in important deals. Social events were an opportunity to make new connections. The British in Hong Kong were not afraid to pursue major financial deals, or amass large fortunes, and there was enormous wealth in the city when Richard and Alex arrived.

Social life was extremely important, with business motives just below the surface. People sometimes went to two or three parties a night, and occasionally a cocktail party provided just the impetus needed to close a deal. The city was seething with activity, economic, industrial, and social, and some saw that the future of industry was in using cheap Chinese labor to produce products at a fraction of the cost of making them elsewhere. The marriage of business and social life was working extremely well, in ways that might have been frowned on in England, but were hotly pursued in Hong Kong. There were sports clubs, traditional clubs, dining clubs, night clubs, parties were constant, all the key players were British, with no Chinese visible on the Hong Kong club scene. There were also fabulous restaurants, and the shopping opportunities for antiques, jewelry, and clothing were supreme.

There were apartments in the tall buildings that had gone up all over the city, and the beautiful old homes, and some important new ones were on the Peak, which was where Richard and Alex would be living in the high commissioner's residence. The governor's mansion was there too.

All social events except cocktail parties were black tie, and there was dancing at almost every party. The French ambassador's wife in Morocco had given Alex the address of a fabulous little dressmaker, who could copy any Paris gown for next to nothing, and Alex was eager to see her for the extensive wardrobe she would need for their busy social life in Hong Kong. Having Paris fashions copied in Hong Kong was common, and every woman had a skilled seamstress to recommend. Their life in Rabat had been slightly more relaxed, and less formal than colonial life in Hong Kong.

The only problems that required closer supervision were those caused by the triads, groups of Communist gangsters originally from mainland China, who worked sub rosa and infiltrated Hong Kong whenever they could, operating with threats and violence to achieve their ends. They were the criminal element in Hong Kong.

The British Red Cross was very active in Hong Kong, and it had been subtly suggested that Alex might like to volunteer, as some of the more social women did. It was considered an appropriate activity, since women were not welcome in any of the clubs, except for special events.

Many dialects of Chinese were spoken in Hong Kong, Cantonese being the most common among the populace and local workers. Mandarin was more widely spoken among Chinese elsewhere. Alex ambitiously wanted to attempt to learn both. She had mastered Arabic and was fluent after her four years in Rabat. Chinese would be a bigger challenge, but as always, she was undaunted, and thought it might be useful for Richard socially, and even for herself, running their home, if she learned Chinese. Knowing her, he was sure she would master it in no time.

They were thrilled when they saw their home on the Peak, with a view of the harbor. They had a full staff, many of whom had come from mainland China after the civil war, and all of whom had been impeccably trained in proper British service by their predecessors. They all spoke English. There were maids, housemen, a butler, an excellent chef who had worked at a French restaurant, and a nanny for Sophie, who looked like a child herself, and was a very sweet young girl. The service they provided was more polished than what Alex and Richard had had before, but Alex still missed the kindness and warmth of Sanjay and Isha in New Delhi. Their help in Rabat had been less formally trained, but they were very kind, and adored Sophie. She spoke to her new nanny Yu Li in French at first. Yu Li giggled and spoke to Sophie in English, and Alex hoped Sophie would learn Chinese as well. She thought a variety of languages would always be useful for her, whatever she chose to do in later life. It had served Alex well so far.

As she always did, Alex reported to MI6 diligently from the day they arrived, and was startled when they almost instantly requested that she take a more active role. Other than her one meeting with the Communist leader in the medina in Rabat, she had never been asked to make contacts in the local population, only to report on who she met and what she heard and saw. This time her contact at MI6 sent her a list of people they wanted her to be on the lookout for, three they wanted her to try to meet, and several they wanted her to include in their dinner parties. Only one of the names was Chinese, the others were British, and all were men, which required some delicacy and ingenuity on her part, so she didn't acquire the reputation of being a flirt or a loose woman. She didn't have access to them in their clubs. It would all have to happen at the cocktail parties they went to, or the dinners they were invited to, and the ones they gave themselves.

Alex was busy setting up the house the way she wanted and she included two of the names on the guest list for the first dinner party they planned to give three weeks after they arrived. The local socialites, businessmen, and diplomats were eager to meet the new high commissioner and his wife, and they had already received a dozen invitations within days of their arrival. Richard wanted her to accept as many as they could attend, sometimes with a cocktail party or two preceding a formal dinner elsewhere afterward. Within a month, their life was a social whirl, and Alex hardly had time for anything else. She had committed to memory the names she was to look out for, and those MI6 wanted her to invite.

She ran into two of the people whose names were on the list at the first cocktail party they went to. One was a Scotsman who worked at the Hongkong and Shanghai Banking Corporation, commonly called "the Bank" by everyone in Hong Kong, and the other was an Irish manufacturer who had made a fortune in textiles since the war. The

Scotsman, Ronald MacDuffy, was her father's age, drank straight scotch, and eyed her with interest. He wasn't particularly talkative except about banking. The other, Patrick Kelly, was an effusive Irishman about her own age. He invited her to lunch when they met, which she declined. Afterward she stood behind him and listened to him talk to a friend of his about a deal he was working on in Beijing. She committed both conversations to memory, and sent them to MI6 in code that night, and then she joined Richard in bed, who was reading reports from his office. He was trying to get up to speed on all the most important dealers and players in Hong Kong, as well as the political issues with Communist China, which was so close at hand.

The two men MI6 had told her to invite both came to their first official dinner party with their wives, neither of whom were very interesting, but beautiful and fashionably dressed. Both men were very influential in Hong Kong, had lived there before the war, returned to England during the occupation, and gone back to Hong Kong as soon as the Japanese surrendered. They had heavy investments in Hong Kong, and one of them quietly invited Alex for drinks the following night. She accepted, based on an instinct that it was what MI6 would have wanted, and she was right. When she reported the invitation to them, they asked her to meet him, and see what he had to say. She had to come up with an excuse to give Richard for skipping a cocktail party they were invited to that night, and meeting him later at the dinner they had accepted at the French consulate. The French were active in Hong Kong too, but not as much as the British.

Richard was so busy at the office that he didn't question her being unable to join him at the cocktail party, with the thin excuse that she had a late meeting at the Red Cross to discuss a blood drive with them that she had agreed to run.

She was wearing a sleek black evening gown when she met Arthur Beringer at the bar at the Peninsula Hotel, and she was mildly reminded of her brief brush with the SS colonel in Paris. He even looked a little like him and was a very attractive man. There was a subtle sexual undertone as he greeted her, and complimented her on her sexy black dress, courtesy of Marie-Laure's Chinese dressmaker who had copied it from a photograph in a magazine in two days. In addition to being ridiculously inexpensive in Hong Kong, they were fast, and the copies were impeccable.

Beringer ordered her a glass of champagne without asking what she wanted. He was drinking gin on the rocks.

"I know you're new to Hong Kong, but I wanted to make you aware of some of the opportunities we have here. There are fortunes to be made. We'll all be rich when we go back to England if we play our cards right." He went straight to the heart of the matter, and the allegory was a good one, since she had heard that he was a serious gambler, and had taken some huge risks to make his fortune. He was a fearless investor and was said to have a few dubious connections. "There are some very interesting deals here, if you're not afraid of unorthodox alliances. Our friends in Beijing understand the merits of capitalism, if conducted discreetly." He wasn't afraid to let her know that he was dealing with the Communist Chinese, which was bold of him. He had no idea whether he could trust her or not, but she looked like an innocent woman, and he saw her as a conduit to the connections she would be making as the wife of the high commissioner. Reaching out to her was a gamble on his part, but could be a good one, and profitable for them both.

"I'm afraid my husband and I aren't in a position to make investments," she said demurely, smiling at him, as she remembered the diamond bracelet she had given back in Paris during the war. In some ways, this was no different. Arthur Beringer was an opportunist said to stop at nothing to get what he wanted.

"I assumed as much," Beringer said smoothly. Most diplomats were not wealthy but extremely well connected with people in high places. "But you'll be meeting many people. If you steer the right ones in my direction, there would be a commission for you, perhaps even a very considerable amount, depending on the results afterward." He had put his cards on the table, and she looked intrigued as she glanced back at him.

"And how would I explain that to my husband?"

"There are banks here that maintain discreet accounts, numbered or in another name. Leave that to me. Trust me, you could be a rich woman by the time you leave Hong Kong."

"I'll have to think about it, Mr. Beringer, but your proposal is certainly intriguing. As long as no one would ever know." She appeared innocent, beautiful, and trusting.

"I have friends in low places," he said, smiling at his own joke. "You have no idea how useful that can be at times."

"The triads?" she asked, referring to what amounted to Chinese gangs, whom she had been told dealt in prostitution, paid assassins, and drug trafficking.

"Perhaps," he said, and signaled for another drink. "You don't need to worry about the details. Lead the sheep to me, and the money will magically appear in your numbered account. No one will ask questions, and your husband will never know." She wondered how many people in their circle did business with him. Possibly more than she would ever suspect. Hong Kong was teeming with honest and dishonest people pursuing their fortunes, some with methods like the ones

Beringer had mentioned. All he was suggesting was a commission for her, which could have been honest, except for the numbered account and the fact that she couldn't tell her husband, and his talk of "friends in Beijing" and allusion to the feared triads of Hong Kong. She glanced at her watch, then slowly picked up her evening bag, smiled at him, and said she had to go.

"Let me know about my offer after you give it some thought. And perhaps we could have lunch sometime." He was too smooth to be blatant about pursuing her sexually as well, but it was implied in the look he gave her, and the way he touched her bare shoulder before she left. There was something dangerous and frightening about him, particularly if he was involved in the underworld of Hong Kong, and it appeared he was.

Her driver took her to the French consulate after that, in the Rolls provided for her, and as soon as she found Richard, she saw Beringer walk in with his wife. She was moderately attractive, slightly older than Alex, dripping with diamonds, and flirted with the French consul all night. Arthur Beringer greeted Alex and Richard with a polite nod, but didn't approach, and there was nothing to suggest that he and Alex had been drinking champagne at the Peninsula half an hour earlier, or that he had any interest in her, business or social. He was a masterful poker player and it showed.

The dinner at the French consulate lasted until one in the morning, and Richard was tired on the way home, after a long day. They talked about the people they had met, and she asked him what he thought of Arthur Beringer and his wife.

"He looks like a shady guy to me," he said without any particular interest, "and she appears to be on the hunt for a little too much fun." Alex smiled at his assessment, and agreed. Richard went right to bed when they got home, and she took her time in her dressing room, as she often did when she felt that her messages for MI6 were pressing. After she undressed, she took out the transmitter she kept hidden in a locked drawer, and sent MI6 the full report of her meeting with Beringer at the Peninsula before dinner. They confirmed receipt of the information with no further comment. She had done her job, and all she had to do now was tell him that she had considered his offer, but felt it best to decline.

When she got up the next morning, she had a message from MI6. She always checked after Richard left for the office. It was part of her daily routine, even if she'd had nothing to report to them the night before. She also checked for messages every night before she went to bed.

The message from her contact was brief. "Don't respond immediately. Stall him for a while." It was easy enough to do. She heard nothing further from them after that, and Beringer called her himself a week later, mid-morning when he knew Richard would be out. He was clever about when to call married women, and Alex suspected he did it a lot.

"Have you given any further thought to our conversation?" he asked, sounding languid and as though it didn't matter to him either way. But he must have cared somewhat or he wouldn't have been calling to press her for a response.

"I have," she said, sounding timid and uncertain. "I just don't want to create a problem for my husband if it ever came out."

"Don't worry. I'm not careless about business matters. No one will ever know."

"And if they do? The Colonial Office is quite adamant about maintaining anti-Communist policies in the colony. You mentioned your 'friends in Beijing.' My husband could lose his job if it became known that I was involved in deals that involved them."

"And his wife could make a fortune. He won't need his job if we do this right, and you can be sure I will." He was pressuring her, which she found interesting. She wondered if later on, blackmail would be part of the deal, with what they'd have at stake. She wouldn't put it past him. "Think about it for a few more days." He hesitated for an instant, and tried to tempt her again. "You could end up with millions if you work on this with me. You'd be wise not to turn it down." Was it a threat? She wasn't sure. She reported the conversation to MI6, and then went out to lunch. She checked for a response from them after her Cantonese lesson that afternoon, and the message was clear.

"Keep stalling or meet him again. Don't let the fish swim away. Do not decline the offer, nor accept, remain ambiguous." They wanted her to play a game with him, which she sensed could be dangerous. He didn't seem like a patient man. She called him in the office, and said that she was tempted, but afraid. She implied that she needed reassurance, and he was happy to provide it.

"Have lunch with me," he said sounding sensual and persuasive, and she agreed, managing to sound innocent and flirtatious. It had been a long time since she had used those wiles in her line of work, and she almost found it amusing, but she didn't want Richard to discover her games. It was different doing espionage work for Military Intelligence, now that she was married. It had been simple reporting who she met, but was becoming more complicated engaging with a man like Beringer. She didn't want Richard to get hurt, or find out. He would never trust her again if he did.

She met Arthur Beringer for lunch the following day at a discreet restaurant he suggested. He was wearing an impeccably cut dark blue suit which looked more Savile Row than Hong Kong, and he never mentioned his offer once. Instead he tried to seduce her and several times brushed her hand, and then finally over tea at the end, he brought up his business proposal to her again, and she sensed a faint desperation in his voice.

"I need someone no one will suspect to work with me, Alex." They had progressed to first names. "You're clean here. I want to move a large sum of money from Shanghai into an account here, which some extremely well-placed people can access without problem. I'm willing to give you a sizable piece of it if you do this for me, simply as a gift. Commissions will come later." She wondered if Communist officials from Beijing would be using the account, and receiving payment from him, or someone in the triads. "I need to do it quickly, in the next few days." She feigned nervousness as he said it, and wondered how far MI6 wanted her to go in stringing him along. Listening to him, she had the feeling that there was a lot at stake, and some very important people involved, whom MI6 were obviously interested in, not just Beringer.

"Give me another day," she said, as he reached for her hand under the table and caressed it, and then rested his on her knee, as she prayed he wouldn't go any farther. He was dangerously close to the edge of her skirt as she met his eyes. "I'm married, Arthur," she said softly, with all that it implied and meant to her.

"So am I. Your husband is too busy to pay attention to you. And he'll have his share of offers too. Hong Kong corrupts people. You haven't understood that yet." She didn't want to. She knew Richard would never be vulnerable to men like Arthur Beringer. "I want to go to bed with you," he said too softly for anyone else to hear him. "You're a beautiful woman and I want you." She wanted to tell him that he couldn't buy her, but knew that silence was the wisest course. This was a job, for both of them. He wanted to convince her, and it was espionage for her, following orders from MI6. It wasn't personal, for either of them. And on his side, it was just a ploy to get her to do what he wanted. If he had dared, he would have forced her and preferred it. She could see violence in his eyes.

She thanked him for lunch then, and stood up, and he grabbed her wrist as she was leaving. "Just do it. You won't regret it," he said intensely. She nodded and walked away, praying no one would tell Richard they had seen her having lunch with another man. She could hardly concentrate on her Chinese lesson that afternoon, and she was quiet when she went out with Richard that night. She had wanted to spend time with Sophie before they left, but they were rushed, and she was happy with her new nanny. Alex felt as though she'd hardly seen Sophie since they'd been in Hong Kong. There were so many other demands on her as the high commissioner's wife.

"Tired?" Richard asked her in the car on the way to dinner. "We go out an awful lot here, don't we?" But he was enjoying the varied facets of his position in Hong Kong and the complex situations that arose more than she was, with Arthur Beringer breathing down her neck. She was grateful that they weren't at the same dinner party that night.

She got a shock when she read the morning paper the next day at breakfast. Arthur Beringer had been murdered by an unknown assassin, possibly linked to the triads. There was a long article in the paper about him, his unsavory connections, some of his more suspicious deals, and his vast fortune. The police called her after Richard left for the office, and asked for a moment of her time in the afternoon. Her heart was pounding when she asked what it was about, and they said that they wanted to speak to anyone who had met with him in the last twenty-four hours of his life, and they had reason to believe that they had met for lunch.

She didn't confirm or deny it, agreed to a five o'clock meeting with them at her home, and flew to her dressing room to send a message to MI6 and hoped they'd respond quickly. She told them that the police wanted to interview her about her lunch with Beringer the previous day. It was sure to cause a scandal if word got out. It was a small city, and there was constant gossip in the circles they moved in, and would be plenty about the high commissioner's wife, if any connection with Beringer was implied. It almost made her want to resign from MI6. They had never said that she would be used as bait, or have face-to-face meetings with dangerous subjects. She was meant to be an information gatherer and nothing more. That had been their agreement and they were stretching that now beyond her comfort level. And this was not wartime, where risking her life seemed right to her. Nor did she want to risk her marriage or Richard's career.

The response they sent her was almost immediate. "We'll handle it from here. Mission complete." An hour later she got a call from the secretary of the chief of police, canceling the appointment, apologizing, and saying that they had made a mistake. They sincerely regretted any inconvenience, and that was the end of it. A month later, there was an article in the paper, saying that Beringer had been laundering money for both the triads and the Communists, and had gotten exposed in a double cross between the two, presumably for a vast amount of money.

Richard said he'd had a bad feeling about him, and Alex nodded, grateful that MI6 hadn't let her down, and had gotten her out of the police investigation. It was the closest she'd ever come to being exposed. She never saw Beringer's wife again. Word was that she had left Hong Kong immediately after his death, and disappeared. And MI6 hadn't asked her to meet with anyone since. They appeared to be content with the reports she sent, and only asked her occasionally to include people at their dinner parties that they wouldn't have invited otherwise, but all of them seemed like respectable businessmen and bankers, despite MI6's interest in them. For now Alex was safe, and glad she was. Richard had no idea how close she came to being involved in a major scandal. It reminded her that her spying activities were dangerous, even in peacetime and even if no one was holding a knife to her throat. The unseen risks could be just as lethal.

Chapter 15

Nine months after they'd arrived in Hong Kong, Alex got another request from MI6 to meet with someone, a Chinese woman this time. The woman had started a massive textile business with factories near Shanghai, and they wanted to know how closely involved she was with the Communists. Alex was fascinated by her when they met. She was somewhere in her thirties, her father had been a major landowner in mainland China and had fled the Communists, but there was concern that she might have maintained or renewed ties with them. Alex only met her once, but it became clear later on that she was the mistress of an important member of the Communist Party, who was facilitating her business. He eventually lost his position and disappeared, and she fled China and moved to England, possibly as a result of the information Alex had deduced from talking to her. She was extremely beautiful and everything about her screamed danger and intrigue.

It was months before Alex was asked to meet anyone again, and each time she did, she had to lie and make excuses to Richard. Only once did she feel that she was in a dangerous situation, with a suspected member of the triads. She had gone to the meeting armed with her pistol and her knife and never had to use them, but she would have if needed. The rest of the time she played the role of gracious hostess and devoted wife, and by their second year there, she had mastered both Cantonese and Mandarin surprisingly well, which impressed everyone who heard her speak them. Only Richard wasn't surprised. He knew how brilliant and talented she was.

And MI6 continued to ask her to meet people of interest from time to time. Hong Kong was teeming with intrigue.

Two years after they arrived in Hong Kong, Victoria wasn't well. Alex went home for a month, and took Sophie with her. Sophie was bored in Hampshire. She said there were too many bugs there, and there was nothing to do. She didn't like riding as her mother had as a child, or any of the classic English pursuits. The foster children were long gone, although they stayed in touch with Victoria, but she was alone now, with only a housekeeper and a man to help around the house. The man running the estate for her came to see her once a week and sent written reports to Alex as well. And Richard always gave her good advice.

Victoria was seventy-two then, and in delicate health. Alex felt guilty about how seldom she saw her, but she was busy as the high commissioner's wife and Hong Kong was far away. Victoria had been widowed for eleven years, and whenever Alex invited her to Hong Kong, she said she didn't like to travel without Edward. She seemed older than her years. Alex was forty-four and thriving in the interesting life she led with Richard. They both loved Hong Kong, and wished they'd never have to leave. They talked about moving back there one day when he retired. Sophie was eight years old and was still bilingual in French and English. Her mother spoke to her in French most of the time to maintain it, and Sophie had picked up Cantonese from the women who took care of her. Being in Hampshire made Alex realize that her daughter had no real ties to England except by nationality. She'd only been there three times in her lifetime, as a small child, and other than her grandmother, she had no one there. Pakistan, where she was born, Morocco, and Hong Kong were the only homes and cultures she knew. It was an enviable life in many ways, particularly for Alex and Richard, but in some ways it was odd for Sophie to grow up steeped in so many cultures that were not her own. Alex's mother thought so too.

"You'll inherit all this one day," she said wistfully about the manor house and their estate, "and maybe you'll come back to live in England then, and enjoy it. You grew up here. And Richard grew up on his parents' farm and in a Scottish boarding school. You both have roots here. But what will Sophie be attached to? She knows nothing of English life, except in the colonies and that's not the same." They all knew people who had grown up in India and other places, and were more English than anyone who had grown up at home, but there was a false quality to it, when you had grown up with an elephant in the backyard, or a camel, her mother insisted. Sophie had loved the camels when they were in Morocco, and she'd probably never go back to Morocco. And Hampshire was more foreign to her than any of the places she'd lived.

"It's an odd way to grow up. But I suppose it's a nice life for all of you, with big houses and many servants. But none of it belongs to you. This does," she reminded her. Alex thought about it sometimes too, and she missed it, but she couldn't imagine living in Hampshire now, and not for a very long time. "I hope you don't sell it. It's been in your father's family for three hundred years, and he loved it so." It was an awesome responsibility, and Alex knew that even if she did keep it, wherever they were living at the time, Sophie might not want the estate when she grew up. If she was living halfway around the world, a house in Hampshire would mean nothing to her. In fact, she couldn't wait to go back to Hong Kong, which was more familiar to her, and Alex felt that way too. It was the downside of the life they had chosen, which suited them so well. They lost their emotional ties to their original homes.

Alex enjoyed the month with her mother and was sad to leave her. Each time she saw her now, her mother had gotten thinner, older, and more fragile, and she was afraid she'd never see her again. She hoped her mother would still be alive when Richard retired and they moved back to England, but that was still a long time away. He was only fifty-two years old and far from retirement. He would spend the last few years in the Foreign Office, after his last post. But they expected to be living abroad for at least another ten years. She wasn't sure her mother would live that long, and hoped she would. She had given up trying to convince her mother to visit them wherever they were posted, and she was an unfamiliar figure in Sophie's life, having spent so little time with her. Being an only child weighed heavily on Alex now. She felt guilty about her mother all the time. Letters and photographs were no substitute for human contact. She saw that her mother saved every one of her letters in boxes, and had for all the years she'd been gone.

Despite the sadness of leaving her mother, Alex was glad to get back to Hong Kong. Richard had been busy, and as always, the parties seemed to multiply. She continued reporting to MI6, and had the occasional meeting at their request, and they never put her in an awkward or dangerous position again. After several meetings at MI6 in London, they sensed that it could prove to be dangerous for her husband, and had chosen to respect that, for now anyway. The last two years flew by faster than Richard and Alex had expected, or wanted them to.

They had dozens of friends in Hong Kong when they left, and this time Alex only had a brief week to spend with her mother in Hampshire. They wanted them settled in their new post quickly. Richard's predecessor had left due to illness, and it was going to be a challenging but plum post for him, one of the more important ones. He was going to be the British ambassador to the Soviet Union, living in Moscow.

It sounded extremely interesting to both of them, though Sophie wasn't happy about it. She wanted to stay in Hong Kong, and Alex promised they'd come back one day. Sophie was nearly ten when they left Hong Kong, and after a week with her grandmother, she flew to Moscow with her mother, where Richard was waiting for them. He told Alex that the ambassador's house was respectable, and had been a luxurious home before the revolution, but forty-five years later, it was a symbol of fallen grandeur, in a Communist country, with a population composed of battered, tired, poor, starving, suppressed people, closely watched by the KGB. It was going to be a challenging, fascinating four years, and as they walked into the house in the same area where all the nicer embassies were, in the Arbat district, and saw the battered furniture, the faded curtains, and threadbare rugs, Alex knew she had work to do. The house was inadequately heated, it was a cold, dreary winter day, and Sophie burst into tears and turned on her mother when she saw it. She hated Moscow on sight. Alex saw it as an important step in Richard's career, and interesting for her too. Sophie was just a child having to adjust to a whole new way of life, again, in an unfamiliar, inhospitable country.

"I hate you for bringing me here!" she shouted at her parents, as Alex and Richard exchanged a look over her head. It wasn't going to be easy. They had known that when they left Hong Kong, which had been the jewel of his career so far, and this might prove to be his greatest challenge.

MI6 was extremely pleased with where Alex had landed, and her contact told her the day they arrived that they had lots for her to do. She wondered if this would prove to be their undoing. She hoped not, and Richard hoped not too, and prayed that he was equal to the task.

Chapter 16

Alex and Richard had been sent to Moscow in 1962, at one of the most interesting times since the Russian Revolution. The Cold War was in full swing, and had been for several years, and the situation had gotten markedly more tense since 1960, when the Russians shot down an American U-2 spy plane, and captured the pilot, Gary Powers. Since then, relations had been strained between the United States and Russia. The incident had threatened to cancel the summit meeting planned in Paris two weeks later. They went forward anyway, with Premier Khrushchev demanding an apology from the American president. When President Eisenhower refused, Khrushchev left the meeting.

Two years later when Richard arrived in Moscow, relations remained tense, and the Cold War had intensified, not only between Russia and the United States, but with Britain as well.

Great Britain had had its own problems with the Russians, who had recruited a number of well-placed English scientists and even diplomats to spy for them, with double agents complicating matters even further by spying for both sides. There was considerable bitterness on the British side about the traitors and defectors who sold everything from highly sensitive secrets to missiles to the Russians.

Spying was an extremely dangerous practice, as Alex had been told by the SOE, and later by MI6. If caught, there was no hope of being rescued. And prison or execution were the norm in Russia for Western spies who were apprehended. Those who chose to spy on Britain for the Soviets, working for the KGB, their secret police, were sentenced to equally unpleasant punishments in England, if caught by the British. The Soviets were known to pay a high price for traitors who defected to the east.

The Cambridge Five were among the most famous spies with high positions in the British establishment, which gave them access to secrets with a major impact on national security. Seven years before Richard arrived in Moscow, the naval attaché at the British embassy in Moscow had been imprisoned in England with an eighteen-year sentence for spying for the Soviet Union.

Nuclear technology was vital to the British, the Americans, and the Soviets. Fortunes changed hands for anyone who would defect to either side.

A year before Richard became the British ambassador in Moscow, a British intelligence agent was sentenced to forty-two years in prison for spying for the Soviets and the British, as a double agent.

The KGB was particularly energetic about trying to steal agents of MI5 and MI6, who were considered a prize. They succeeded in a number of instances. British Military Intelligence was extremely sensitive about it. The game of stealing spies and intelligence agents and luring them from one side to the other had become an almost common feature of the Cold War.

In spite of it, the appearance of diplomacy continued, with the ball being carried vigorously by the Americans whose embassy, Spaso House, hosted many of the most glittering social events in Moscow, and whose invitations were the most prized. Their July Fourth party every year was legendary. In 1935, they had added a ballroom onto the house where they held balls, dances, concerts, movie screenings, and some of the best diplomatic parties in Moscow. Premier Khrushchev was notorious for showing up and attending every event he was invited to by the Americans, although the KGB spied on them relentlessly.

The American ambassador and his wife were Richard and Alex's first visitors the day after they arrived. Alex was trying to decide how to make the house more attractive for the receptions they planned to hold there. She had found some extra furniture and rugs rolled up in the basement, and when the Americans arrived, Alex apologized for how she looked.

"You look lovely, my dear," the ambassador said warmly, as his wife handed Alex a beautifully wrapped gift, and he pointed to the street outside, as he spoke to her, and Richard immediately understood and nodded. The American ambassador put a finger to his lips as he looked at Alex. "Why don't you let us show you your neighborhood. There are some charming old houses you'll enjoy seeing." He smiled at her, and his wife nodded, smiling at them.

"I'll get our coats," Richard said and disappeared, and returned a minute later, and handed Alex her coat, as he put on his own. Sophie was getting acquainted with the young girl at the embassy who was to care for her. She was Russian but spoke relatively good English, and Sophie hadn't warmed to her yet. They were unpacking some of her toys in her large, chilly bedroom upstairs, where Sophie had taped movie posters to the walls.

They were on the street a moment later, appearing to stroll toward Arbat Square. "I'm sorry to kidnap you," the ambassador said, smiling at Richard, as his bodyguard followed at a discreet distance behind them. "I'm sure you've been warned by your own government, but our homes are riddled with listening devices, put there by the KGB. We found over a hundred microphones and cameras when we combed it when we moved in. In fireplaces, in plants, under couches, in the walls, in the air vents, in the garden, they're everywhere. You can't say anything in the house you don't want the Soviets to hear. I thought you should know how extensive it is." Alex and his wife were chatting as they walked, and she invited the newcomers to a formal dinner at Spaso House the following week, and Alex thanked her.

"They're always after our operatives from MI5 and MI6, quite successfully at times, unfortunately," Richard said wryly.

"We all have the same problems," the American said. "They'll have bugs in your daughter's room, and don't trust any of your servants. It's an entire nation of people taught to spy and report on each other. It's quite sad really," but the Crisis in Suez and the American U-2 disaster had intensified the Cold War. "And they'll go through your personal belongings several times a day."

They discussed the diplomatic situation in Moscow then as they walked. British and American goals were much the same. To provide information about Soviet domestic and foreign policy, to promote British trade, and American in their case, and develop scientific and cultural exchanges, and to influence Soviet foreign policy on broader international issues. It was all very straightforward, but when you added espionage and counter-espionage to the mix, it became complicated. And being an ambassador to the Soviet Union, from whatever country, was both an honor and a challenge.

They walked around the square in a leisurely way for about half an hour and then the Americans left them.

Before they did, the ambassador had offered to lend them their "decorator," who was actually a superb agent trained in detecting listening devices and debugging the house whenever possible. Richard accepted gratefully. The agent brought in a team that claimed to be "interior decorators," a clever ruse the KGB hadn't caught on to.

"Thank you for sharing the information," Richard said pleasantly. He had heard much of it before, but the American ambassador had added to it very usefully.

"You'll get used to it. We all do. And it's a good group here, in the foreign community. We all got here for a reason. If we do well enough everywhere else, they reward us by punishing us here." The American laughed and Richard smiled ruefully. "They like to have a good time though. And they love coming to the embassy."

"We've got some work to do with ours," Richard said. He knew Alex wasn't happy with the condition they had found the house in, and Sophie hated it. The transition was difficult, particularly coming from the luxurious comforts and sophisticated delights of Hong Kong, which was infinitely more civilized than the conditions in Russia.

He and Alex walked for a few more minutes once they were alone, and she tried not to show how discouraged she was. "You might want to hide your pistol, Alex, if they haven't seen it already." He was worried about it. "They might wonder why you have it."

"I thought of that too. That and my knife are in a safe place." She smiled at him.

"Where's that?" He was puzzled. Nowhere was safe, if they searched their belongings constantly, as the American ambassador said.

"On my body." They weren't allowed to search a diplomat's wife, by reciprocal agreement, unless they had proof that she was a spy, which they didn't.

"And your bigger, uh . . . accessory . . . ?" he asked her, referring to the Sten gun she said she kept as a souvenir of the war.

"It comes apart and folds up nicely in a leather bound Bible." He looked impressed and smiled at her.

"Why do you still need to carry that? You're not a volunteer in wartime anymore." He didn't know if she'd ever used it and thought it unlikely.

"You never know when it might come in handy. I got it during the war and I just kept it all. You may be glad I have that one day."

"You don't want the Russians to think you're a spy," he warned her.

"I'm not a spy," she lied to him, "I'm just careful."

"Just make sure no one finds it. I guess I should be grateful you left your other submachine gun with your mother," he teased her. He had never believed that when she said it. And how could she have one? The Sten gun she had with her was ominous enough and some kind of fetish for Alex, along with her pistol and knife.

"It's annoying that the house is so heavily bugged," Alex said thoughtfully. "I'll warn Sophie. How will you work if your office is bugged too?"

"That's for our technicians to solve. It's what they get paid to do." And he told her about the team of decorators the American ambassador had offered. "It's all a big game here, about who is spying on whom." And everything they could find out or overhear went straight to the secret police in Moscow, the KGB.

They discovered that night that their cook was surprisingly good, although he had never left Russia. They had a fine meal and went to bed early. Richard had a lot to think about and read late into the night, trying to get up to speed. His post in Moscow was the greatest challenge of his diplomatic career so far. The next morning Alex had a message from MI6. It gave her a time and a name, in code, for a meeting, and a code phrase that would tell her the person was a British operative, but didn't mention a meeting place. She decided to wait to see what would happen.

At precisely eleven A.M., as she sat at her desk in the small office she was going to use at the residence, one of the Russian maids came to tell her that the wife of the Finnish ambassador had come to visit. The name matched the one she'd received from MI6. And she went downstairs to be handed a bouquet of flowers by a pretty blond woman.

"I love daisies in the winter, don't you?" she said to Alex with a warm smile. It was the code phrase, and Alex was intrigued to realize that she was a British agent for MI6 too. She was English, and the wife of an ambassador. They had much in common.

"Yes, I do. That's so kind of you." Alex smiled at her as a knowing look passed between them. They exchanged pleasantries and womanly information about Moscow, where Alex could get her hair done, where the best shopping was. Sophie was going to be tutored at the embassy, and Alex was planning to take Russian lessons. Many of the diplomatic families hadn't brought their children to Russia but Alex didn't want to leave Sophie with her mother, where she'd be lonely and unhappy, nor put her in boarding school, so they had brought her. Alex wanted to take Russian lessons with her. It would keep them both occupied.

After they chatted for a while, Alex walked the wife of the Finnish ambassador back to her car. On the way, Prudence Mikki said softly, "Don't trust anyone or anything, not even in your car. I think our friends in London will keep you busy. They do me. There's a lot to do here." Alex didn't comment, but she hoped not. Soviet Russia was the last place on earth where she wanted to make a mistake, and be imprisoned as a spy. The thought of it made her shudder. They kissed on both cheeks, and Alex waved with a smile as Prudence was driven away by her chauffeur, and Alex called after her thanking her for the flowers. At least she had a friend here.

Alex was able to buy some fabric at a market Richard's secretary told her about and got new curtains made for the reception rooms, and she discovered that there was more furniture in a warehouse. The last ambassador hadn't liked it, and they had brought their own. What was stored was infinitely better than what was in the residence now. She made a list of things to ask her mother for. She rolled out the carpets she'd found, and brought some of the spare furniture to the house, and asked the housekeeper to order flowers for them twice a week. The residence started to look better. She asked Richard's secretary for the most recent embassy guest lists, and planned their first dinner party. As they had in Hong Kong, MI6 gave her a list of who they wanted her to entertain. The list was long here. Alex didn't question it, she just added the names, and she knew the KGB would see a copy of the list anyway. She planned to invite most of the members of the diplomatic community to their first party, and they had room for dancing if they moved the furniture. The wife of the American ambassador had said Alex could use their band. It seemed vital to meet the most important people as soon as possible, although entertaining seemed clumsier here, and more awkward, than in Hong Kong where everyone was so social, and it all went smoothly. Hong Kong was far more sophisticated than the Soviet Union, but she had expected that.

A week before the party, MI6 added two more names to the list. Richard and Alex were going to the party at the American embassy that night and she was looking forward to it, and Richard said he was too when he came home to change.

When they got there two very proper Chinese butlers were checking in the guests, worthy of Buckingham Palace in their precision and decorum. The ambassador's wife had told her about them. They were Chinese, married to Russians, and couldn't get visas to leave the country, so they were trapped there, and worked for the Americans. They were well known in Moscow, and Alex envied how smooth and professional they were. The help at the British residence was far less efficient, and seemed more intent on listening to them and spying on them than providing proper service.

The atmosphere at the party at Spaso House was a breath of fresh air. The house was beautifully decorated in an elegant, modern American way. The ambassador and his wife had brought their own paintings, and everyone seemed relaxed just being there, as though they weren't even in Russia. It set an example that Alex wanted to emulate. She wanted to show the locals and the rest of the diplomatic community what a proper British home looked like, and how it was run. She decided to give a series of high teas, proper luncheons for women, and cocktail parties like the ones in Hong Kong, as well as formal dinner parties for important guests. She had a dozen new ideas when they left the party that night, and she had loved their band and planned to use it. There was a singer who sang jazz like Billie Holiday.

"You look happy," Richard said, pleased. He had enjoyed meeting so many of his fellow ambassadors in one room, and a number of important Soviet officials, whom he had wanted to meet.

"I'm planning our social life for the next six months," she said. They never spoke of anything more important anymore unless they were walking down a street. They tried to take a walk together every day so they could catch up on what really mattered. "I loved the singer."

"I did too. Maybe we should try for something a little more British," he suggested and Alex dismissed the idea.

"When the Americans get it right, they really do." It had been a beautiful evening.

She was in great spirits until she retrieved her encoded messages, and was given the name of someone they wanted her to meet with, within the next few days. She had to hire him as a guide at a museum. It was all she knew, that and his name. She looked much less happy when she got to bed. Richard was already half asleep. The man she was supposed to meet had a Russian name. MI6 was putting her to work, and it was delicate here. They hadn't pressed her about many meetings in Hong Kong after the Beringer incident, but in Moscow, they needed all their agents to be active. They had warned her of it when Richard was transferred, and they were already moving into action.

She went to the museum the next day, and asked if they had any guides who spoke English, before she asked for him by name. They called someone on the phone, and a short thin man appeared, gave his name, and it was the same name she'd been given by MI6, which seemed fortunate. He was carrying a recording device in his hand, he explained after she introduced herself. And he said he had the entire tour recorded in English on the machine, but would accompany her to explain it. She nodded, and they began their tour of the museum, and he turned the machine on for her when they reached the first room and she put on headphones. All of the art dated from after the Bolshevik revolution and had themes of work. Most of it was in a crude style, and none of it was pretty. And as she looked at the first paintings, the recording began. It had nothing to do with the art. It was a lengthy message for MI6 about nuclear arms meetings that were taking place, in violation of a recent treaty. She showed no reaction or surprise, and continued to listen to the recording and look at the art, as they went from room to room. The recording ended long before they finished the tour, and she pretended she was still listening, and when they reached the last room, she thanked him and handed the machine and earphones to him. She had committed all of it to memory, as she'd been trained to do, and the tour guide erased the message as soon as she handed back the machine. She had listened to it a second time to be certain that she would remember it all. He was obviously one of the Russians who was spying for the British, and could even have been a double agent. Although she was sure that MI6 knew he was secure, if they had her meet with him, given her delicate position because of Richard.

It wasn't up to her to evaluate the information, only to pass it on. She left the museum, went back to the residence, and encoded the entire recording she had committed to memory verbatim, naming the source before she did so. He had offered to give her the recording and she had refused it, so he erased it instead. It was too dangerous for him to keep. She had been trained for this, the transmittal of information. It was what she had done during the war, and it had been no more or less dangerous than this.

She waited for a response after she sent it. She had turned the taps on in her bathroom as though she were running a bath, to drown out any minor sound of her tapping on the transmitter. The response came two minutes later.

"Received. Well done. Thank you." She stared at the transmitter for a minute, hating what she had gotten herself into, yet still compelled to do it.

"To hell with you too," she said softly, as she put the tiny machine away, in its case, which looked like a first aid kit. No one would have guessed what was in it, what it was, or what it could do. Like Alex herself, it looked entirely innocent, and was anything but. The lives of the people affected by it, and her own, were on the line every day. She realized now that their stay in Moscow was going to be much more dangerous than she'd expected.

Chapter 17

Realizing how delicate her situation was, and not wanting her to quit, MI6 didn't ask her to do too many missions for them. Fewer than they had others do. They saved the really important meetings and inquiries for her, so they didn't waste her with risks that weren't crucial. Mostly, they stuck to their agreement of having her gather information she gleaned socially in diplomatic circles, but every now and then, they sent her out to meet someone she assumed was an operative of MI6. She never saw the man from the museum again. But there were others. She had to meet one woman in a butcher's shop and stand in line with her for hours, and she was late for a dinner party they were going to at the Turkish embassy. Richard was annoyed with her for being late and having to change when she got home. She said she had gone to the butcher to pick their meat herself since the cook bought such poor cuts on his own. He complained that she could have done it in the morning, and she didn't argue with him. He was tired and stressed a lot of the time, trying to maintain the balance between defending Britain's interests and not adding to the hostility of the Cold War, which was a juggling act at best, particularly knowing that the KGB was watching them at all times. It was a constant source of stress, even for Sophie.

Within six months, Alex was speaking Russian, which was even more useful for the eavesdropping she did for MI6. Richard couldn't get the hang of it and had a translator with him constantly. He used several of them, all sent from England with Russian skills, but he never fully trusted them. He believed his secretary to be trustworthy but anyone in Russia could be a double agent, and many were. He didn't even fully trust the Brits there, which added constant stress to his job. He could see why his predecessor had gotten sick. One had to be on the alert every moment of the day and night. Alex felt that way too. MI6 was in constant contact with her, and she hated hearing from them here. Every time she did an assignment for them, however small, she felt the weight of responsibility on her shoulders, and was torn between her duty to her country, and responsibility to her husband, and was afraid of hurting him in some unseen way that would blow up in their faces later. but quite remarkably, nothing did. It all went smoothly, however tense things were.

The year after they arrived, in November of 1963, the assassination of John F. Kennedy shocked the world, and dreams were broken when he died. An innocence had been lost, if it had ever existed. The days of Camelot seemed more than ever like an illusion now. Alex cried with the rest of the world at the tragic face of Jacqueline Kennedy behind her widow's veil as she held her young children's hands.

It reminded everyone of the evil forces that came into play every day. Even the Soviets were deeply moved by his murder. It was hard not to be. The American ambassador and his wife had gone to Washington for the funeral.

Their time in Russia seemed to pass more quickly than any of their other posts, because the days were so chock full, the stakes were so high, the tension so constant. It was like living in a minefield, and Alex was glad when their next assignment came, and Richard admitted privately that he was too. Russia was one of the most important posts the Foreign Office could assign, and he knew he was close to his last ones before they brought him home. He had been assigned from one foreign post to another for exactly twenty years. Alex had just turned fifty, and Richard was fifty-eight. He guessed that he would have one more assignment, and then they would assign him to a desk job in the Foreign Office for a few years, offering sage counsel based on experience until he retired. But they had one more post coming their way, and he smiled when he read the communique. He had earned it, and he was gratified that his superiors recognized it. He had won their gratitude and respect for his four years in Russia. His next assignment, and probably his last, was Washington, D.C. He told Alex after dinner when they took their nightly walk around the square.

"I have something to tell you," he said, tucking her hand tightly into his arm. He loved their few private moments together and valued her advice.

"You're in love with your secretary," she said, grinning at him.

"Please God, no. Have you looked at her?"

"You're joining a religious order?"

"I would if we stayed here much longer. No, we're going to Washington."

"For a holiday?" She looked pleased, and he laughed.

"Do you think I re-enlisted here?" They couldn't do that anyway, but he would have died first. Four years was enough. "No, my darling. I think it's probably our last assignment, given my age, and they saved the best for last. Or one of the best. It's a plum post, and will be a taste of Heaven after Moscow, the Cold War, and the KGB."

"You're going to be the British ambassador to Washington?" She almost screamed it, as he nodded, stopped walking, and hugged her close. For all the difficult moments, and sometimes frightening times and occasional disappointments, they were closer than ever, and their marriage had stayed solid. The diplomatic corps had torn asunder more than one marriage. It was not an easy life, and infidelity was common, but Alex was well suited to Richard's career and they had grown to love it over the years.

"I am going to be the ambassador to Washington. And we are going to eat hamburgers and go to baseball games, and probably go to dinner at the White House from time to time. Happy days are here again." He beamed at her, and they walked back to the house to tell Sophie. Richard didn't want the KGB knowing before it was officially announced, so Alex wrote it on a piece of paper and handed it to Sophie, and she screamed when she read it. She was almost fourteen years old and thought that America was the coolest place on earth, although she'd never been there. She loved Elvis and had all his records, although she loved the Beatles too, Nat King Cole, and Frank Sinatra, Rock Hudson, and Doris Day.

"When?" Sophie whispered.

"In a few weeks, I imagine."

"And for once, I speak the language, thank God." Sophie still remembered her Cantonese, her Russian was awkward and she hated it, and her French was perfect. She hoped never to use any of it again, except maybe French. She grabbed the paper out of her mother's hand, and scribbled on it rapidly. "Can I go to a normal American high school?"

"Yes." Her mother smiled at her, and went back to Richard. Sophie wanted to start packing that night. Russia had not won her heart.

"You have a *very* happy daughter," she said.

"She'll never want to leave once we get there," he said, looking worried. "I want her in England with us, when we go home."

"That won't be a problem. She's English, not American."

"She's never lived there," he said.

"All colonials go back 'home' eventually. So will she."

"Don't be so sure. But at least she'll have fun for the next four years." Russia had been dreary for all of them. Alex was leaving the residence in better shape than she'd found it, and he had done a good job as ambassador, but they were very ready to leave.

Alex sent a message to MI6 that night to inform them that they would be transferring to Washington shortly, she wasn't sure if MI6 had been advised yet. Their response came back swiftly.

"Congratulations to the ambassador. Well done."

She went to bed that night dreaming of Washington, and the delights waiting for them there.

There were countless dinners for them at all the embassies before they left. It was a closed community, particularly in Moscow, and they were all sorry to see Richard and Alex leave.

The Russian officials came to visit him one by one, and thanked him for his help in trying to achieve detente. He couldn't ask for more. And he thanked his entire staff warmly when he left. He had been respected and admired in every part. He spent two days with the new ambassador to brief him, left everything in good order, and then they departed.

They flew from Moscow to London, spent a few days there so Richard could be briefed by the Foreign Office, and stayed with Victoria in Hampshire for a few days. Alex did some shopping in London with Sophie, and then they flew to New York on BOAC. It felt like a dream to all three of them.

The embassy on Massachusetts Avenue, designed by Lutyens with extensive gardens, was magnificent. It was built in 1930 with primarily British materials, marble, wood, glazing, with new offices in a building in front of it, completed only two years before they arrived. The staff was superb. Richard paid an official visit to President Johnson, and the White House was even more impressive than he had imagined. The previous ambassador had left everything in impeccable order. They settled into the ambassador's residence. Alex assumed that she would have very little to do for MI6 for the next four years. The British did not spy on the Americans, they didn't need to. They shared information liberally. It was an enormous relief not to be in a hostile country, surrounded by danger and risk.

Alex and Sophie went to look at schools days after they arrived. She hadn't been in a proper school since Hong Kong and had been tutored for four years in Moscow by an English teacher married to a Russian.

She fell in love with the Sidwell Friends School, one of the finest private schools in Washington. Richard went to see it too. He wanted to be sure that she went to a school that would prepare her for the British university system when they went back. But they all agreed that it was a wonderful school, and she passed the equivalency and entrance exams without problems, in all subjects. They accepted her, despite her previously unorthodox schooling. She would be starting a "real American high school" in September, just as she had wanted to.

Her parents had never seen her happier, and Alex was just as happy. She felt as though she had dropped a thousand pound weight off her shoulders when they left Russia. She had worried about every one of her missions there, and had been afraid of being caught and arrested as a spy. But she had stuck it out anyway. She was planning to leave MI6 in four years when they went back to London, after thirty years of espionage work. It was a more than respectable career as a spy.

The time had expired on her twenty-year vow of silence on her work for the SOE while they were in Russia. Technically, she could have told Richard and was tempted to but since she was still working for MI6, she decided not to, so as not to arouse his suspicions.

As they had in Hong Kong, they were caught up in the social whirl of Washington immediately, and went to embassy dinners, state functions, parties of every kind almost every night. The highlight of their social life there came in the form of the invitation to Luci Johnson's, the president's daughter, wedding to Patrick Nugent, two weeks after they arrived. The reception in the East Room for seven hundred guests was dazzling, and Richard and Alex thoroughly enjoyed it.

They made friends easily in the international community in Washington, and among the locals, some of them the parents of the girls Sophie went to school with. Sophie was thriving in an American school. It was like her reward for the odd upbringing she'd had from Pakistan to Morocco, China, and Russia. She never talked about it to her friends. She told Alex she wanted to forget about it, and settle down in one place for the rest of her life.

Alex's work for MI6 in Washington was almost negligible, which was a relief too, and felt like a vacation. She told them about the politicians and diplomats she met, and dinners at the White House. It was all very tame, with no crisis whose resolution rested on her.

They were privileged to attend their second White House wedding when President Johnson's daughter Lynda Bird married Charles Robb sixteen months after her sister's wedding just after Alex and Richard had arrived. There were six hundred and fifty guests, and Alex and Richard knew most of them by then. They were frequent guests at the White House, for state dinners, and smaller, more intimate ones.

The time went too quickly. They had a battle royal with Sophie when she was a senior in high school, and it wasn't one Richard wanted to lose. She wanted to go to an American college like her friends. She didn't want to go back to England with her parents, and go to university there. She said she felt American now and wanted to stay.

"That's absurd," her father argued with her. "You're not American, you're English. You've only been here for three years."

"I don't care. I want to stay here. I don't know anyone in London. I don't want to live with Grandmama in Hampshire. I don't want to go to an English university. I want to go to college here. I have to apply this year, Papa." She pleaded with him, and begged her mother to convince him. But Alex didn't like the idea of leaving her in the States either.

"We have no relatives here. What if you get sick?" Sophie was headstrong. Alex wanted to be near at hand to guide and watch her.

"Then you can come over and be with me. Please don't make me go back, Mama. I want to stay here." She'd had assorted minor boyfriends by then, but that wasn't her reason for staying. She loved her friends, and everything about America, and all her friends were applying to college in the States. She thought England was dreary and felt no bond to it since she'd never lived there. Being English was just a passport to her and nothing more.

Alex and Richard talked about it constantly, and he offered a compromise.

"You can go to college here, if you get in. But after you graduate, you come back to England and go to work there, without question. I don't want you staying here, and I'm not going to live three thousand miles from my only daughter in my old age," he said firmly, and after Sophie left the room, squealing with delight, Alex turned to him with a serious expression.

"That's what my mother did. She's been alone, thousands of miles from her only daughter, for twenty-three years, and totally alone ever since my father died." She felt sad as she said it.

"We'll be home in a year. You can make it up to her," he said gently. But Alex knew she couldn't give her mother the years back. She and Richard had been gone for all that time in the diplomatic corps. It had been a good decision for them, but not for her mother, and she felt terrible about it.

The final months flew by. They were leaving in June, right after Sophie's high school graduation. She was planning to travel around California with friends, and spend August with one of them in Martha's Vineyard. The girl's parents had a house there.

She had been accepted at almost every school she'd applied to, and decided to go to Barnard at Columbia University in New York. She was going to live in the dorms. She would be seventeen when she started college in September, and turn eighteen in December. She was coming back to England for Christmas and her eighteenth birthday, and Alex was going to visit her in school in the fall for a parents' weekend. She already missed her and hated the idea of her being three thousand miles away. It gave her a taste of what her mother's life had been like.

Richard and Alex had one last dinner at the White House. Richard Nixon had become president, and Richard had a good rapport with him.

Sophie's graduation was bittersweet for them, but joyous for Sophie. She couldn't wait to leave for California with her friends. She left Washington before they did, and the morning she left, Alex turned to Richard. They were packing to leave themselves.

"I feel as though I've lost her," Alex said with tears brimming in her eyes, and he put an arm around her.

"You haven't. She'll come home after all this, like a good English girl." Alex wondered if her father had said that to her mother when she and Richard left for India. But she'd been married, which was different. She had to follow her husband. Sophie was following her dreams, which was more dangerous.

Two weeks later, they left Washington and flew to London. She and Richard stayed at Claridge's for a few days, and found an apartment. He had the summer off, before he had to report to the Foreign Office, and Alex had promised her mother they would spend the summer with her, except for a few short trips they wanted to take around England to visit old friends, and maybe a short trip to Italy or France. Richard hadn't seen his farm in years, and didn't even know the renters anymore. A management service at the local realtor handled it for him. He was thinking of selling it. The property wasn't valuable, and he was never going to live there. There was no point hanging on to it.

They drove down to Hampshire, and Alex was shocked when she saw her mother. She was thin and pale and emaciated, and could barely walk. It was obvious that she was ill. Alex went to see her mother's doctor, who told Alex that she had stomach cancer. She hadn't wanted to tell Alex and worry her, and had been sick alone for months. She talked to her mother about it when she got home.

"Why didn't you tell me? I would have come home." Her mother seemed peaceful about it, as she looked lovingly at her daughter.

"You couldn't leave Richard and Sophie alone in Washington," her mother said generously. So she had been alone here. The housekeeper took care of her, but she'd been alone at night and insisted she didn't mind.

She slept a lot once Alex was home. They walked in the garden together, and visited her father's grave, and her brothers'. Her mother was eighty-two, and most of her friends were gone. But at least Alex was home. At last. Her mother had waited so long for this, and now it was so close to the end. They had missed more than two decades together. It was Alex's greatest regret about her life. That and the little boy she had lost. It had been a good life other than that.

Victoria died in her sleep, peacefully, three weeks after Alex came home. It was as though she had waited for her. And once she saw her again, she could leave.

Alex called Sophie to tell her, and she flew back from California for her grandmother's funeral. Only a few people were there in the small church. Sophie stayed until her friends got to Martha's Vineyard, and then she flew to Boston to join them. Alex took her to the airport, and hugged her tight before her flight.

"Be careful. I love you, Sophie." As she watched her go, running to catch her plane, her dark hair flying behind her, Alex realized for the first time that a mother's greatest gift was to let her children pursue their dreams, wherever they took them. Seeing Sophie go was one of the hardest things she'd ever done. It gave her new respect for her mother, who had lost two sons and let her only daughter fly away to the other side of the world.

Alex drove to London after that. She had an appointment she'd been planning to keep for a long time. She had nothing left to do for them. She had done very little for the past four years. She had spent the war years working for the SOE, and had worked for MI6 for twenty-four years after that. It was long enough. The money they had paid her had never been remarkable, intentionally. She had done it for the love of queen and country. There was no other reason to do it.

She handed in her letter of resignation, and her contact shook her hand and thanked her.

"You've done a fine job for us for a long time." It seemed odd that thirty years as a spy ended with a letter and a handshake, but she had done her job. It was up to others now.

She drove back to Hampshire feeling nostalgic but lighter, and as though she had come full circle. She still missed her mother, and all the years they hadn't had together, but she had followed Richard on his path, and had had her own too. She had managed both, and had been there for Sophie too.

He was just coming back from the lake with his fishing pole when she got home, and he looked like a boy playing hooky as she smiled at him.

"Was her flight delayed?" he asked Alex. She was late coming home.

"I had a meeting in London. Long overdue."

"Medical?" He looked worried, and she shook her head. It was time to be honest with him at last. She had kept secrets from him for most of their life together, but she'd had no other choice.

"I retired from MI6 today," she said, expecting him to look shocked.

But he wasn't surprised. "I've worked for them for thirty years." There were tears gleaming in her eyes as she said it. And she knew she would miss it. It had given added meaning to her life for so long. More than half her life.

"I always knew." He smiled. "I just prayed that you wouldn't get arrested, or get us thrown out of wherever we were living at the time. You scared the pants off me in Moscow a few times."

"I scared myself too," she admitted and laughed. He knew her better than she thought. "You never said anything?"

"I thought it was bad form to ask my wife if she was a spy. Most women don't drag a submachine gun around or carry a pistol. I suspected something during the war, but I knew you couldn't tell me."

"I worked for the SOE then. Espionage and sabotage behind enemy lines. It was much rougher stuff."

"I hate to think of it," he said seriously. He walked over and kissed her then. "So you're not a spy anymore?" She shook her head. "Well, that will be different. You'll have to tell Sophie about it one day."

"Maybe. I'm not sure she'd want to know." She had her own life to lead now. Her own secrets to keep.

"You're quite a woman," he said as they walked into the house that was hers now. They had some repairs to do, and a few things Alex wanted to change. They had a good man managing the estate. They were planning to live in London during the week, and use it on weekends. Alex had been involved in running it for many years, and Richard took an interest in it too. It would be easier dealing with it at close range now that they were back. "You'll have to find something else to do now, without weapons, I hope." She had loved the house and considered it home all her life, no matter where she had lived in the world. She regretted that Sophie had never gotten attached to it. Maybe when she was older she would.

Alex could feel her parents near her at the Hampshire house. She and Richard had had a fabulous life together, living all over the world, but she was glad they were home. And she hoped Sophie would consider it home one day too.

Chapter 18

Alex's predictions about her daughter were more accurate than Richard's. She graduated from Barnard and didn't want to come home to England. Her friends were all in the States now, from Washington and Columbia. She wanted to stay in New York, at least for another year. She had fallen in love with a boy who graduated from Columbia Law School when she got her undergraduate degree, and the romance looked serious to Alex.

They met Steve Bennett at Sophie's graduation, and had lunch with him and his parents. Steve's father was a West Point general, and Steve was an only child and had been an army brat, and had grown up all over the world too, and he had hated it as much as Sophie had their travels. He had just joined a law firm in New York and wanted to live in one place now too. Richard enjoyed talking to Sam Bennett, Steve's father, about their war experiences, and the places they had lived. And his mother was a warm woman, who had followed her husband around the world whenever possible. Sam was still in the military, currently stationed at the Pentagon, and they lived in Washington, D.C. He was four years younger than Alex, and a dozen years younger than Richard, and a vital, dynamic man. They both enjoyed him and his wife and liked his son.

Steve represented stability to Sophie. They wanted the same things, a solid life, in one place forever. Steve seemed overwhelmed by his father, and had hated what he'd seen of the military, which his father privately admitted to Richard had been a disappointment to him. Sam was third generation West Point. But Steve had done well in law school and had joined an excellent firm.

Sophie had already lined up a job for herself at the United Nations after graduation, as a French-English translator, and had listed Chinese and Russian as languages she spoke adequately. Steve was enormously impressed with how mature she was, as were his parents. He was twenty-seven, and had worked at a bank for two years before going to law school. He had gotten a joint law and MBA degree, and was obviously solid and serious and just as in love with her as she was with him. They were young, but mature for their ages and crazy about each other.

Richard strenuously objected to her staying in New York, but it was a losing battle and Alex knew it. She convinced Richard that they had to let Sophie do what she wanted. She was almost twenty-two, and knew her own mind, just as Alex had when she left Hampshire and moved to London at twenty-three, and never came home to live again.

"That was different, there was a war on."

"I'm not sure that would have made a difference to me. I was ready to leave the nest. It was a good excuse. She's ready too," Alex said with resignation.

Steve and Sophie came to Hampshire for two weeks in August, and Steve spoke to Richard, and asked his permission to ask for Sophie's hand in marriage, and there were tears in Richard's eyes when he gave him his blessing. He hated the idea of her staying in the States but knew he couldn't stop her. He hated that Alex was right.

They got engaged at Christmas and married the following summer in New York. Alex and Richard wanted her to get married in Hampshire, but all of their friends were in New York, so they agreed to let them get married there. They liked his parents, they were good, solid, respectable people with good values. Steve and Sophie seemed so young to get married, but Alex pointed out to Richard that they would have gotten married sooner too if there hadn't been a war on.

"Instead we snuck around to cheap hotels, pretending to be married, terrified every day that one of us would get killed. I'd rather see them happily married," she said with a sigh. "She is young, but she knows her mind. I think we frightened her, dragging her all over the world because that was what we wanted to do. All she wants is to put down roots and never move again. It's what's right for her." And Steve felt that way too after his own childhood. Both sets of parents had chosen lives and careers that didn't suit their children, even if it had been interesting, filled with rich experiences.

"The diplomatic corps was the only job I could think of after the war," Richard said apologetically to Alex.

"It was right for us. I don't think it was for her. She's happier now. And Steve will be good to her. He's a nice boy. She doesn't want the adventures we had. And he doesn't want the life his father had in the military." Listening to her, Richard knew she was right. She so often was, and knew their daughter well.

They married in June 1975, a year after they both graduated. She was twenty-two, and he was twenty-eight. It seemed young, but not too young. And their babies came quickly after that. Steve and Sophie felt ready for it. His parents had married young too. Steve and Sophie had three daughters, Sabrina was born a year to the day after they got married. Alex flew to New York the minute the baby came. She looked just like Sophie, and was a beautiful baby, and they were proud and ecstatic. Alex cried when she held her. She hadn't expected to feel as much for a grandchild as she did.

Elizabeth was born two years later, with blond angelic looks, like a princess in a fairytale. And Charlotte was an accident, but warmly welcomed, a year after Elizabeth was born. They had three children in four years, and moved to a house in Connecticut. Steve was doing well at the law firm. Sophie hadn't worked since her first pregnancy, and Steve didn't want her to. She was happy at home with her babies, and a young Irish girl to help her. Sophie loved her husband, her babies, and their home. She became an American citizen after Charlotte was born, which really broke Richard's heart. But she maintained dual nationality, which appeased him somewhat.

Alex wished they lived closer, but New York was only a plane ride away. She wasn't going to make the same mistake her own mother had made, never visiting them, but they had been in more difficult places halfway around the world. New York was an easy trip. And it warmed her heart to see Sophie looking happy and fulfilled. She finally had the life she had always wanted, that suited her, and she was at peace.

Sophie dutifully brought the girls to visit her parents in Hampshire for a month every summer, and Steve came for two weeks. He worked hard, and they liked spending time in Maine every year after Hampshire. Alex loved her time with her granddaughters, and visited them in New York two or three times during the year. She thoroughly enjoyed how different they were, with distinct personalities from the moment they were born. Sabrina was very serious, and seemed very conservative and traditional as she was growing up. She was as horse-mad as Alex had been as a young girl. She spent as much time as she could on the horses Alex and Richard had bought when they moved back to England. Alex still rode a great deal herself, and rode with Sabrina when she visited.

Elizabeth was the princess in the family. Her sisters teased her about it. She loved pretty clothes, going to parties, having fun. She always had a flock of boyfriends and admirers and said she wanted to get married and wear a beautiful gown. She loved going through Alex's photographs of her presentation at Queen Charlotte's Ball, which Alex thought looked ridiculously old fashioned now, but Lizzie loved them, and wished she could do it. Sophie had come out at the International Ball in Washington her freshman year in college and her parents had flown over for it.

Charlotte was the adventurer in the group, always up to mischief, daring, afraid of nothing, wanting to explore beyond the horizons of her world. As she got older, she loved hearing her grandfather talk about the places they had lived. She thought it was exotic and exciting.

The girls were fourteen, twelve, and eleven when Richard told them and their mother one summer during their annual visit that their grandmother had been a spy for thirty years. They were stunned and fascinated and wanted to know all about it. Sophie was horrified and realized how little she knew her own mother. Sabrina was filled with admiration for her. Elizabeth thought it sounded scary and awful, and Charlotte drank it all in, and hounded Alex to tell her about it. She wanted all the details. Their mother was shocked by some of the stories, particularly of the SOE during the war. She'd had no idea that her mother had been an intelligence agent during her father's entire diplomatic career, although she knew a little about her war experiences. But Alex had always underplayed it.

"Why didn't I know about all that?" Sophie asked her mother about her years with MI6.

"You weren't supposed to. I couldn't tell anyone about the SOE for twenty years. Your father didn't know either, or I thought he didn't. I told him when I retired from MI6 after we came home from Washington, and he said he'd known all along. He never told me." At Richard's insistence, Alex showed the girls her war medals, which made it more real to them.

Richard was eighty-two and retired then, but still healthy and strong. They had kept the apartment in London, but didn't go often anymore. He preferred life in Hampshire, and Alex went to the city alone sometimes, to shop or see old friends. Bertie had died a few years before but they had stayed good friends and had had lunch from time to time. Alex had the leisure time to do things now that she hadn't for years. At seventy-four, she looked ten years younger. She enjoyed her month with Sophie and her granddaughters every summer, although she could see that Sophie had no real attachment to the house in Hampshire. It was a place she visited and dutifully brought her daughters to see her parents. But her heart was with Steve and in the States. And she felt more American than English. It was her country, by choice, and she'd lived there since she was fourteen, after they left Moscow.

It was Sabrina who loved coming to England, and ultimately went to Oxford. She came to see her grandparents regularly, and spent weekends with them, and eventually brought the boy she had met at Oxford and fallen in love with along with her. He was the classic British aristocrat, and everything Alex's mother had wanted her to marry. It had taken two more generations for that to happen. His father was a marquess, and he had a big family property of his own, and a title, that he would inherit as the oldest son.

Like her mother, Sabrina married young, and she married at Wickham Manor, much to Alex and Richard's delight. She was twenty-two when she married, and Anthony twenty-five. Having their wedding in Hampshire meant the world to Alex. Richard had just turned ninety, and was slowly becoming frail, and going to New York for the wedding would have been too much for him. But he could be at his granddaughter's wedding, since she had it at Wickham Manor.

Not to be outdone, Elizabeth married a year later. She seemed less serious and more frivolous than her older sister. Sabrina was taking a course for a master's degree in archaeology at Oxford. Elizabeth married a man ten years older who treated her like a princess, and spoiled her. Her husband, Matthew, was from a New York banking family, and Sophie had to plan an enormous New York wedding for four hundred. She enjoyed it, and had nothing else to do. Elizabeth had just finished college and wanted to sail straight into marriage, before going to work for a fashion magazine in the fall. Matthew worked at the family bank and Lizzie wanted a huge wedding. They were in all the magazines regularly as the golden couple, and Sophie sent all the clippings to her mother. Elizabeth had grown up to be very much like Sophie as a little girl.

Alex and Richard both agreed that he wasn't strong enough to attend the wedding in New York. A society wedding for four hundred people would have been too much for him, and he urged Alex to go to see their granddaughter married.

She spent a week in New York helping Sophie before the wedding, and stayed for two days after. It gave Alex a chance to spend time with Charlotte, who had just finished her last year at Harvard, graduating a year early. She had been in a rush to do things all her life.

"Don't tell me you're getting married too," Alex said when she arrived in New York, and Charlotte laughed.

"Not a chance, Grandmama. I have other plans. I want to travel. Actually, I have an idea. Would you go to Hong Kong with me one day? I want to see where you and Grandfather lived, and my mom grew up, or one of the places anyway. She still remembers it, and she loved it. She hated Russia."

"We all did," Alex admitted. "I'll go with you one day, but I don't think I should leave your grandfather right now." Charlotte nodded. He was ninety-one, and had seemed very frail at Sabrina's wedding. She and Anthony were living in London, and flying in for Lizzie's wedding. "What are your plans?" Alex asked her youngest granddaughter. Charlotte was the boldest and most adventuresome of her granddaughters. She had majored in political science at Harvard.

"I want to get a job in Beijing," she said without hesitating. Interesting things were happening there, and China was the wave of the future. Charlotte had taken Chinese in college and spoke Mandarin very well. "I want to go there, and to Hong Kong with you one day."

"I never went to Beijing when I lived there. It wasn't open then. I'd like to see it with you," Alex said thoughtfully. At eighty-three she was still hungry to travel, but Richard wasn't up to it anymore. He didn't even like going to London. They hadn't used their apartment there all year, but Alex liked having it, in case she wanted to go to town and spend the night, although she worried about leaving Richard. Their housekeeper took good care of him, but Alex didn't like leaving him for more than a few hours.

Sophie joined them then with her table seating charts for the wedding in her hand. "What are you two up to?" she asked them, looking distracted.

"Planning a trip to China," Charlotte answered.

"Now?" She looked surprised.

"I can't leave your father. We're just dreaming." Alex smiled at Sophie.

"Maybe next year," Charlotte said hopefully, as her mother looked at Alex intently.

"Do you mind sitting next to my father-in-law, Mama?" Her mother-in-law had died the year before, shortly after Sabrina's wedding. "You'll both be alone. I have nightmares every night about the seating."

"That would be fine," Alex said easily. "You can seat me wherever you like." They had rented an enormous estate in the Hamptons, and were tenting the lawn for the reception. And there were buses to take people back and forth to the city so they didn't have to drive. The logistics were like planning an invasion. Alex said it reminded her of D-Day but Sophie had it well in hand and enjoyed it.

The wedding was as beautiful as Alex knew it would be. Elizabeth wore a dress made for her in Paris and she really did look like a fairy princess as she came down the aisle on her father's arm. It had none of the British country feeling that had characterized Sabrina's wedding in Hampshire. Lizzie's wedding was pure Hollywood glamour. She wore a slinky white satin dress that showed off her figure, with a twenty-foot train behind her, and a lace veil. She looked like a movie star, and everyone gasped when they saw her. *Vogue* was covering the wedding. Both of her sisters were bridesmaids wearing pale blue satin gowns. Sophie was wearing emerald green organza, and Alex had worn navy lace that showed off her trim figure too, but was appropriate for her age. The groom's mother was more theatrical, and was wearing gold.

It was a seven o'clock black-tie wedding, and everything was perfection. There was a twelve-piece dance band for the beginning of the evening, and a disco with a famous DJ was being set up later in a separate tent. The lighting and sound system alone had taken two days to set up, and the white orchids on every table were exquisite. Alex smiled when she saw Sophie dancing with Steve at the wedding. They were still in love after twenty-four years. Alex and Richard had been married for fifty-four years.

Alex enjoyed her seat at the wedding. General Bennett, Steve's father and grandfather of the bride, was good company. He had retired from the army a few years earlier, but still consulted at the Pentagon, and was on numerous military councils. He had taught a class at West Point the year before, which he told Alex he had thoroughly enjoyed.

"Our granddaughter Charlotte told me something interesting last year," he said, smiling at Alex, pleased with his seat too. It had been an adjustment losing his wife the year before, and he said he was keeping busy.

"Charlotte always tells me interesting things," Alex said, smiling. "She was trying to talk me into a trip to Hong Kong and Beijing with her when I arrived. I loved it in Hong Kong when we lived there. I think it's the only place we lived that Sophie enjoyed, other than Washington. She's American at heart."

"Charlotte tells me you were a spy," he said with a smile. "Is that true?" He wasn't sure if she'd been exaggerating or not.

"I suppose so," she said, looking mildly embarrassed. "I worked for the SOE during the war, doing espionage and clandestine missions behind enemy lines. And I worked for MI6 in British Army intelligence from 1946 until 1970."

"Did Richard know?" He looked profoundly impressed. He'd heard a lot about the SOE in military circles and had collaborated with MI6.

"Not when I worked for the SOE, he said he always suspected when I told him when I retired from MI6. They recruited me when I married Richard, and he joined the diplomatic corps. They approached me right before we left for India, and I agreed, but he didn't know for certain until after I retired. I couldn't tell him. He suspected. He knows me too well. And I suppose the submachine gun I was rather fond of was a clue." She laughed.

"That's an interesting time to have been working for Military Intelligence," Sam commented. "The independence of India and Pakistan, and later, the Cold War."

"I scared myself a few times in Russia," she admitted with a grin. "I was always afraid I'd get caught and shot as a spy. There were a lot of defectors from England then, some of them working as double agents for the Russians. It was impossible to know who you could trust. We were both relieved when he got transferred to Washington. That was great fun."

"Working behind enemy lines during the war can't have been easy either."

"It wasn't," she confirmed, but offered no details.

"I don't think I've ever known a spy," he said, smiling at her, "at least I wasn't aware of it. I always think of spies as men."

“There were some astoundingly good female agents during the war,” Alex said staunchly.

“Charlotte says you have two medals.” Alex was embarrassed then. She wasn’t used to talking about it. She never had before except to Richard, Sophie, and her grandchildren.

“Bouncing around in a drawer somewhere,” she said about her medals.

“You should be very proud of your service to your country,” he said respectfully, and she was touched by how earnestly he said it.

“Coming from a general, that’s very generous of you. I’m sure my contribution was far less impressive than yours.”

“I doubt that. Would you like to discuss it on the dance floor? I’d like to get a dance in, before they switch to the disco.” She laughed at what he said, and joined him on the dance floor. He was an excellent dancer and she had a good time. He was seventy-nine years old, looked younger, and was in great shape. They talked about politics and the many places they had both lived, and they rode one of the buses back to the city together that evening and he dropped her off at the St. Regis Hotel in a cab.

“I enjoyed the evening, Alex,” he said. “There aren’t a lot of women I can discuss espionage with, or who understand about living through a war.”

“It’s all a long time ago now.” She smiled at him, but she had enjoyed it too. “Call us if you ever come to England.”

“I will.” He was still living in Washington, and enjoyed the consulting he still did at the Pentagon. It kept his hand in on military affairs.

There was a brunch for family and close friends at the Carlyle the next day, which Alex attended. Sam had gone back to Washington, and the bride and groom left for their honeymoon early that morning.

They were going to Paris and the South of France. Alex congratulated Sophie on putting together a beautiful wedding. The next day, Alex flew back to London, and arrived in Hampshire just as Richard was going to bed. She had called him the day before with all the details.

"I missed you," she said as she kissed him, and he smiled.

"Who did you sit next to?"

"Steve's father. He said to say hello. Charlotte had told him about my work for the SOE and MI6, so it gave us something to talk about."

"He had no problem finding something to talk to you about last year at Sabrina's wedding. He has an eye for you, my dear."

"Don't be silly. I'm an old woman. He's not chasing after me."

"I'm sure he would."

"I hope this means you're jealous. That would be much more interesting to me," she said, kissed him again, and helped him up the stairs. She didn't like how tired he seemed. He had been slowly running out of steam for several months. He was like a candle beginning to flicker, which tore at her heart. She helped him get ready for bed, and then told him more about the wedding as they lay there together, and while she was talking to him, he fell asleep, and she lay next to him, holding his hand.

He seemed better the next morning, and they went for a nice walk. Richard's mind was still crystal clear, but his body was failing. The eight-year age difference between them now seemed vast, when it never had before.

The following week he caught a cold and stayed in bed. She called the doctor, who came to see him, and said he was fine, and to keep warm and rest for a few days. Alex made him stay in bed, and brought his meals up on a tray. Day by day he seemed to be growing weaker.

She was frightened when she looked at him. He seemed to have aged years in a matter of weeks. She sat by his bed in the afternoons and read quietly while he slept, and she stayed close and kept an eye on him, and was right there next to him if he needed anything. But mostly, he slept.

"Let's go for a walk tomorrow," he said one night as she helped him back into bed. "I'm tired of lying around here." He looked very pale and thin.

"Good. We'll go for a walk tomorrow," Alex said as she tucked him in. She kissed him on the cheek, and he held her hand when she got into bed. She could hear him breathing softly a few minutes later. She lay next to him, wishing she could give him back some of his energy and vitality, or give him some of hers. She gently stroked his cheek, and then fell asleep herself. When she woke in the morning, he looked peaceful, and he was gone. Richard had slipped away in the night, lying next to her. She'd been at his side until the last moment, and she was grateful he hadn't died when she was in New York for Lizzie's wedding. She lay next to him for a little while longer, and then she got up, kissed his cheek, and quietly left the room. She had known this moment would come, but she wasn't ready for it, and knew she never would be. After fifty-four years, she couldn't imagine a life without him. They had been so perfectly suited to each other. It took the breath out of her, thinking of going on without him.

She sat down in the kitchen and called Sophie, and told her what had happened.

She was shocked, not prepared for it either.

"I'm so sorry, Mama. I'll fly out today." Alex nodded, as the tears rolled down her cheeks.

"I can't imagine my life without him. I never could." The pain of it reminded her suddenly of when they had lost Edward, only this was infinitely worse. They had been life partners for more than half a century.

Alex called the vicar and the funeral home after that. She stood by in a plain black dress when they took him away. She went for a long walk after they left, all the way to the lake, and she could feel him with her. She knew he always would be, they had shared so much, and she was going to miss him so terribly. It was a deep pain and a loss like no other.

Chapter 19

Alex slept alone in their bed that night, for the first time in years. She got up at six and made herself a cup of tea. Sophie arrived a few hours later. She had taken the night flight from New York, and Charlotte was with her. Sabrina had promised to come down from London that afternoon, with Anthony. And Lizzie and Matthew were flying in from Paris from their honeymoon. Steve was coming from New York in time for the funeral, to be with Sophie. And by that night, the house was filled with voices and people, her daughter and granddaughters, her son-in-law and two grandsons-in-law. She wished that Richard were there too. It was how the house was meant to be, alive and vibrant with youth. She was glad they were there. Two days later, they buried him next to her father and mother, and the headstones for her brothers. She'd had a small one put there for Edward when they came back from Pakistan. Her grandparents were there too.

After the burial, they went back to the house and had lunch. Sophie organized it with the housekeeper, and the girls helped. They chattered and talked and they all took a walk that afternoon, just as Richard had wanted to right before he died. They stayed another day, and the house was agonizingly empty when they all left.

For the next six months, Alex felt like a marble in a shoebox, rolling around the empty house, not sure what to do with herself, without him. She went up to London, and used the apartment, and that felt strange too. It still felt unbelievable that he was no longer there. She couldn't get used to it and not having Richard to talk to. Sophie invited her to New York for Christmas, but she decided to stay home, with her memories of Richard.

A year later, Charlotte got a master's degree from Harvard in political science. Alex was very proud of her, and went to the ceremony.

Sam Bennett was there too and asked how she was doing. He told her how sorry he was about Richard.

"I'm all right," she said halfheartedly.

"It's strange at first. And very hard. The world feels off kilter without them, and then you get used to it and you go on living," he said wisely and she nodded. He had described it perfectly, and had gone through it when he had lost his wife two years before. Alex was eighty-four then, and Sam was eighty. They were each half of what had once been whole, and now no longer existed.

"When are we going to China, Grandmama?" Charlotte asked her at lunch after graduation, and Alex looked wistful. She wondered if it would be too painful now to go. "I'm starting a job in Beijing in November," she said, and Alex was startled. "I have some training to do before I leave. We should go over this summer." It would be hot then, and Alex was curious about her job in Beijing.

"What kind of job?" she asked her.

"With a newspaper," Charlotte said vaguely. "They had a spot for one foreigner and I got it. If you don't want to go now, you can visit me when I'm there, working. I could meet you in Hong Kong."

"I might do that," Alex said, looking intrigued. "What sort of training will you be doing?" Charlotte looked away as she answered.

"You know, the usual kind of thing, before you take a job in a foreign country."

"Your Chinese is fluent," Alex reminded her as she watched her granddaughter's face. And she saw Sam watching her too. Their eyes met for a minute afterward. Charlotte went off to talk to some of her friends then, and Sam and Alex were alone for a minute. "What sort of job is it?" she asked him quietly, and he smiled at her.

"Your security clearance was probably higher than mine, so I guess I can tell you. She's going to Quantico."

"Quantico?" It rang a bell, but she wasn't sure what it was for a minute.

"CIA," he said so no one else could hear them, and Alex looked shocked. "They train FBI agents there too, but she's interested in international, not domestic. Like your MI5 and MI6."

"She's training for the CIA?" she whispered, and he laughed at her.

"You of all people should understand. I think it's genetic. She's following in your footsteps," he said gently.

"But that's so dangerous!"

"And it wasn't for you? They all have to follow their own paths, just as we did. Steve hated the idea of West Point, and Sophie hated growing up all over the world, and cares nothing about England. Sabrina is more English than the English and her children will be too, with Anthony. And Lizzie wants a glamorous life in New York, which you and I don't care about. Now Charlotte wants to be an agent of some kind, maybe a spy, just like you. And who knows, maybe one day we'll have a great-grandson who will go to West Point. They are who they are, in spite of us, not because of us. But of all of them, Charlotte is the most like you. She's a bold, brave, passionate, incredibly bright girl, and if she is a spy, she'll be a damned good one, like you were. And whatever it is she's doing in Beijing, she's not going to tell us much about it, just like you never did." As she listened to him, Alex knew he was right, and if Charlotte was going to work for the CIA, she'd be a terrific agent. Alex was proud of her just thinking about it. And when Charlotte came back to the table, Alex smiled at her.

"I think I'll come and see you once you're working in Beijing. It's too hot there now. We'll go to Hong Kong if you can take a few days off." She didn't ask her any more questions. She knew now.

Charlotte came to see her that afternoon at her hotel before she left, and Alex turned to her with a smile. "I have a graduation present for you." She had already given her a small pair of diamond earrings, which Charlotte was wearing, and Alex reached into her purse, and handed her something from the palm of her hand. Charlotte saw immediately what it was and looked shocked. "Is that yours?" It was the pistol Alex always had on her person or in her purse.

"I've been carrying it for more than fifty years. It's an antique, like me. Now it's yours." She handed her the bullets separately. She had removed them when she got back to the hotel. "Good luck at Quantico," she said softly.

"How did you know?" Charlotte asked her, cradling the small pistol in her hand.

"Your grandfather told me. I was a spy, not a clairvoyant. It actually shoots quite well, by the way. I've always been a fairly good shot." She sounded young again as she said it, and Charlotte laughed. "And whatever you do, don't do anything to be like me. Follow your own dreams, and your own heart."

"I've always wanted to do something like this, especially once Grandpapa told us about your being a spy. I'm not ready to settle down like my sisters, and I don't think I will be for a long time. I've got a lot of flying to do and I'm ready to spread my wings." She looked at the pistol again then and at her grandmother. "You don't need it, Grandmama?"

"I think at my age, it would be a little unseemly if I go around shooting people. My judo is still pretty good." Alex was grinning at her, proud to be her grandmother.

"You're dangerous, Grandmama." It was a compliment and Alex took it that way.

"I used to be. I don't need to be dangerous anymore. Just be careful. Learn your lessons well, and always follow your instincts." It was good advice for life, not just espionage. Alex kissed her then, and Charlotte left a few minutes later, with the pistol and bullets in her purse. Her grandmother still amazed her. She wished she knew more about her life, but probably no one ever would. It was her personality, and the nature of her work.

Alex flew back to London that night, and was back in Hampshire on a beautiful summer day.

She went for long walks every day, and felt better by the end of the summer. Her granddaughters didn't come in the summer anymore. They had their own lives to lead, their partners, and their careers. Charlotte was in Quantico in training, which her parents didn't know. Sam and Alex were the only ones who knew, and the "newspaper" job in Beijing was a cover for her first job with the CIA.

Alex was thinking about it one afternoon when the phone rang. It was Sam Bennett, calling from London.

"What are you doing here?" She was surprised to hear his voice.

"I'm speaking at the Royal Military Academy, on the war in Vietnam, and where we went wrong. Can I buy you dinner?" She liked the idea. They always enjoyed talking to each other at family events. Richard had liked him too.

"You can. We can trade war stories. Would you like to come to Hampshire after that? You've seen my friendly old place here, with hundreds of years of family history to bore you, some good walks, and a lake." He had been there for Sabrina's wedding, and liked it a lot.

"It seems like a very nice place for two old warhorses like us to hang out. I'd like to come. The girls love it, and even Sophie grudgingly admits that she does too. Dinner in town tomorrow?"

"It sounds wonderful. I have a flat in Kensington, so I'll spend the night. Where are you staying?"

"The Connaught." It was a very distinguished, small, elegant hotel, suitable for a general.

"I'll pick you up at your hotel, if you like," she offered.

"Perfect. Eight o'clock?"

"Wonderful. And, Sam, thank you. For the good advice about Charlotte and letting her spread her wings and do what she wants . . . for taking me to dinner . . . I was getting bored here."

"We have lots to talk about," he said, sounding buoyant. "The general and the spy. It sounds like a plot for a book."

"I'm not sure I still have a book in me." She laughed. "But a chapter or two perhaps."

"We'll just see where the story goes. I've waited a long time for this.

I've had my eye on you since Sophie and Steven's wedding, but my wife was a good woman and your husband was a good man." Richard was right. He had said that Sam had an eye for her, and he wasn't wrong. She didn't know where it would lead. Maybe nowhere, but he had questions to ask her, and she had stories to tell, and she wanted to hear his. "Tomorrow at eight then."

"I won't be armed. I gave Charlotte my pistol as a graduation present. I still have an old Sten gun here somewhere." She was laughing.

"I come in peace." He was laughing too. They were having fun, and there was no harm in that.

"So do I," she assured him.

"See you tomorrow, Alex."

"Thank you, Sam." She smiled as she hung up.

Danielle Steel

Have you liked Danielle Steel on Facebook?

Be the first to know about Danielle's latest books, access exclusive competitions and stay in touch with news about Danielle.

www.facebook.com/DanielleSteelOfficial

MORAL COMPASS

Saint Ambrose Prep has been the school of choice for the sons of the great and the good for over a hundred years. Now, for the first time, Saint Ambrose has just enrolled its first female students. While many of the kids on the campus have all the privilege in the world, some are struggling to deal with family, insecurity and loneliness. In such a heightened environment, even the smallest spark can become a raging fire.

The day after a Halloween party, a student lies in the hospital, seriously injured and with a dangerous level of alcohol in her blood. Only the handful of students who were there when she was attacked know what happened, and they have closed ranks. As parents, students, staff and the media attempt to establish the truth, no one at Saint Ambrose will escape the fallout.

As the drama unfolds, those involved will reach a crossroads where they must choose between truth and lies, between what is easy and what is right, coming to rely on their own moral compass.

Available for pre-order